Freeing
Grace

Written By

Laura Powell

Cover Design: Pixel Studios

ISBN: 978-1-7353597-4-8

Dedication

This book is dedicated to my voice teacher at Illinois Wesleyan University, Jody Kienzler. Your influence went far beyond the music studio and the stage. Thank you for shining Christ's light and modeling a vibrant relationship with God during such a crucial time in my life.

For the grace of God has appeared, bringing salvation for all people.

-Titus 2:11

Acknowledgements

Anne and Jerry Engelhardt, Rebecca England, Lynn Jackson, and Patricia Powell, thank you for being such an outstanding editing team! Thank you for shaping this novel. I'm so grateful.

Thank you to Ray Boosinger, with the state of Illinois, for your help understanding safety regulations in businesses. And thank you to Phil Johnson, firefighter for the City of Springfield, for answering many questions on firefighting logistics. Your service to our community is invaluable.

To my six-person "bulk sales team," Sue and Al Alexander, Patricia and David Powell, and Shelly and Joe Wheeler, thank you for supporting my writing and sharing these books with so many people.

Just as with the first two books, *Freeing Grace* features Springfield, Illinois area businesses. Bella Milano, Crowne Plaza, Incredibly Delicious, Joe's Italian Pizza, Papo's Café, Three Twigs Bakery, and WLUJ Christian Radio Station are a few of the many quality businesses serving our community, and I am thrilled to spotlight them.

Chapter One

SEPTEMBER 2013

"Love is a choice," Ethan recited to himself, as he had dozens of times over the course of the week. "Love is a choice, not just a feeling," he repeated again, bending over to light the first of ten pillar candles he'd placed around the sunroom.

He'd decorated the glass table in the four-seasons room with a bouquet of exotic lavender orchids. Being a landscaper, Ethan liked unique plants, and he'd gone to great lengths to have the orchids shipped for the special evening. Next to the flowers sat a platter of grilled steak covered with foil, and the side dishes he'd made were resting at a warming temperature in the oven while he waited for Jezmeen to arrive home.

They'd only moved into the brand new two-story, set back a mile on Ethan's twenty-three acres, a few months earlier, and Jezmeen had decorated the place from bottom to top. Ethan had a big night planned, but he needed the afternoon alone to pull it off. So, he'd sent her on an errand to purchase home furnishings. It was her favorite hobby.

Months ago, he'd opened a joint savings account with Jezmeen, depositing $30,000 so she could purchase all the furniture needed for the place. After all, they had moved from a 300 square-foot camper on the property to a spacious 3,000 square-foot home. The original budget hadn't covered nonessentials for the laundry room, and Jezmeen had

1

already drained the account. So he sent her away with a little more of his hard-earned cash.

He imagined Jez would come back with artwork, organizational items, and knickknacks. Even if he didn't think they were necessary— to him, a laundry room was just a place for washing clothes—he knew the space would look lovely when it was done, and the covert mission would have served its purpose. "Project Perfect Proposal" was underway.

Two weeks earlier, Jezmeen had shocked him when she announced that she was pregnant. Technically, a pregnancy test and a note left on the counter did the job. He'd gotten the steps of an honorable relationship out of order when he had allowed Jezmeen to move in with him almost a year earlier. Much had changed, just like the seasons.

Ethan finished lighting all the candles and headed to change his clothes. They still smelled like smoke from the grill. After putting on a navy-blue polo and khaki pants, he went into the bathroom to shave. Leaning over the granite countertop, Ethan brought his cheek to the mirror, curious if he could see signs of the port-wine stains he had removed three years earlier.

Twice a year he went to St. Louis for maintenance laser treatments. Jezmeen had lived with him through the recovery process of his most recent one last winter. She was horrified when he got back with small purple dots all over his face. It was normal, but she'd never seen him that way. Back then, the dots faded quickly.

Now, a tiny patch of pink had begun to appear between his right eye and the bridge of his nose, and he knew it was time to make another appointment. He sighed, wishing his appearance was perfect, but he knew Jezmeen wasn't in a relationship with him because of his looks.

Sure, if he stood up straight and squared his shoulders, he was almost six feet tall, and he had more than normal upper body strength because he lifted heavy objects for a living. However, Jezmeen's beauty put her in a league of her own. Ethan understood she was attracted to him because he had money—along with a growing status in the community as a small business owner.

Ethan lathered shaving gel onto his cheeks. "I got myself into this mess, and this is the right thing to do," he said to himself. Between swipes with the razor, Ethan checked his watch. It was almost five-thirty, and Jezmeen had been gone for over two hours. How long could it take to buy trinkets for the laundry room? The knot in his stomach began to tighten, knowing dinner was near.

"Ethan?" Jezmeen called from the first floor.

She has a nice voice, Ethan thought as he wiped his cheeks with a towel. I could live with that voice for the rest of my life, he reassured himself. "Coming," he bellowed back.

Moving quickly downstairs, he hurried into the kitchen to greet Jezmeen. When he saw her, he pulled her into a hug.

"What was that all about?" Jezmeen asked, as she pulled away. Ethan hadn't made any physical advances for weeks. Afterall, their relationship had been on the rocks. "Are we having company?" she asked, bewildered by the smells in the kitchen and Ethan's attire.

"You're the guest of honor," Ethan replied, putting on the charm he barely knew he had. Obviously, the adrenaline of the night was overtaking the introverted behavior he'd fought with his whole life.

"What's the occasion?" Jezmeen asked suspiciously.

"Our future," Ethan replied. "Why don't you go have a seat in the sunroom, and I'll get you a glass of sparkling cider."

"Okay," Jezmeen said, drawing out the word. "But don't you want to see what I bought?"

"Umm, sure, why don't you take the bags in there. We can look at everything while we eat."

Jezmeen lifted the sacks and carried them into the room that adjoined the kitchen. "Wow," her voice echoed as she stepped inside. "It's beautiful in here."

"Thanks," Ethan called, as he poured the amber liquid into two champagne glasses.

He carried them into the room and found Jezmeen digging through the tissue paper in her shopping bag.

"Do you like this?" she asked, holding up a crystal-clear round container.

"What's it for?"

"Laundry soap."

"Oh."

"So, what do you think?"

4

"It's…nice."

Ethan went back into the kitchen to get the twice baked potatoes and corn casserole out of the oven. Why couldn't she just use the box the laundry flakes came in?

"I got this for half price," she said excitedly, holding up a wicker basket as he entered the room again, balancing two dishes.

"Looks…sturdy," he replied.

"Did you make this?" Jezmeen asked, eyeing the corn casserole as he set it down.

"Yes, it's my mom's recipe."

Ethan took the seat across from her.

"Do you mind if I pray?" he asked. As a new Christ-follower, he was beginning new practices, but Jezmeen didn't share his faith.

"Sure," she replied casually.

After uttering an 'amen' he lifted the foil off the platter of steaks, and steam rose into the air. Nerves made his appetite diminish, even though the smell of the meat was tantalizing.

"Did you see half the town while you were out?" he asked, trying to make conversation. Ethan often heard about how many people she ran into when she was out and about.

"Maybe a fourth," she teased. Jezmeen watched Ethan put a steak on her plate. "So, we're celebrating our pregnancy?" she asked, bewildered.

"Kind of," Ethan replied, wondering if this was his opening. He'd rather get the question out of the way, so he didn't have to think about how it would go throughout the rest of the dinner. Wiping his hands on his pants, he pushed his chair back, eased to one knee, and heard Jezmeen gasp.

Breathing out a burst of air, Ethan pulled a notecard out of his back pocket. "As you know, I'm not very good with words," he said, repositioning the card so he could read it.

"Have you heard of the purple saxifrage?

Jezmeen laughed and shook her head 'no.'

"It's the hardiest plant in the world. It grows in the arctic, surrounded by sea ice and snow for eleven months of the year. It thrives where most life would shrivel up and die. I want that to be us," he read from the card with a controlled voice.

"Even though we've had some difficult times, I want our baby to have the foundation we didn't—two parents living under one roof, working together and loving each other through thick and thin. I know I'm not there yet, but I want to become the man you feel safe with, confide in, trust, and love with your whole heart. Jezmeen Marie Williams, will you be my wife?"

Ethan reached into his pants pocket and pulled out a maroon velvet box. He pried open the hinged lid revealing a brilliant two carat round diamond. The jeweler told him this particular cut had fifty-eight facets, the most of any shape, and Jezmeen's eyes told him he picked wisely.

Jezmeen just sat there looking at the ring.

6

"It's beautiful," she whispered.

Ethan wiped his free hand on his pants leg.

"Is that a 'yes?'" he asked nervously.

"Are you sure this is what you want?" she asked.

"I'm certain." Ethan smiled.

"Okay then," Jezmeen said hesitantly, eyebrows furrowed. She took the diamond out of the box and placed it on her finger. "Oh," she laughed. "I think you were supposed to do that."

Ethan rose from the ground and loosened his knee from its locked position. Relief flooded his soul. The proposal was presented, and she said 'yes.' He reached behind his seat and grabbed a gold-colored gift bag.

"I got something for you."

"Besides this?' Jez replied, admiring the ring with delight. She ruffled through the white tissue paper until her hand touched a book. Holding it up she read the title, "*What to Expect When You're Expecting.*"

"Did you have something like that when you were pregnant with Ace?" Ethan asked, remembering her first pregnancy, twelve years prior, that ended in adoption.

"I think so, but it's long been thrown away. So this is very thoughtful."

"I figured if you left it out on the counter, I'd read it, too. When I was at the store, I flipped through the pages, and it said the baby is about as big as an orange at fourteen weeks. I figured correctly, didn't I?"

"Fourteen weeks? Umm, yeah, I think so. I haven't made an appointment with a doctor yet."

"Do you want me to do that for you?"

"No, I'll do it. I've just been too busy...or too tired."

"I can start a bath for you after dinner," Ethan said.

"And then you'll want to sleep in the same bed tonight, too," Jezmeen replied, figuring the bath was the indicator of things to come. They'd been sleeping in separate rooms for weeks.

"No, Jez. This is going to sound backwards, but that's how everything in our relationship has gone so far. I want to wait until we're married to pursue that kind of intimacy again with you."

"You've got to be joking," Jezmeen laughed heartily.

"I've been learning God loves purity, Jez, and I really messed things up."

"But we've already...you know...consummated the relationship. And we're living together, Ethan."

"I get that. But I want our marriage to start out right. Afterall, we were both raised by single moms. We didn't know our dads. We're both only children. Now we're pregnant. I think we're starting with some severe disadvantages."

Jezmeen's mocha brown hand reached out and stroked the pale skin on Ethan's arm. "Won't you get...lonely?" she asked seductively.

Ethan didn't pull away but looked into her striking yellow-green eyes, while placing his free hand on top of hers to quiet its movement. "Jez, you can drop the act. You don't have to do that to secure your place with me."

"What do you mean?" she huffed, pulling her hand out from under his, looking hurt.

Ethan busied himself cutting his steak, ignoring her question.

"Have you had a chance to put in your notice at Finnegan's Taphouse?" he asked, switching subjects.

"No. Why does it mean so much to you?"

"I just don't want my pregnant fiancé to be bartending. It's too hard on your body, and the hours aren't conducive to a family. We talked about this last week."

"I know, but I didn't agree to anything."

"Well, I found a job online that seemed like something you'd be good at. Assistant Interior Decorator for that store downtown, *Style Street*."

"You were looking for jobs for *me?*"

"I was actually posting a position and came across it. We're trying to hire a new mowing guy... 'lawn maintenance specialist,'" he smiled.

"I don't have any experience."

"Just take some pictures of the rooms in this house, Jez. I think your work speaks for itself."

Jezmeen warmed at the compliment. "Wouldn't I have to have a degree?"

"I don't know, but you could always take some classes online. Just think about it."

They ate in silence for a few moments.

"So, do you like the steak?" Ethan asked, noticing she hadn't eaten much.

"It's delicious."

"You're eating for two now, and somehow you still look like you're not even a day pregnant."

Jezmeen laughed uncomfortably. "Good genes, I guess. I barely showed with Ace until I was six months along."

"I still can't believe you kept the pregnancy a secret for three months."

"Well, I wanted to be sure. Most miscarriages happen in the first trimester."

"And we're past that now, right?" Ethan asked.

"Did you learn that from the book, too?" Jez teased.

"Well, I certainly didn't get it from VJ or Mark," Ethan replied, referring to his two landscaping assistants. "When are we going to start telling people anyway?"

"About this or this?" Jez asked, holding out her ring finger and then pointing to her belly.

"Either. Both."

"I think we should start with the engagement. Let people get used to that for a while."

"Okay, but we're not going to be able to hide it much longer. After all, in two months the baby will be as big as a coconut," Ethan said with a twinkle in his eye.

"I think you have the book memorized," Jezmeen laughed.

Jezmeen twisted the engagement ring around her finger as she slowly walked the perimeter of the store. Bins of fake greenery, lamps, pillows, topiaries, candle holders, and lanterns were tastefully grouped in separate displays atop varying pieces of furniture at *Style Street.* She half-heartedly picked up a hardcover coffee table book featuring beautiful beaches, too preoccupied to really look, knowing that the owner, Monica Taylor, would step out of her office any minute to greet her for an interview.

It wasn't long after Ethan mentioned the position that her mind began to weigh its potential. After bartending for seven years, she was ready for a change. And even though she wouldn't admit it, she was glad Ethan had thought about her when he saw the job posting.

When she called *Style Street* for more details the young lady that answered said she needed a portfolio and a "natural eye for creative design." Jezmeen hoped she had the latter. As for the former, she took Ethan's advice and snapped photos of the rooms she'd designed at their home.

If she got the job, and that felt like a big 'if,' she told Ethan she'd enroll in an online program to earn certification for interior decorating. He'd brought up combining their incomes, so they could have a better handle on their budget. But Jezmeen wasn't about to reveal her sizable dowry. Afterall, she didn't really intend to get married…ever. The diamond did exactly what she'd wanted. It secured her place in Ethan's life, not a trip down the aisle.

"Jezmeen Williams?"

Jezmeen recognized her potential boss from the website. She estimated Monica to be in her late fifties. Dressed in a tailored red blazer with black accents on the breast pockets, black slacks and black heels, Ms. Taylor looked sophisticated.

"Nice to meet you," Monica said, extending her hand. "My office is this way."

The first thing Jez noticed, once inside the small, windowless room, was the exposed shelving holding samples of a wide array of wood and granite. Then her eyes scanned the opposite wall where a row of hooks held fabric swatches. Books of wallpaper were in a large basket on the floor, and a color wheel sat on Monica's white desk. She felt like it was the first day of elementary school art class with all the creative materials surrounding her.

Jezmeen sat down in a contemporary, white plastic chair, which was surprisingly comfortable, and smiled to cover her jitters. Now that she had been enchanted by the delightful workspace, she wanted the job more than ever. Monica eased into the chair behind her desk and pushed her champagne blonde bangs to one side.

"So, what did you think of the store?" Monica asked with a Cheshire grin.

"It's beautiful," Jezmeen replied truthfully, resting her portfolio on her lap.

"You probably know that the *Style Street* store in Schaumburg is one of the top decorating outlets in the Chicago-area," Monica gloated.

"I read that on your website," Jez replied, hoping to show that she'd done her research.

"I have built this company from the ground up. Not many designers own a franchise."

"This store came first," Jezmeen interjected to prove she knew the history.

"Correct," Monica said, nodding her head in agreement. "I was raised here in Springfield, you know. I opened this one, and then I met my husband. Well, now ex-husband. He saw my talent and just knew I had to go bigger." Monica replied. "Of course, it benefited *him* when I moved to the suburbs, because he was working there at the time. He turned out to be a really selfish-" she stopped herself from saying a foul word. "But let's not talk about him. Let me see your portfolio." She reached out her hands towards Jezmeen's book.

Monica opened the top drawer, pulled out glasses with striking red frames, and put them on. "Ahh. I did a very similar room," she said, pointing to the picture of Jezmeen's living room. "Have you heard of Robert Barlow?"

Jezmeen shook her head 'no.'

"Famous lawyer up in Schaumburg. He owns Barlow, Weston, and Keys?"

"I'm not familiar with them."

"I did his living room in all white. He loved it. Said I was the best decorator he's ever worked with."

Monica flipped the page. "I use a lot of greenery in my rooms, too," Monica said as she viewed the picture of the plant on a side table in a guest bedroom. "You've heard of Matt Ellis, right?"

"Sorry, no."

"He was a relief pitcher for the White Sox for one season. I can't believe you've never heard of him," she glanced over her eyeglasses disapprovingly. "He didn't want any plants he had to maintain…being on the road and all. I used fake greenery, and do you know what he asked me?"

Jezmeen shrugged.

"How often do I have to water them," Monica laughed. "He was joking of course. Matt is so funny."

Jezmeen chuckled in false comradery.

"He's such a personable guy. You know the really famous ones can be quite hard to work with. So, he was a pleasant surprise."

Monica quickly thumbed through the rest of the pictures and shut the book. "I know you haven't done this as long as I have, so I can't expect your rooms to demonstrate my level of expertise, but I just really need someone who can follow instructions. I need someone who will be loyal." Monica looked up, directly into Jezmeen's eyes.

"My last five assistants were horrible," Monica continued drawing out the last word. "I'll give you some free advice. If you get this job, just do what I ask. It's so simple."

Monica took off her glasses and put them back in the drawer. Then handed back Jezmeen's portfolio. "The assistant decorator is an entry level position. All you have to do is meet with clients, write down their expectations, likes, dislikes, that kind of thing, and then get me the information. I draw up the design, and then you fulfill my vision. Seeing that you don't have any *real* experience, you could really learn from me."

Jezmeen had never been so silent at an interview. She wondered when she'd be asked questions, but quickly gathered Ms. Taylor was more into talking about herself. Thankfully, she'd become a good listener through her years of bartending.

"I interviewed two others earlier today, but you have the right image for my company. I only come to Springfield a few times a month, so you are my eyes and ears here. Daniel, my last assistant, said the job was '*too stressful.*' So, here's some free advice, don't take the job if you aren't willing to work an occasional night or weekend."

"Are you offering me the position?" Jezmeen asked, hopeful she wasn't reading too much into the conversation.

"I'm assuming you want it," Monica said curtly.

"Yes, I do."

"Then I'll need you to come back tomorrow morning at nine, so we can go over your paperwork, and I'll teach you about the software program I use."

"Thank you very much," Jezmeen said, extending her arm for a handshake.

"Don't let me down," Monica replied.

Chapter Two

Jezmeen glanced at her phone. It was exactly nine o'clock, and she had been standing outside *Style Street* for ten minutes. Dressed in black form-fitting capris, a white blouse, and cheetah print heels, she hadn't taken into account how quickly the shoes would become uncomfortable.

But that was secondary to her concern about disappointing Monica. The last thing she wanted to do was appear tardy on her first day of training. Since she didn't have Ms. Taylor's number, she decided to knock on the glass door. First timidly, then more loudly, Jezmeen rapped until she saw Monica through the glass. Monica approached and fumbled with a set of keys.

"Sorry. The door was locked." Jezmeen said as she passed Monica's slender frame, while she held the door open for her.

"Why yes," Monica said bluntly. "The store doesn't open until ten."

"How did you get in?"

"There's an entrance in the back," Monica replied. Jezmeen noted Monica's chin length hair was perfectly fixed, and she dressed similarly to the day before in black pants, black heels, but this time she wore a sapphire blue blazer.

"Is that the way you want me to come in?" Jezmeen asked, trailing behind the woman.

"No, I'll get you a key to the front. You should have called when you arrived."

"I would've, but I didn't have your number."

"Well, you should have asked me for it yesterday."

"Sorry," Jezmeen said humbly. She hoped putting in her two weeks' notice at Finnegan's Taphouse was a good idea. Monica didn't seem to like her, but then again, most women didn't.

Monica assumed her position behind the white desk, and Jezmeen picked the same seat she sat in the day before.

"I'd like to go over the current projects before we do paperwork and the software program," Monica said, pulling a sapphire rimmed pair of glasses out of the top drawer.

Jezmeen wanted to ask Monica how many different colors of glasses she had, but she didn't know how Monica would take the question. When she was bartending, Jezmeen made conversation easily—especially with the male clientele. With Ms. Taylor she felt uncomfortable, bumbling, and awkward. Jezmeen pulled out a notebook and pen from her oversized cheetah print bag.

"Daniel left me high and dry with these first clients. Randall and Teresa Amani," Monica said, getting right to work. "We're doing a baby's nursery for them. The wallpaper's been ordered, and the Amani's have the furniture, but here is the brief." Monica handed Jezmeen the paper. "And here's the floorplan."

Jezmeen took the papers and began to look them over, but Monica continued.

"Client number two is the Bank of Springfield. They love me. Every time they open a new branch, Brent calls me. He's the V.P. We're doing a lobby for the Wabash location. Boring. Straightforward. You'll just have to hang a few pictures, purchase a few plants, a floor mat. That kind of thing."

Monica handed Jezmeen another paperclipped set of papers. This time Jezmeen didn't even bother to glance at them.

"And, last but not least, our newest client, Charles Noble. The first two clients are repeat customers. My reputation is well-known here, as I'm sure you are aware," Monica peered over the rim of her glasses and stared at Jezmeen. "But Charles is brand new to Monica Taylor and *Style Street*. He's moving to Springfield and is opening a counseling practice. He's hired us to design his space, and we've got to do it well. We *need* more customer retention."

Monica pushed the brief across the desk to Jezmeen.

"Daniel did *nothing* to help my standing in the community."

"How long did he work for you?" Jezmeen asked, thinking it must have been years.

"Three months, but he never brought in a single client. It's not like I can run the shop in Schaumburg and do all the work here, too. But that's exactly what he expected of me."

Monica looked down at her notes.

"Now, Jezmeen, if you do a good job with," she paused to look at the name on the list, "Charles Noble, he may want you to decorate something else—perhaps his personal residence. Upsell. Upsell. Upsell. You do know what that means, don't you?"

"Absolutely, Ms. Taylor, as a bartender, that was a standard part of the job."

"Good. And I imagine you know that we get more business by doing good business. All you have to do is follow the brief and the floor plan, and it's magic."

"So, I don't do any designing?" Jezmeen had hoped she would get to create, too.

"Oh no. You are *not* to deviate from my plans. After all, I'm the one with the degree and thirty years of experience."

Monica took a drink from the mug on her desk before continuing.

"One thing you *can* do is sell. Clients get ten percent off all their purchases from *Style Street*. When we use our own products, we make more money on the project."

"I get that. My fiancé owns Adams Landscaping. He grows and sells his own plants for the same reason."

"Speaking of, I noticed your ring yesterday. I would strongly encourage you to leave it at home."

"Oh?"

"Let's just say, I believe you'll have more success without it." Monica busied herself, straightening the papers. "Plus, it can scratch things. Bill and I were married for three years, but I figured both of those things out in only a matter of months."

Jezmeen liked her ring. It was a reminder that she no longer had to constantly capture men's attention. For ten years she had bounced from one man's home to another, just like her mother.

"Ms. Taylor, which of these projects is the priority?" Jezmeen asked, burying her thoughts about the ring.

"All of them."

"And how do I know where we're at with each project?" Jezmeen questioned, flipping through the three stacks of papers.

"This is what Daniel left me. Call him if you need more information." Monica replied as she opened her laptop computer.

"I better get his number then, and yours, too, while I'm at it." Jezmeen swiped open her phone, not wanting to be unprepared again.

"Free advice, you'll need Gabrielle's, too."

"Who's Gabrielle?"

"She's the cashier at the front desk, and she'll relay potential clients to you."

Monica fed Jezmeen the numbers.

"Now, Jezmeen…" Monica paused, looking like she swallowed a lemon. "Your name does *not* roll off the tongue."

"My mom wanted a fancier version of Jasmine," Jezmeen replied apologetically. Nothing she did seemed to please this woman.

"What's your middle name?" Monica drummed her pen on the desk.

"Marie."

"Perfect. Soft. Cerebral. I wouldn't take my ex-husband's name, you know. Szymanowski. Think how that would have looked on the advertising," Monica chuckled. "You do what you have to in this business to make it. I could write a book about that. Actually, people have told me I *should*."

"Go for it," Jezmeen said cheerfully, trying to gain positive traction in the conversation.

Monica clucked her tongue and shook her head. "Oh, Marie, you'll soon learn, there's no time for that. Now…let's talk about the floor planning software."

Ethan had stalled long enough in the restroom. He trusted the small talk in the Sunday School class would be over. It was his first morning to attend, and he couldn't stand the idea of trying to make idle chit-chat over a cup of coffee. Even though he was free of his birthmarks, he still felt like a turtle wanting to hide in its shell.

But his hunger for knowledge was stronger than the temporary discomfort he might feel being new to the class. He had hoped that Jezmeen would come with him and not just because he could blend into the background while she did all the socializing for the two of them.

When Ethan first met Jez at Finnegan's Taphouse, more than a year earlier, he was instantly captivated by her hazel eyes, which seemed to glow yellow in the right light, and her flawless light brown skin. The father she'd never met was from Colombia, and her mother, Sherry, was from Illinois.

He was also drawn to her outgoing personality. As a bartender, Jezmeen was confident and friendly. Given that he could be content taking care of the plants in his greenhouses for days at a time, without saying a word, they were opposites.

But he should have known, when Jezmeen asked to move in after being evicted by her male "roommate," that their personalities were more polarizing than he'd realized. If God hadn't given him a sign, he wasn't sure he would've asked for her hand in marriage—even though she was pregnant.

Afterall, he was raised without a mother and father living together in holy matrimony. He hadn't met his dad, Wayne Copeland, until Jezmeen connected them back in June. But two weeks ago, while Ethan was pulling weeds, God made it clear that he had to give Jezmeen a chance.

And he needed to love her well. So, he headed to room 104 to check out "Foundations of Faith." He wanted to grow in his new relationship with God, and he figured this would be a good place to start learning about love.

When he opened the door, the associate pastor, David, was already leading the group in prayer, so Ethan took a seat in one of the two chairs that were available at the long table, close to the exit. After an "amen," the man next to him passed a handout his way, and Pastor David continued.

"You may think that we're going to begin with talking about the birth, death, and resurrection of Jesus. And those would be a good starting point, but we have to go farther back to even understand why He came. In the book of-"

Ethan heard the latch on the door unhook, and he glanced back. He instantly recognized the attractive woman with the porcelain skin and dark-brown hair. She sang on the praise and worship team during the first service. She picked the seat next to Ethan and gave him a smile, bringing out the deep dimples in both of her cheeks. The man next to Ethan slid him another set of notes, which he pushed along to the singer.

With the interruption, Ethan lost track of what Pastor David was talking about, and he tried to focus again. For the next forty-five minutes, Ethan listened intently to the discussion on Adam and Eve and original sin. He didn't feel bold enough to ask a question, so when class ended, he felt unsettled with racing thoughts.

"Ethan, could I see you for a minute," Pastor David said, as he was about to bolt out the door. Ethan wondered if he was in trouble for coming in late. The pastor only knew his name because they'd gone around the room doing introductions shortly after he arrived. If he was getting called out for being tardy, he wouldn't be back. Ethan made his way towards the front of the class. He was too preoccupied with worries about wrongdoing to notice the singer was following him.

"Hey, Ethan, nice to meet you," David said, extending his hand. Ethan took his grip. "I was just wondering if you want to put down an email," David said, pointing to a clipboard that held a paper with names and email addresses. "We sent this around, but I don't think it got to you, or Ariana. Have you met Ariana?" David asked, gesturing to the woman who was standing an arm's length behind him.

Ethan turned to look and nodded a greeting.

"I'm just getting emails, so I can send out additional discussion questions and articles during the week, if you're interested. No pressure. I just wanted to let you know," Pastor David continued.

"Thanks," Ethan replied. "That would be great." He bent down, picked up the pen on the table, and wrote out his name.

"So, where do you want to go to lunch today?" Ethan overheard David ask Ariana while he was writing.

"I'm game for anything," she replied in a sweet, feminine voice.

Ethan could see how David and Ariana would fit together. David was a good-looking guy in his mid-thirties, and Ariana was...Ethan wondered if engaged men should find other women attractive.

"So, did you enjoy class this morning?" Pastor David asked as Ethan stood up.

"Yeah," Ethan replied.

"What is it you're not saying," David laughed.

Ethan felt his hands get clammy. "I had some questions. That's all, but I could email them to you," Ethan replied, hoping David would let it go at that.

"Well, I'm still waiting for my wife to get here. She teaches an elementary Sunday School class at the same time I'm doing this one, and Ariana and I can't leave to go to eat without her," David smiled.

Ethan should have noticed David's ring, but he hadn't until he made a pointed effort to look.

"Hey, would you like to join the three of us? I'm sure Ariana wouldn't mind," David said.

"Yes, please join us," Ariana chimed in, knowing that handsome, single men...who went to church...were hard to come by.

Chapter Three

"Thanks for the offer, but I have plans," Ethan replied, grateful for the lunch appointment with Jezmeen, his dad, and half-sister, Izzy.

"Maybe another time then," David replied, picking up the clipboard. "Is there anything you'd like me to try to answer before you go?"

Ethan hesitated. Ariana was standing there looking at him, and he felt uncomfortable.

"I've been a Christian for twenty-three years, Ethan, and I still ask questions," David said.

"Okay," Ethan began. He shifted his weight and tried to sound more confident than he felt. "How do you know Adam and Eve were real? How come you feel so certain that the Genesis account isn't mythology or allegory?"

"I'm glad you're fielding this one," Ariana laughed and then sat down in one of the plastic maroon chairs that lined the tables.

"Great question. But before I answer that, I'd like to ask you something. Do you believe that Jesus lived on earth?"

"Yes."

"And do you believe He ever lied?"

"I don't know? I guess not."

"When Jesus spoke about the book of Genesis, He referred to it as history. Jesus told lots of parables, but not about Genesis. Jesus quoted the passage, 'God created us male and female.' If He wanted us to know something different about our origins, He gave Himself the opening."

"Okay," Ethan replied, "but couldn't we reason that he created lots of men and women, and Adam and Eve are just the archetype?"

"Another excellent question," David said. "But did you know that the book of Luke traces Jesus' lineage all the way back to Adam? The actual Adam of Genesis. And the Jews were known for being meticulous record keepers. Luke wouldn't have been referring to a group of people in a genealogy."

David wrote something down on the clipboard. "I just made myself a note to send you a video I watched recently. I think you'd find it really interesting. Scientists have traced humanity back through mitochondrial DNA to a *single* individual they dub "Mitochondrial Eve.""

"I'd like to watch that."

"Me too," Ariana chimed in from the chair.

"I'll send it to both of you," David said.

"Thanks," Ethan said. The lag in the conversation gave him the opportunity to make his exit. "I better get going."

"No problem," David replied. "Don't forget to send me any more questions. I love talking about this stuff."

By the time Ethan got to his truck in the church parking lot, it was nearly noon. He was relieved that he hadn't been in trouble for being late, but his heart was still elevated from choosing to stay and talk with Pastor David and Ariana. He was impressed with the way Pastor David fielded his questions, and he was glad he asked them. Thankfully Jezmeen would be home to let his dad and sister in, if he wasn't on time.

Sharing a Sunday meal was a tradition Wayne started as soon as he met Ethan. Only recently had Jezmeen been able to join them. Ethan was relieved that she'd put in her resignation at the bar and delighted that she'd been selected for the assistant decorator position.

With a baby on the way, a new work environment with primarily daytime hours seemed healthy. Jezmeen certainly didn't look pregnant, but now beginning sixteen weeks, the little one was no bigger than an avocado. At least that's what the book said. Jezmeen had kept it on the counter. He hadn't caught her reading it, but he appreciated being able to skim the pages.

Advice for fathers this week was to attend all the doctor appointments and ask questions. When Ethan mentioned he wanted to go with her to her next one, Jezmeen said she didn't know when it was, but she'd find out. She'd been keeping everything about the pregnancy very private.

Ethan was bursting to share the news, but Jez asked him to wait. She said they were barely out of the first trimester, and she was still worried about miscarrying. Ethan knew his half-sister, Izzy, would be thrilled, so it was hard to keep it secret. That reason alone made him wonder why Jezmeen was so silent on the subject. Jez and Izzy had a special bond, and Jezmeen had to know Izzy would be overjoyed.

But Jezmeen had been pregnant before, so he trusted that she knew what she was doing, Ethan reasoned. Only weeks earlier, he learned that Jez had given up her firstborn child when she was a senior in high school. Her adopted son, Ace, attended *Cornerstone Church,* the same place Wayne and Izzy attended. And for the last nine years, Jez never missed a Sunday.

She never went inside but waited in the parking lot just to see him. Ethan hoped her church attendance would change. If his actions showed her another dimension of love, maybe she'd be drawn to the Source.

As he pulled into the circular driveway in front of the house, he saw Wayne and Izzy were just getting out of Wayne's truck. He pulled his beat-up work vehicle, sporting Adams Landscaping magnets on both doors, behind Wayne's.

"It was my day to choose lunch, and I was craving pizza," the blond-haired thirteen-year-old rambled as she ran over to Ethan and wrapped him in a hug.

"I could use a little help here," Wayne hollered.

"Oh, yeah, I was supposed to carry in the salad. We texted Jezmeen, and she said she wanted something healthy," Izzy said.

Ethan wanted to say something about how she had to feed the baby nutrients, but he caught himself and refrained.

"How'd you like your new church?" Izzy asked. "I sure wish you would go to *Cornerstone* with us."

"Well *Living Hope* is closer to my house," Ethan replied, knowing that was only half the truth. Jezmeen hadn't told anyone but him about Ace, and he didn't feel like it was his place to share. He switched churches hoping one day Jezmeen would attend with him, and if he stayed at *Cornerstone,* he didn't think Jezmeen would ever go inside.

They walked towards Wayne who was standing by the truck with two boxes of pizza in his hands. Izzy grabbed a plastic container of salad out of the back seat. As they headed towards the door, Jezmeen flung it wide open.

"I heard your truck," Jezmeen said.

"Whose?" Wayne asked.

"Well, yours is quieter," Jezmeen replied, "so I guess it was Ethan's," she laughed.

"When are you going to replace that old thing?" Izzy asked. Then her hand flew to her mouth. "Sorry, was that rude."

Ethan chuckled and patted her on the shoulder. "No, you're right. That truck needs to go."

"Maybe when your next check from Tryton Building Products arrives, you can upgrade," Jezmeen said, as they joined her in the house.

"I still can't believe a company bought your pergola idea, and you get paid every time a kit is sold," Izzy replied. "If I didn't want to be an actress or a news anchor, maybe I'd be an inventor."

"Or maybe you'd be an interior designer like Jezmeen," Ethan said, hoping Jez didn't mind that he was leaking her big news.

"Decorator," Jezmeen corrected, as they entered the kitchen and began picking seats at the table. "I'm just a decorator. A designer has to have formal training. In Illinois, at least a two-year degree. They know more about architecture, construction, building codes, that kind of thing."

"Jez got a job as an assistant decorator at *Style Street*," Ethan interjected.

"That's so exciting, Jezmeen," Izzy bubbled. She got up, even though she had just sat down, and ran and threw her arms around her.

"Oh, you can't call me Jezmeen anymore," she replied.

"What do you mean?" Izzy asked.

"My boss, Monica, doesn't think it 'rolls off the tongue,' so she's calling me by my middle name, Marie," Jez replied.

"You can't be serious," Izzy declared. "That's so stupid. I would've just told her, 'It's my name, get over it.'"

"It's not that big of a deal. I want the job, so I'll do what it takes. So, how's school going?" Jezmeen asked Izzy.

"We had fall play try-outs this week," Izzy replied, as she grabbed two pieces of pizza, cheese stringing from the edges of the slices.

"How'd you do?" Jezmeen questioned.

"I was pretty nervous, but I'm hoping it didn't show. The cast list goes up on Monday."

"What part do you want?" Ethan asked.

"Either the oldest princess or the youngest because they have the biggest parts."

"What play are you doing?" Jezmeen asked.

"*The Twelve Dancing Princesses.* There are a lot of roles for girls, but only a few for boys, but that's okay because it's always harder to get guys to try out. Actually, one of the guys who tried out gave me a ride home. Well not him—his mom. He's not old enough to drive." Izzy rambled.

"Why didn't your grandma pick you up?" Wayne interjected, knowing it had been her responsibility.

"I think she forgot. She was sleeping in her chair when I got home. I asked her why she didn't answer her cell phone. She said she didn't hear it. I checked it, and the volume was turned off. She's so bad with technology," Izzy groaned.

"Why didn't you call me?" Wayne asked.

"I knew you were working, plus Brady offered, and he's cute," Izzy smiled. "If he gets the part of the soldier, and I get the part of the oldest princess, then we get married—in the show of course, not in real life. Speaking of getting married, when are you two tying the knot?" she asked between a bite of pizza.

Everyone in Ethan's family had already learned of their engagement a week earlier, after she said 'yes.'

Ethan glanced at Jezmeen. "I hope soon."

"And I say, 'no rush,'" Jezmeen replied.

"But, Jez, if you get married then I can have you as a sister forever," Izzy pleaded.

"Sister-in-law," Wayne interjected.

"Sister-in-love," Izzy corrected. "What kind of wedding do you want?"

Jezmeen speared a forkful of lettuce as she thought about it. She didn't need to tell the group she had no desire to be married.

"Simple. Intimate. Understated."

"A girl who likes a ring like *that* wants to do 'understated?'" Wayne teased.

"You will invite your mom, right?" Izzy asked, ignoring her dad's comment.

"I don't know," Jezmeen replied, concentrating on her salad.

"Oh, you've got to. I mean it just wouldn't be right if you didn't. Even if she was a stinky rotten mother, she'd want to know about it."

Jezmeen had shared pieces about her past with Izzy. Izzy's own mother was in jail, and they both felt great disappointment in their mother-daughter relationships.

"I think Jezmeen should do what's the best for her," Ethan interjected.

"Thank you," she said earnestly, casting her gaze towards him.

"Well, whatever you do, I hope I get to be a flower girl or something," Izzy continued.

"Aren't you too big to be a flower girl," Ethan bantered.

"You'd be my maid of honor," Jezmeen replied.

"Seriously?" Izzy burst out. "That's like for your best friend. I'm your best friend? Oh, that is so sweet. I'll do it."

Izzy jumped out of her chair for the second time and hugged Jezmeen's shoulders again.

"Now we can go shopping for dresses! I can't wait."

"Slow down, Isabella. Jezmeen said she's in no hurry to plan anything, so don't rush her," Wayne interjected.

"You can rush her," Ethan whispered loud enough for everyone to hear.

Chapter Four

Like a child, Jezmeen swirled around in Monica's desk chair—then thought better of it. Maybe Monica had cameras in her office, so she could observe "the help." That seemed like something she would do. It was Jezmeen's first day with clients, and she hadn't been so happy since...well she couldn't think of when. She'd taken Monica's advice and left her engagement ring at home. Nick's diamond necklace, too.

She hadn't seen her former boyfriend, Nick, since their "overnight" back in August when Ethan had kicked her out. Sure, she'd over-medicated Ethan's office manager, Claire, but it had been an accident. Thankfully, she had an ally, and Ethan's half-sister, Izzy, reasoned with Ethan to take her back. Jez was back to Ethan's home within a day, but it didn't erase the time she'd spent with Nick. She hadn't told Ethan where she went that night, and she didn't plan to.

Dressed in cream pants, cream heels, and a sleek mauve top, she felt attractive but wondered how long she could pull off the tight clothes. She'd make it work as long as she could. Her body had always been one of her greatest assets. Jezmeen was meeting with Charles Noble at ten-thirty, and she was ready with a list of questions from Monica. After her training with Ms. Taylor, Jez wondered if Monica would micromanage her client appointments, but she hadn't called...yet.

Jezmeen heard a knock on the door, and as it swung open, she saw the store manager, Gabrielle, next to a lean man in his fifties with a round face, tortoise shell glasses, and thinning light brown hair.

"Marie, this is Mr. Noble. He's here for the consultation," Gabrielle smiled.

It took Jezmeen a second to respond to the new name. "Hello," she replied, standing up and walking over to shake his hand. "I'm Marie Williams. Nice to meet you, Charles."

"My clients often ask me where they should sit," Charles smiled, as he peered at the two white chairs facing the desk. "Now I'm wondering which one to choose."

"Either is fine," Jez replied warmly.

"That's exactly what I say to my clients," Charles chuckled.

Any nervousness Jez had melted away. "I'm excited to work on your space, Charles. I hear you are new to Springfield, so welcome."

"Actually, I'm just returning. I grew up here. Moved away for college. Got married and settled in the St. Louis area. My wife, Katherine, passed away a year and a half ago, and my parents are in an assisted living facility, so I came to be near them," Charles said, picking the seat on the right.

"I'm so sorry to hear about your wife, but it sounds like you are a wonderful son," Jez replied.

"I don't know about that. I felt led to come."

Jezmeen didn't know how to respond, so she forged ahead.

"Tell me about your new office space."

"It's in the Lindbergh Plaza, so it's not exactly new construction. The last owners were accountants. It's about 2,000 square feet. There are two separate offices and a reception area."

Jezmeen jotted down notes as fast as he shared them. "What colors do you like?" she asked, looking up with a smile.

"Well, you're the expert, but I think blues and greens are calming."

Jezmeen nodded in agreement as she wrote. "So, if you have two offices, what do you plan to do with the second one?"

"For right now, I'll be working alone, but I'd like to hire another counselor to join me in practice. So, I guess you'll need to decorate both."

"And what's important to have in the offices?"

"In my last location, I had a desk off to one side. I don't sit at it when I'm with clients, but I use it when I'm alone. A few comfortable chairs would be nice. And I'll need a couch. Could I be a counselor without one?" Charles joked.

Jezmeen laughed simultaneously. "How long have you practiced?" she asked, deviating from the brief, out of curiosity.

"Thirty years."

Jezmeen felt young, or Charles was old, she rationalized. She was almost twenty-nine, and Charles had been in the same line of work her whole life.

"You either have a lot of discipline, or you really like what you do," she replied.

"It's probably a bit of both. There were some clients I'd worked with for over ten years in St. Louis. So, I'm sad to discontinue the journey with them, but I'm excited to start over here managing my own private practice."

"Do you work with certain age groups?' Jezmeen asked, thinking about the design again. She was veering from Monica's list of questions, but she thought the information would be helpful.

"Mostly adults. Some teenagers. I don't work with children."

"We'll make sure the design style reflects your clientele," Jezmeen said aloud as she wrote. "And is there artwork you'd like featured?"

"I'm not sure who I talked with on the phone when I made the appointment, but I mentioned I'm a Christian counselor. I use scriptures with my clients, so that kind of thing would be nice." Charles put his forefinger into the air. "I'll need a bookshelf," he added suddenly. "Just thought of that. I have quite a collection."

Jezmeen bit the end of the pen with her teeth, thinking. She wanted to veer off the brief again. "Could you walk me through a typical workday?"

"Usually I'm the one asking the probing questions," Charles laughed. "But I will happily do that. First I grab myself a cup of coffee."

Jezmeen jotted a note about creating a drink station for him.

"Then I pull up the notes I have for the day's clients on my computer. Then my client will come in, I'll work with that person for fifty minutes, and repeat the process until I have a break, or the day is done."

"Do you eat lunch at your desk?"

"Mostly, yes."

"So, would it be helpful to have a mini refrigerator or a microwave?"

"Absolutely."

"It sounds like a 'break area' would be helpful to have."

"Definitely, but I don't know where that would fit within the floor plan."

"Well, our next step is to tour the space itself, so I'll have a better idea after that."

Jezmeen continued down the list of questions from Monica, touching on lighting, the reception area, budget, and timeframe. The hour passed quickly, and when Jezmeen glanced at the clock on the wall, she was surprised it was almost noon.

"I'm sorry we ran long," Jezmeen apologized. "I had hoped to go through the store with you, so you could point out things you like and dislike. That helps me get a feeling for your style preference." Jezmeen also knew if she could sell Charles on *Style Street's* wares, Monica would be pleased.

"I'm meeting my sister for lunch today, but I'd be glad to do that another time. My schedule is fairly free until the office is complete."

"Oh, you have a sister in town?"

"Yeah, one of those older, bossy ones," he joked. "Actually, she's pretty great. One of the advantages of moving closer is that I get to see her more often. Do you have any siblings?" Charles asked, standing up.

"Nope. I'm a lonely only."

"Did you ever wish you had a brother or sister?"

"More times than you can imagine. That or a different mom," Jezmeen laughed.

"Hmmm. Sounds like an interesting story. I'd like to hear it sometime."

"Sure," Jezmeen said with casual indifference as she walked Charles towards the exit.

Ethan opened the bedroom door and quietly made his way to the office on the second floor, across the hall from where Jezmeen slept. It was his third autumn running Adams Landscaping, although the first season barely counted. He'd come so far, personally constructing five greenhouses, a storefront, and overseeing a staff of four.

Having been through all four seasons multiple times, he knew the ebb and flow of the work calendar. The month of October was particularly busy, with trees losing their leaves and homeowners looking to get projects done before winter. The stress of the long hours made setting his spiritual foundation in the morning crucial.

Ethan had become a follower of Jesus Christ two months earlier, after God spared his business when a tornado ripped over Farmingdale Road, touching everything else in its path. But he had been wrestling spiritually for years before his conversion. Finding out that he was to be a father made his newfound faith even more of a priority. There was so much to pray about now that he was engaged and would soon become a father.

When Jezmeen first shared that she was pregnant, he was angry. They'd been broken up at the time, and Jezmeen was looking for a new place to stay. Ethan had discovered she'd stolen money from his business and lied to him about it, tried to manipulate the neighbors into selling their home so she could turn it into a Bed and Breakfast, and even interfered with his assistant Claire's insulin pump one night when she happened to be their guest. It could have caused Claire to end up in the hospital—or worse, but thankfully God alerted Claire to the danger.

Claire had been forgiving, which made it easier for him to do the same. But he still wouldn't have coupled himself to Jezmeen had she not been pregnant. Even then, it took God's leading.

Ethan had been pulling bindweed that attached itself to the air-conditioning unit, one evening while he was thinking about what to do. There was so much overgrowth of the emerald vine he almost didn't notice the *Rosa Carolina* hidden underneath. The beautiful Carolina Rose was a "species rose," naturally occurring with no help from man.

With five bright pink petals and a saffron-colored pistil, it was a stunning surprise. He stopped to inspect its beauty, and as he cradled the flower, he remembered the exact verse he'd read that morning. "Let the wheat and the weeds grow together until harvest."

Ethan wasn't sure if Jezmeen was wheat or weed, but he knew God wasn't done with her, so he wouldn't be either. Since that day, he'd recommitted himself to Jezmeen. He just hoped that the feeling of obligation would pass, and a deeper love would form in its place. As he eased into his black leather chair at the desk, he bowed his head to pray when he heard a rapping at the door.

"Something's wrong," Jezmeen said with concern.

Chapter Five

Ethan looked up in alarm. "Are you okay?" he asked.

"The zipper on my suitcase is stuck," Jezmeen replied.

"That's all?"

"Well, I can't get dressed until I open it."

Ethan followed Jezmeen across the hall into the guest bedroom. A big, black suitcase lay on the double bed.

"Why haven't you hung them in the closet?" Ethan asked, while he tugged at the toggle.

"It's going to be cold out today, so I need to get into my fall stuff."

"No wonder you brought four suitcases when you moved in."

"One for each season."

Ethan put his weight against the bulging bag and tried the zipper again—this time with success.

"Come to think of it, when you moved into the trailer with me all you brought was suitcases," Ethan said, as he pointed to the three bags on the floor of the closet.

"I travel light."

"How is it that you always look like you have an endless wardrobe?"

"I'm good at mixing and matching," Jez said as she ruffled through the clothes in the open case.

"Why are you up so early?" Ethan asked. The bedside clock read six, and Jezmeen didn't usually get up with the sun.

"I have an appointment at nine, and I wanted to do some sketching before I go."

"I thought Monica was doing all the designing?"

"She is, but it can't hurt to offer some of my ideas."

"I know she'll see your talent," Ethan replied. "Hey, do you mind if I pray for you and the baby?" he asked.

"I guess it's okay," Jezmeen said warily.

"Why don't you sit down?"

"Is it going to be a long prayer?" Jez asked with a cocked eyebrow.

Ethan laughed. "None of mine are."

Jezmeen plopped onto the end of the bed and closed her eyes. Ethan rested his hand on her shoulder.

"Father, thank you for Jezmeen and the new life growing inside her. Please watch over them both today. Help me be aware of what she needs and help me show her how much I care about her and this baby.

46

Give her wisdom for her client appointment this morning and help her to feel your peace wherever she goes. Amen."

When Ethan finished, he noticed Jezmeen was rubbing her temple.

"You okay?" Ethan asked.

"I just have a headache, but there's aspirin in the medicine cabinet."

"I thought you weren't supposed to take that stuff when you're pregnant."

"Oh right," Jez replied hastily.

"I read that you could use a cold or warm compress. Do you want me to make you one?" Ethan asked from the doorway.

"Nah. I'm sure it will go away after I eat something."

"Okay, but if that doesn't work, let me know."

Ethan turned to go, glancing again at the suitcases in the closet and wondering how many times Jez moved with just her clothes.

"I'm going to go take a shower, but I'll make us some eggs when I'm done," he said.

Jezmeen felt bloated from the big breakfast Ethan prepared, but her headache was more troublesome. The throbbing in her temple wouldn't stop. After she grabbed her new briefcase, a gift from Wayne and Izzy, out of the backseat, she hit the automatic lock button to her car. She was ten minutes early for her meeting with Charles, and it felt like her first day of high school—fear and excitement mingling together.

Her black heels clicked against the peach-colored tile as she entered the atrium that was shared between the three offices in the building. Each business had their name listed on the glass doors that separated the spaces. An investment company and a lawyer were to be Charles' new neighbors. *Tony Weshko, C.P.A.,* was still stenciled on the glass door where Charles would practice.

Jezmeen tried the handle, but it was locked. There was a padded bench next to the door, so she sat down. She'd gotten a copy of the floorplan from the realtor who sold the place, and she'd spent the first few hours of the morning mapping out where furniture could go and how lighting could be used to create the right ambiance. The walk through with Charles would help her see if her vision matched reality.

She heard the whirr of a leaf blower outside and thought about Ethan. He'd been so sweet to her—making her breakfast and praying for her. It was the first time, since elementary school, that she was in a committed relationship, and it wasn't about her appearance…or what she could provide. And that made her uncomfortable. If she didn't owe Ethan anything, where was her value? Jezmeen reached to find the file for the Noble project when she heard a voice.

"Marie?"

She continued to search for the folder.

"Marie?"

She looked up.

"Charles," she exclaimed, still not used to her alternate name. "Good morning."

"I'm sorry to keep you waiting," he said, putting a key into the lock.

"I just got here myself."

He held the door open for her, and she walked past him into the small reception area. The first thing she noticed was the faded maroon carpet with a gold fleur-de-lis pattern running through it. Charles must have noticed her stare.

"I wish my budget allowed for new flooring," he said apologetically. "It's pretty bad, isn't it?"

"I'm sure Monica and I can come up with something," Jez replied. She had a feeling if Monica was there, she wouldn't be happy that Jez tried to take any credit for the project.

"Now will I be working with Monica, too?" Charles asked.

"She'll be here in three weeks to check out the final reveal, but don't worry, we'll be working hand in hand to help your space become exactly what you want it to be."

"I trust you and Monica explicitly. If Katherine was here, she'd be the one to help me with all this."

"Was she a counselor, too?" Jez asked sensitively.

"No, but she could have been one," Charles smiled. "She was a writer for the St. Louis Post-Dispatch. Every day she asked people questions, and she was good at it."

"I bet you miss her."

"Terribly."

Charles worked to hide the sadness in his voice. "But you seem to be pretty good at asking questions yourself. Where'd you learn the skill?"

"Bartending," Jez replied, taking out the file she had been looking for and the fancy laser measuring tool.

"How long have you been an interior decorator?"

Jezmeen put the laser measure against the corner of one wall and pushed a button. "I've enjoyed designing since I was a kid," she replied, hoping that Charles wouldn't press further. "And you told me the other day you've been a counselor for many years. How'd you get into the field?"

"I always enjoyed analyzing relationships and understanding how the human brain works with the body. It's been very challenging. But I've stayed with it because it can also be really rewarding."

"How so?" Jezmeen asked and then jotted down the length of the wall before moving to the next corner.

"It wasn't until my wife died, when I went through intense therapy of my own, that I realized how healing it can be. So many people lack hope and joy, and I get to help restore those."

"That is a gift," Jezmeen said, as she slipped the measuring tape into her pocket. "Well, I've got what I need here, how about we move into the offices," Jez said. "Which one do you want—the office with one window or two?"

"I thought you hadn't been here before?"

"Your realtor emailed me a copy of the floor plan."

"Impressive," Charles replied as they walked into the small hallway. "Two windows, please."

"Good choice," Jezmeen said, heading to the right.

"Did you grow up around here, Marie?" Charles asked, making small talk as she went to work measuring the room.

"Born and raised."

"Do you have a lot of family in the area?" he asked.

"Not anymore. My grandma died when I was little, and Sherry moved to Texas quite a while ago."

"Who's Sherry?"

51

"My mom. If you could call her that."

Jezmeen stopped measuring and pursed her lips. "We'll need light-filtering blinds in both rooms, won't we? I hate to block the view, but I know you mentioned at our consultation that everything's about privacy."

"Excellent catch. I didn't even think of that until you brought it up."

Jezmeen resumed getting the dimensions of the windows.

"Where does your mom live?" Charles asked, resuming the conversation.

"San Angelo."

"Is that close to Dallas?"

"I don't know. I've never been. My mom's not much of a hostess." Jezmeen jotted some notes onto the file. "I remember on my tenth birthday she pulled out a box of Little Debbie snack cakes from our pantry and stuck a candle in one of them. At least she remembered that year," she laughed.

"You probably didn't laugh back then," Charles replied.

"No, but at least I stopped crying." Jezmeen scanned the room. "Well, I think I'm done in here, let's head to the other office."

For the next half-hour Jezmeen wrote down all the numbers she'd need to pass along to Monica and discussed some of her own ideas with Charles. As he locked the front door behind them, he asked, "So, where do we go from here?"

"Monica will draw up a plan in the next few days, and then we'll need to touch base either here or back at *Style Street* to finalize approval."

"I'll be looking forward to seeing what you come up with," he replied. "Oh, and Marie, when's your birthday?"

"It's actually in a few weeks, why?"

"It seems that you deserve much more than a Little Debbie snack cake, and I wondered if it was nearing."

Chapter Six

"Ethan," called a sweet voice.

The first Sunday in October was crisp. Ethan had been staring at the clear blue sky as he walked to his truck, but he turned at the sound of his name.

"Ariana," he replied, catching sight of the gorgeous worship leader.

"You really scooted out of there this morning," she said breathlessly. Ariana handed Ethan a set of stapled papers. "Pastor David wanted me to give these to you. He said it would help answer your question about the genealogy of Jesus. He would have brought it himself, but one of the members of the class asked for prayer."

"Thanks," Ethan replied, taking the papers from her. He noticed Ariana undo and redo the top button of her red shirt methodically and wondered if she was nervous. He felt flattered if that was the case. That never happened before his laser surgeries. "Well...thanks," he said again, not knowing what else to say.

"Did you enjoy class today?" Ariana asked, pulling him back into conversation.

"Yes, did you?"

"Most of it I've heard before. I'm taking the class because I like David's teaching style. And he and his wife have been so kind to me since I moved here."

"How long ago was that?" Ethan asked as Ariana strolled with him down the row of parked cars.

"I moved here two years ago. I got a divorce. Bad situation. But I have a nice apartment and a good job here, now."

"Where do you work?"

"Koke Mill Medical Center. I'm a 'patient coordinator.' You know everything these days has to have a fancy title. Basically, I'm a medical receptionist."

"Well, as a former medical transcriber, I feel your pain," Ethan grinned.

"What? You were a medical transcriber? That was one of the careers I was thinking of going into when I moved here. I'd love to hear more about your experience in the field."

"Sure, anytime."

"What do you do now?" she asked as they stopped by the side of his truck.

Ethan pointed to the magnetic sign on the door.

"You run a landscaping company?" she said in awe.

"Entering my third year."

"How far do you travel?"

"Depends on the job."

"Well, my parents live in Staunton, and they have been wanting to have some bushes removed and new ones put in."

"That's about an hour away?"

"If you're going the speed limit," Ariana winked.

"Let me grab you a business card," Ethan said, opening the driver's side door and reaching into the middle console. When he turned back around, he found Ariana picking at the skin on her hand.

"I have a job in Hillsboro in a few weeks, and that's not too far from Staunton. So, if your parents want a quote, tell them to give me a call," Ethan said.

"Thanks. I'll do that," she smiled broadly. "I was hoping you'd ask David some more tough questions after class. I've been a Christian since I was teenager, and you really made me think."

"Well, there's more where they came from," Ethan said. He glanced at his watch.

"You have a lunch appointment again?"

"Every Sunday."

"That's too bad. I was going to ask if you wanted to grab something with me...and Pastor David and his wife. They're really lovely," Ariana paused as if she wanted to say something more and then thought better of it. "Well, I'll let you go. See you next week."

Sitting across from one another at the kitchen table, Ethan glanced at the article from Pastor David while Izzy took her time studying the chess board. The dishwasher whirred quietly in the background. Wayne had left to run an errand, and Izzy had begged him to let her stay after lunch. Wayne was to come and get her when he was done. Jezmeen was laying down upstairs, after complaining of a stomachache at lunch.

Izzy made a move, so Ethan set down the papers to take his turn. "So, how's play practice going?" Ethan asked, as he moved his rook.

"Great. I still can't believe I got a lead role."

"I can. You're a natural."

"Aww. That is so sweet. You and Jezmeen have to come to opening night."

"When is it?"

"Friday November fifteenth."

"I'll tell Jez."

"I still can't believe Brady is my *father*. Can you believe Noah Carstone got the part of the prince? He's only a seventh grader."

"He must be talented."

"He is, but he's nowhere near as good-looking as Brady. But the good news is that my grandma is letting me get a ride home from Brady's mom every week."

"How come?"

Izzy captured one of his pawns, picked it up, and laid it on her side of the board.

"You really need to brush-up on your skills, bro. You left that guy wide open."

"Hey, I'm an only child. Who do you think I had to play chess with?"

"If you do recall, I am an only child, too," Izzy retorted.

"Well, where did you learn to play?"

"My Grandma," Izzy replied. "She hasn't played in a long time though. Can you believe she says I cheat? That is so not true. I *don't* cheat. Never have. Never will. She just keeps forgetting the rules, so we don't play anymore. That's why she's letting me go home with Brady's mom."

"Huh?" Ethan asked, not following.

"I think she's forgotten the way to the school or back or something, and she doesn't want to admit it. I told Dad that, but I'm not sure he believed me. He said every time he talks with her, she seems fine. He said she forgets a word now and then or the name of a place, but he said that's normal at seventy-nine."

"How long has she been like that?"

"I don't know. Since I rotated between you and my dad at the end of the summer, I guess it seemed really noticeable once I got back."

"Do you want me to do anything about it?"

"What can you do?"

"I don't know? Talk to Wayne."

"Maybe. Let me think about it. What's up with Jez?"

"What do you mean?" Ethan took one of Izzy's pieces. "Left it wide open," he teased, and she punched his arm playfully.

"She just hasn't seemed like herself," she replied, studying the board.

Ethan longed to tell her about the baby, but he knew Jez would be furious. Jez told him they could consider sharing the news after the ultrasound in a few weeks.

"Could be stress from her new job," Ethan offered.

"Yeah," Izzy replied, sounding unsure. "Just keep taking good care of her. I need her to get healthy, so we can go pick out dresses."

Jezmeen blankly stared at the decorating magazine. She sat propped up in bed against two pillows. They'd eaten fried chicken for lunch, but she had felt sick to her stomach since Ethan's prayer over her before they both left for church.

Sure, going to church for her meant watching her adopted son walk in and out of the building, but she never missed a Sunday. There were times in the past that seeing Ace was all that kept her going. Being pregnant at seventeen hadn't been easy, but it got harder when her boyfriend, Steven, left her three months before the due date. They'd been living in his apartment, so she quickly became homeless, forcing her to move back in with her mom and her mom's "flavor of the month."

She'd planned to keep Ace and even decorated his nursery in the apartment. When Steven left, all the trust she'd placed in humanity departed with him. She'd met Steven when she was a freshman in high school, and he was a senior. The band of red and black ink tattooed on his bicep, like a ring of fire, caught her eye in art class.

Just like her, his homelife was tumultuous, and they easily found solidarity with each other. He was her safe place from the storms, and when he held her in his arms, all her worries seemed to fade away. She loved him deeply, and all would've been fine, if she hadn't gotten pregnant. At least that's what she told herself.

Jezmeen put down her magazine and opened the top drawer of the nightstand, retrieving a flowery spiral-bound notebook with an inner pocket. She pulled out the three pictures inside. The first one was of her and Steven at her freshman homecoming dance. They never went to another dance again. He said it wasn't his "thing."

The next picture was her ten-year old self hugging Patches, a mutt with brown spots muddying his white fur. Patches moved in with Tom. One of only two guys her mom dated that she actually liked. Tom was always nice to her…even attentive just because he cared, not because he was trying to impress Sherry.

Patches left with Tom a few months later. He gave her a fashion drawing set when they said goodbye. She sketched hundreds of outfits using that present before it got lost in a move.

The final picture was the sonogram of Ace at twenty weeks. She could see Ace's rib bones and the outline of his lips, nose and forehead. Jezmeen had forgotten the date was typed in white against the black background at the top. If she was going to share it with Ethan, she'd need to cut that part off. At the thought, her nauseous stomach spoke to her again.

With Ethan being so attentive and kind, it felt wrong to lie to him, but she couldn't admit the truth. Not when everything she wanted was falling into place. She finally had a ring on her finger, a beautiful home, a hard-working man, and for the moment he didn't even require anything from her.

Filing the pictures back into the pocket, Jezmeen noticed "the list." All the men she lived with after Steven were on it. Somehow keeping a record made it seem more legitimate. She'd grown up watching her mom prostitute herself in exchange for a place to stay. "The list" duped her into believing she hadn't become a carbon copy of Sherry.

Jesse was number one—the first boyfriend after Steven. But he turned out to be an alcoholic. It didn't matter much until a bottle came flying one night and cut her forehead. Jesse thought she came home too late from work and convinced himself she was with another man. While that hadn't been the case, the ten tiny stitches in her hairline still reminded her why she moved on to number two, Mario.

Flirtatious Mario was obviously as good at attracting the ladies as she was the gentlemen. He cheated on her for months before he said she'd been replaced. She'd known about the others but had no place to go. Staying, and being used as a disposable item, made her feel invisible. Those memories were ones she wished she could erase, but even if she removed names from "the list," the scar tissue was on her heart.

Ten years of these "relationships" formed so many callouses, nothing could touch her now…so she thought. Only her stomach hurt. At least she hadn't married Chad Angermann, she giggled silently. Chad hadn't actually been an angry man. He'd just moved. She thought about Monica and how she'd refused to take her ex-husband's last name. Adams was a nice, sensible last name though, she reasoned, thinking of Ethan… then the phone rang.

Chapter Seven

"Marie? Monica Taylor. We need to go over the Noble project," she said without even a hello.

"Sure, let me grab the file."

Jezmeen scurried over to her briefcase and retrieved the folder and a pen before returning to the call.

"Just some advice, Marie, you didn't need to go get the file. I'm going to send you an attachment *right now* so we can look at the floor plan together," Monica said coolly.

Jezmeen groaned inwardly at her incompetence while she silently opened her email.

"Now you'll see we're going to go with the Cortland blue on the walls. I think that will be perfect once we paint the woodwork white. I've decided to have Charles and his future partner share a desk area in the waiting area. It can double as a reception desk to take payments and also be their workspace when they're not in their offices."

Jezmeen wondered what Charles would think of that—he seemed to prefer a workspace in his own office. But Monica was the expert, and it was a creative use of space.

"You'll notice I put a beautiful sideboard and hutch at the end of the hallway between the two offices. That's going to act as their break room of sorts."

"Oh, you used my idea!"

"What are you talking about?"

"That was in the floorplan I sent—"

"I don't need help from a rookie, Marie."

Jezmeen felt confused. Surely Monica wouldn't have thought to put in that feature without her notes. And Monica picked the exact sideboard and hutch she sent with *her* design.

"But what about—"

"Let's move on Marie," Monica curtly cut her off. "When I did all the office spaces for the Jaguar dealership in Naperville...You have heard of Jaguar, haven't you?"

"Of course," Jezmeen replied, trying to hold in her frustration.

"Well, when I designed their offices, I didn't need your help. And it all went just fine. They loved the design. They especially loved their chairs, so I'm going to go with the same executive high backs for the counselors, only in a stationary version."

Jezmeen scanned the picture included on the email and was conflicted. Charles asked for a chair with good ergonomic support. While the one Monica picked looked nice, it didn't seem like it would be kind on the back.

"Monica," she interjected. "Charles mentioned it was really important to have excellent lower back support since he sits all day."

"Yes, *dear*, I saw that," she replied condescendingly. "I know you're still new at this, so here's your lesson for the day. The client doesn't always know best. Our job is to make the room look good. And like I said, *everyone* at Jaguar just raved about these chairs."

"Okay," Jezmeen replied with doubt.

"Just keep in mind that you were hired to *follow* my lead. I give the plan. You execute it. Don't make it so hard on yourself."

Over the next ten minutes, Monica continued to explain her choices, and Jezmeen listened dutifully.

"I think Charles will be very pleased when you present the design to him. I'm going to email you a link of *me* doing a client presentation, so please watch it before your appointment with him," Monica said, wrapping up the conversation.

Jezmeen wondered what to do if Charles pushed back on anything, but she was too afraid to ask.

"On a different note. I'm happy to see you've learned from me how to recruit new clients," Monica continued. "Gabrielle sent me your work schedule for the week, and of course I don't miss a detail. I noted the two new jobs ahead. Did the clients mention they saw my work featured in the Naperville Sun?"

"No," Jez replied, fully aware she secured the business all on her own.

"Well, the article ran in the paper a few months back, but word travels. Now Marie, my trip to Springfield is in three weeks. So, if you have any hang-ups about finishing the Noble project or the Amani's nursery at that time, let me know. I'll do a *thorough* walk-through of the spaces. I hope you're capable of following directions."

"I went down the list step-by-step," Claire said from the cash register in the new storefront.

Ethan's administrative assistant was trying to get the credit card reader to work. It had gone offline mid-morning, and Ethan stopped by to help her get it running again during his lunch break.

"Did you press the 1,5, and 9 all at the same time?" Ethan asked, looking over her shoulder.

"I thought I did."

Ethan tried it, and the screen asked for a password.

"You have the golden touch," Claire smiled. She entered the password and then pressed one to recalibrate the machine. "Sorry you had to come back just to do that."

"No worries," he replied. "How'd the morning go?"

"It was pretty slow, so I got caught up on sending out invoices."

"It won't be too long before I lose you again," Ethan said, remembering how Claire had pursued a teaching job in China the year before.

"I'll be here until Christmas," she protested.

"I'm thankful for that. I never handle my accounts as well as you do. When is Tyler coming home?" Ethan asked, glancing at her engagement ring.

"He'll be in Springfield a few days before Christmas. After that we'll spend a week with his parents in Iowa."

"And then you both fly to Tianjin?" Ethan asked.

She nodded an affirmation.

"Have you and Tyler decided where you'll live once you're married?" he asked.

"Not yet."

"I think we may-" Claire was interrupted when the chimes above the double doors rang.

"Ariana," Ethan said, recognizing the dark-haired beauty.

"Ethan! I didn't expect to see you here," Ariana replied, striding towards the cash register. "I'm on my lunch break from work. My parents wanted me to stop by and check out your inventory."

"Claire, this is Ariana...Thompson, isn't it?"

"Good memory," she said as she shook hands with Claire.

"Claire's my office manager, even though I can't get her a proper office," Ethan chuckled.

"And I know Ethan from church," Ariana interjected.

"Ariana is a worship leader," Ethan added.

"Do you mind showing me what you have in the way of shrubs?" Ariana asked Ethan.

"Sure. They're in 'The Green Jungle,'" Ethan said.

"Creative," Ariana remarked.

"All the hoop houses have names. Just something I did when I built them," Ethan said as he led her towards the exit.

"Nice to meet you, Claire," Ariana called over her shoulder.

The October afternoon was cloudy, and the sky hinted at rain, as they headed to the first greenhouse in the row of five.

"I hear you're headed to Staunton in a few weeks," Ariana said.

"I'm glad your parents decided to go with Adams Landscaping."

"They said you offered a fair price."

Ethan swung the door to the "The Green Jungle" open for Ariana.

"If I remember correctly, your parents have some overgrown blue holly, and they want to plant something new."

"I grew up in that house, and that's all I can remember being out front."

Ariana and Ethan headed down the first row of black containers brimming with life.

"Since you'll need something that can handle full sun, I'd recommend boxwoods or burning bushes."

He led her toward the back corner. The boxwoods were still small. With a growth rate of only about an inch per year, most people passed them over in favor of larger plants.

"It will take a few more years to get a mature look with these," Ethan said as Ariana eyed them. "However, the spirea does well in full sun, and I have some nice sized ones over here."

"Maintaining all this must take a lot of work," Ariana said.

"Thankfully Claire takes a huge burden off me, so I can deal with the client jobs, and I have a younger sister who works on the weekends when she can."

"I didn't know you had a sister," Ariana exclaimed. "I have a younger sister, too. We're two years apart. How about you?"

"Twenty-two years."

"What?"

"My mom and dad were young when I was born, and Izzy, Isabella, is my half-sister. I only recently met her…and my dad."

"Wow. What's that been like?"

"Getting to know my dad and half-sister?"

"Yeah."

"Pretty incredible, actually. My dad is a Christian. He's been a great influence. And my sister, well, everyone who meets Izzy loves her."

"That's great," Ariana said, continuing down the row. Ethan noticed her pull at the hair on her arm but didn't think much of it.

"Oh, these are beautiful!" Ariana exclaimed, stopping in front of the hydrangeas that still held a few late blooms. "Would these work?"

"They're meant for partial shade, but they could go along the side of the house."

"I'll show my parents." Ariana pulled her cellphone out of her pocket, snapped a few pictures of the plants, and glanced at the time. "I better be getting back to work. I only get an hour, and the drive will take at least ten minutes."

"How do you like working in the medical field?" Ethan asked as he led her out the door.

"It's okay. It's a job. How'd you like transcribing?"

"Same. Paid the bills."

"I majored in psychology in college, thinking I'd become a counselor, but after I did my internship, I realized it wasn't for me. So, I have a pretty piece of paper in a frame, and I'm still clueless about what I want to do with my life."

Ethan didn't know how to respond, so he remained silent.

"Pastor David and Laurie have been praying for me, and I pray too, but I haven't had any new direction."

They reached the storefront.

"You're a good listener. Thanks for taking me around. You'll be at church Sunday?"

"That's the plan," he smiled.

Ethan brought a plate of microwaved leftovers into the family room to be near Jezmeen, even though she was engrossed in a work project. He'd arrived home late—too many yards with leaves, so they hadn't eaten dinner together.

A year ago, when she first moved into his trailer, the rhythm and flow of their shared time was much different. Back then, she hung on his every word, massaged his neck, and claimed his lips were delightful. But then Ethan realized her affection was only a cover-up, so she'd have a place to stay and money to spend. Once he saw through the act, and realized he was the victim of her attention and affection only for her own manipulative means, he told her repeatedly to drop it. Now neither of them knew what to make of their relationship, and it showed. It was almost as if they were roommates. Not that Ethan minded. It felt more honest than her false seductions.

As he sat down in the recliner, he silently asked, "How can I show her love, God?" It was his latest plea and passionate goal. *Ask her about her day.*

"How was your day?" he asked, breaking the silence.

"Tiring. I hung wallpaper for the Amanis' nursery."

"Ever done that before?"

"No, but the pattern was pretty forgiving."

"I bet we both have sore arms. Mine are from raking leaves out from behind a shed. And yours are from wallpapering. How are you liking your new job?"

"It's good," she said flatly. She'd always been a private person. Opening up to someone else meant connecting on a deeper level, so she didn't want to reveal how much she enjoyed it despite Monica's demeaning attitude.

"And how are you feeling?" he asked, aware that she had another headache in the morning.

"Fine. Oh, thanks for the ginger candies that you put in my briefcase. I ate one after breakfast, and it helped my stomachache."

"You're welcome," Ethan said, wondering if she found him remotely attractive, as he stared at her captivating face. He knew she liked the house they lived in and the salary he provided, but did she feel anything for *him*? "Do you think we should start coming up with a birth plan?" he asked. "We just have a couple more weeks before the sonogram, and then we're halfway there."

An uncomfortable expression briefly crossed Jezmeen's face. "I had an epidural with Ace. I guess I figured I'd do the same thing."

"Is that safe?"

"Lots of women get them."

"What day is the ultrasound? I don't think you told me what worked out with your schedule."

Jezmeen looked away. "I think it's on a Tuesday. I don't have my phone down here."

"It's with Dr. Wallace, right?"

"Huh?"

"Your doctor's last name is Wallace, right?"

"Oh, yeah," she said.

"Well, just let me know so I can get it on my calendar."

"Sure," she replied, looking back to her computer screen.

Ethan wondered why she seemed so troubled whenever they talked about the baby but reasoned it could be because she felt nervous about the birthing process or maybe she felt shame about giving up Ace but keeping this child. Whenever he opened the conversation, she became distant and tight-lipped.

"What now, God?" he asked the Unseen while he took a bite of his dinner. *Serve.* Serve? Ethan was used to being taken care of by his mom when he was little. And when he got older, he waited on himself. This was new.

"I'm going to get myself a drink. Can I get you one while I'm up?"

"Umm, sure. Water's fine."

Ethan set his plate on the coffee table.

"Guard my food from Chewy, okay?" Ethan knew his copper-colored cat, named after the famous Star Wars Wookie Chewbacca, probably wouldn't try to eat his rice and beans, but the chicken was a different story.

When he returned with their beverages, Chewy was curled up on the couch next to Jezmeen, aware of the plate, but not trying to pounce, thanks to Jezmeen's hand scratching his neck.

"I noticed you haven't been wearing your ring," Ethan said.

"Oh, yeah. Monica told me to leave it at home. She said it gets caught on things when you're working."

Ethan wondered about the validity of that claim but moved on. "What do you think of Monica?" he asked. "You haven't said much about her."

"She's okay. Really into herself. My clients seem to like me—but Monica, well, I never seem to please her."

"She's probably intimidated."

Jez laughed. "By me?"

"You're really beautiful," Ethan said sincerely, managing to be bold enough to hold eye contact. "And you're good at this stuff," he continued, pointing at her laptop.

"Thanks," she replied with warmth in her voice.

"That could be threatening to her."

Jezmeen was silent, as if absorbing what he said.

"Well, I guess I'll take this to my office, so you can get your work done." He picked up his plate. *Love her.* The Voice resonated in his mind.

He put down his food again and walked behind the couch where she was sitting. Acting impulsively, he pulled back her hair with one hand and rubbed her slender neck for a few minutes, easing out knots he hadn't seen with his eyes.

Taken aback by his movements, Jezmeen swung her head around. "Is this okay?" he asked nervously. It had been so long since they'd touched.

"It feels good," she said softly.

He continued his gentle movements until she seemed relaxed and then bent down and kissed her cheek.

Joy perched in Jezmeen's heart. The feeling was still so foreign to her, it caused her pause and introspection. Was it because Ethan ran a bath for her again and rubbed her sore neck the night before, or because he kissed her gently on the cheek and something within her stirred?

Either way, as she left the house, she was thankful for the spring in her step and temporary relief from the headaches and stomachaches that had been plaguing her the past few weeks.

She was meeting Charles at *Style Street* to present Monica's powerpoint and her own touch—a design board with fabric and texture samples. She knew Monica had asked her specifically not to add in her own ideas, however showing Charles his space over the computer didn't seem nearly as helpful as letting him see and touch what he could.

The afternoon would bring working on the Amani's nursery and two potential client consultations, but fresh morning energy was upon her as she pulled up Monica's power point while waiting for Charles to arrive.

As she waited for the computer to power up, she looked at the design board, and anxiety crept upon her. She was offering Charles two different choices for office chairs and an alternate example for a desk he wouldn't have to share. Certainly, it would be easier if he picked Monica's ideas because then she wouldn't have to figure out how to defy her boss, but in the end, she wanted Charles to be satisfied.

Seeing the home screen, Jezmeen clicked on Monica's presentation, then felt the dull throb of a headache forming again in her temple and groaned just as Charles walked in with a bag from the *Three Twigs Bakery.*

"I brought you some doughnuts," he said, setting the sack on her desk.

"That was so thoughtful. Thank you," Jez replied.

"The s'mores one is my favorite." Charles sat down in his usual chair. "You okay?"

"The groan?"

"Yeah."

"Oh, it's nothing. I just keep getting these temple headaches."

"Sounds like stress. Too many projects lately? Is a certain counselor working you too hard?" he grinned.

"No, and definitely no. You are a delight to work with, and I *love* my job."

"Are there any major changes in your life?"

Only a new job and lying to my boyfriend— make that my fiancé—about this pregnancy, she thought to herself.

"Why do you ask?" she questioned.

"I just know the body can be signaling warning signs with recurring aches and pains. Sometimes it's from being overwhelmed. Sometimes it's from shame or guilt. Or you could check in with your doctor to make sure it's nothing physical."

"Or I could just take two of these," she laughed, pulling out a bottle of pain medicine from her purse. She wouldn't tell Ethan and taking them in front of Charles wasn't a concern. Swallowing the pills without a glass of water, she continued. "How about we move on to the fun stuff."

Chapter Eight

The days of tight-fitting clothes were over for Jezmeen. At "week nineteen" in her pregnancy, she knew a baby bump *should* be showing—and she had to keep up the act. It had been a week since Ethan kissed her, and since then they'd had no physical contact. But even with her new wardrobe of loose-fitting clothing, the look in his eyes betrayed his distance.

He'd continued with his routine of making her breakfast and praying over her and the baby each morning, and on this day, it was no different. He hadn't acknowledged that it was her birthday, but it was likely he didn't know. They'd only been dating a short time when it had come around the year before.

His prayer was nice, Jezmeen thought as she drove to Charles' office. He didn't use flowery language or drone on and on, and she felt a calm wave wash over her while he spoke. Something about being surrounded by Christ-followers…Wayne, Izzy, Ethan…made her curious about its appeal.

The last few weeks she'd been listening to sermons on the radio. Whenever she rode with Ethan, he'd play Christian radio, so she'd come to enjoy it. Words like "everlasting peace, divine joy, and never-ending love" came up, but "sinner and salvation" were spoken too, and those references made her uncomfortable.

She'd never read the Bible, but she imagined stealing (money and men), lying, and sleeping with dozens of men would exclude her from God's "good list"—if he had one. There was something about not being wanted that felt familiar. Jezmeen certainly didn't desire to put herself in a place to receive one more rejection.

As Jezmeen pulled into the parking lot, she turned off the radio and sighed. She was fighting sadness that had become customary every October fifteenth. The majority of her birthdays had been anything but celebratory, with a mom so selfish she'd exchange Jezmeen's gifts, given by Sherry's boyfriends, to buy clothes for herself. Then, in Jezmeen's adult years, no one around her ever seemed to care or remember. At least her expectations for the day were low, and she looked forward to work.

When she entered the reception area of Charles' office space, the first thing she noticed, after inhaling the pungent odor of fresh paint, was the outdated carpet. Why was it, she wondered, that the imperfections seemed more apparent than the upgrades? To save money, Charles opted to paint the walls and trim himself. He'd already applied the Cortland blue, and he'd finished painting the baseboards for the reception area. She was inspecting his work when she heard a baritone voice in the hallway bellowing "happy birthday to you!..."

Before long, Jezmeen could see Charles approaching carrying an exquisite looking cake frosted with dozens of pastel pink roses. Walking slowly, to keep the flickering candles lit, Charles arrived in front of Jezmeen just as the song ended. Taken aback, Jezmeen wished there were chairs for the front entry so she could sit down.

"Make a wish," Charles said.

Jezmeen shut her eyes, thinking, then opened them and gently extinguished the candles, causing little billows of smoke to curl into the air and with it came the smell of burned wax.

"How did you know?" she questioned.

"I asked Gabrielle at *Style Street*. Told her you'd mentioned your birthday was coming up. Asked her if she could find out when it was, and she looked in your file."

Charles, still holding the cake that was resting inside its bakery box, looked around for a place to set it.

"I brought plates, napkins, and utensils, but I didn't think about the lack of furniture. I guess the little ladder in my office will have to do."

"What if I hadn't come in today?" Jez asked, still in shock, as she followed Charles down the hall and into his empty office.

"I know how hard you work. I figured once I texted you the baseboards were done, you'd be right in to check out my work. How'd I do with them?"

"Great. I think if you got tired of counseling, you'd make a fantastic painter."

"When Katherine and I moved into our first house, we wanted to paint every room. We'd lived in an apartment for eight years, so it felt good to be able to put our stamp on something."

"Did she help?"

"Absolutely. We were always a team."

Charles balanced the box on the second rung of the stainless-steel step.

"I'd ask if nine o'clock is too early to eat cake, but I'm curious if this tastes as good as it looks."

Charles retrieved a plastic sack in the corner of the room and pulled out the serving utensils. "I didn't know if you liked chocolate or vanilla better, so I decided to get something unique...lemon raspberry."

Charles cut into the creation, revealing tantalizing layers of bright yellow and deep red filling in between spongy white cake. Handing her a plate with a generous slice, Charles then cut himself a piece. Jezmeen took her plate and sat down against the wall. Then Charles followed suit.

"Delicious," she sighed.

"It should be. It's from *Incredibly Delicious,*" Charles chuckled.

"You mean the bakery downtown?"

Charles nodded approval.

"Thank you," Jezmeen said, looking into Charles' eyes.

"You're welcome." He held her gaze. "I figured this might be a step up from the Little Debbies," he said sincerely, slicing his cake with his fork.

"Katherine was a lucky woman. I bet you two had the best marriage."

Jezmeen licked the frosting from her fork before going in for another bite.

"The interesting thing about grief is how your brain processes all the memories. For the first few months, all I could think about was the pain in the last few days of her life. I kept remembering the feel of her bony hand in mine and how thin her face had become."

He scraped at the frosting on the side of his plate.

"But then after the fog lifted, all the happy moments poured in. Katherine almost seems more ideal in death than in life. But don't get me wrong, we weathered tough times, too."

"Listening to people from my bartending days, it seems like most marriages do."

"Probably the hardest thing, besides Katherine's cancer, was infertility. It was so unexpected, and we both dreamed of having kids." Charles looked uncomfortable, having shared personal information. "Do you want to have children one day?" Charles asked, trying to draw the focus away from himself.

"I have one," Jezmeen said softly.

"Oh, sorry, I shouldn't have assumed–"

"That's okay. I got pregnant when I was seventeen. Had him at eighteen. A couple in town adopted him."

"Is that hard?"

"Yes and no. I go to see him every week."

"Oh, it's an open adoption?"

"No," she laughed. "I just found out where he attends church, and I watch him walk in. That might seem silly to you."

"It sounds to me you're trying to connect to him in the best way you know how."

"I guess. I felt so guilty for months after giving him up. Like I was the worst person in the world. I mean who does that, right?"

"I'd say brave people do."

"It felt pretty cowardly. Like I was running from taking care of my own flesh and blood just because I was so selfish."

"Maybe you recognized that you didn't have the support system or the mental capacity to parent at the age of eighteen, and you probably found a very competent family to raise him."

"I hope so. You only know so much from paper and pictures. I met them once. They seemed nice, and he looked happy."

"Did you ever go through any sort of counseling afterwards?"

"I probably should have. Maybe my whole life would have turned out differently."

"From what I gather about your mom, she probably didn't help you process your grief."

Jezmeen laughed. "You got that right. My mom doesn't seem to have anything but selfish bones in her body."

"Why do you think she's like that?"

Charles had set his empty plate down beside him and pivoted his body to continue looking at Jezmeen.

"I don't know. Her parents were older when they had her. They had two boys much earlier in life. One of them passed away in a car accident, and I think my mom said they never really got over it. Maybe they didn't have time or energy for her? Maybe she raised herself? I don't remember much about my grandparents. I was really young when they passed away."

"If your mom was here today, what would you say to her?"

Jezmeen stared up at the ceiling, caught up in the impromptu counseling session, not minding the questions. "Why? Why couldn't she be there for me— ever. I tried to be an obedient daughter. I tried to please her. Why'd she push me to the side all the time? Never chose me over a boyfriend? Never give me the time of day? Was I really so bad to be around?"

Jezmeen felt a lump settle in her throat. Charles was silent. He noticed a tear trickling down the side of Jezmeen's nose and handed her his unused napkin.

"Is this what happens to all your clients?" Jezmeen laughed while she wiped her cheeks.

"You're not a client. You're a new friend."

"Why do you care?" she asked, searching his eyes for an answer.

"You've been carrying a heavy load for so long. It must be quite burdensome...even now."

Jezmeen cradled the cake box in her arm as she opened the door leading into the house from the garage. It was a little after five o'clock, but thanks to the fall season, it was already quite dark outside. So, when she walked into the mudroom, passing through into the kitchen, she wondered what was casting a light up ahead.

Flipping on the switch, she nearly dropped the cake, as three figures popped out from behind the island.

"Surprise!" Wayne, Izzy, and Ethan shouted.

Izzy ran over and gave Jezmeen a hug around the waist, while Ethan scurried into the sunroom, retrieving a sheet cake filled with dancing candles.

"I guess you brought your own cake to your party," he teased as he threw his gaze at the box she'd set on the counter.

"From a client," she said.

"That was thoughtf-" Izzy began before Ethan started singing. The trio sang "Happy Birthday," and for the second time in one day, Jezmeen exhaled a breath and a wish.

"As much as we'd like to start with the cake," Ethan said, as he waved away the smoke with his hand, "my dad picked you up some three-way pasta from *Bella Milano.*"

"My favorite! How did you remember?" Jezmeen asked.

"Same way I remembered your birthday," he said, tapping his head.

"Let's do presents right after we eat," Izzy interjected. "I can't wait to give you my gift."

After they'd eaten their fill of Italian, and Ethan had cleared away the dishes, Izzy handed Jez a small box decorated with marker drawings and stickers.

"Okay, I know I'm not in kindergarten, but I didn't want to give you a plain box. My grandma moved the gift bags and tissue paper, and she couldn't remember where she put them. I looked all over before giving up and deciding I'd just improvise."

"This is perfect," Jez replied.

She flipped the lid and pulled out two tickets.

"They're for my show in two weeks. I spent my own money. They were eight dollars apiece. But I wanted to treat you."

"She didn't even buy me a ticket," Wayne said.

"That's because it wasn't your birthday," Izzy retorted.

"Isabella Nicole Copeland, you are the sweetest young lady in the world," Jez said, getting up to give her a hug.

When she sat back down, Wayne slid a card across the surface of the kitchen table.

"Who would've thought all those years ago, when I met you at Finnegan's Taphouse, that you'd be my future daughter-in-law. At that time, I didn't even know I had a son," Wayne said, shooting a glance at Ethan.

Jezmeen opened the envelope and pulled out a gift card. "Money for *Bed, Bath and Beyond*. Thank you! You know how much I like shopping there."

"I'm just glad you now have a job taking other people's money and spending it on home furnishings," Ethan joked as he handed her a gift bag.

She gently removed the tissue paper on the top and lifted out a box. "*Home Designer Suite 2013*," she read.

"What is that?" Izzy asked.

"It's a computer program that lets you design floor plans," Jez explained, knowing exactly what it was.

"Her boss, Monica, doesn't let her do any of her own designing, even though she has access to the company software," Ethan said, explaining his gift choice to Izzy and Wayne.

"Why?" Izzy questioned.

"Designing is Monica's job. Implementing is mine," Jezmeen parroted.

"One more," Ethan interjected, pulling a small, wrapped box out of his jeans. "Sorry," he said, pointing to the wrinkles in the wrapping paper.

Jez gladly opened another gift, this time gasping at its contents.

"When Izzy told me she was getting you the tickets, I knew if you wore the necklace your grandmother gave you, and your engagement ring, all you'd need to complete the ensemble was diamond earrings," Ethan explained.

"These are gorgeous," Jezmeen said.

"Are those real diamonds?" Izzy asked.

"Isabella," Wayne said firmly.

"Sorry, dad, you know how things just fly out of my mouth."

Ethan laughed. "Yes, Izzy, they are real diamonds."

"I don't get to wear anything that nice for the play. All the stuff we're wearing is just costume jewelry," Izzy replied.

"Then maybe you'll have to borrow these," Jezmeen replied.

"I don't think so," Wayne quickly interjected.

"How come?" Izzy pouted.

"What if you lose them? Costume jewelry seems fine for the stage." Wayne stood up and stretched his legs. "I think I'm going to step outside for a moment."

"Everything okay with him?" Ethan asked Izzy, after he left the room.

"Yeah. He's just taken up smoking again. He used to do it all the time, but when he gave up drinking, he gave up cigarettes, too."

"Wonder why he started again?" Ethan mused aloud.

"Who knows?" Izzy replied. "At least he's not drinking."

"I think I'll turn thirty every year," Jezmeen sighed with contentment.

"But if you keep staying the same age, and I keep on counting, our age gap will be wider than five years," Ethan replied while he rubbed Jezmeen's feet, as they sat on the couch in the family room.

"You're not thirty-five yet," Jezmeen said.

"I know, but I'm close. The age difference between Izzy and the baby will be fourteen years," Ethan mused. "I wonder if Izzy will become our permanent babysitter?"

Jezmeen pulled the foot he was rubbing with a jerk. "Sorry that tickled," she replied.

"I don't know. I haven't thought about it," she said curtly.

"The sonogram is next week. Then we can tell people, right? I can't believe how many times I've almost slipped up and said something to VJ or Mark at work."

"I can't believe you haven't told Claire," Jezmeen replied. She used to be so jealous of Claire, thinking that Ethan liked her. But once Claire got engaged, she was no longer worried.

"It's actually been easier to keep it from her than my dad."

"You really don't have to go to the sonogram," Jez said.

"Are you kidding? I've been waiting for this day since I found out the news."

"But you're so busy at wor–"

"I'm going to be there."

They sat in silence for a few seconds, while Ethan's hands gently worked out tension in her muscles. The hem of Jezmeen's dress lay at her ankles, and he pushed it up slightly to begin rubbing her calves. Jezmeen took this as a sign that Ethan wanted more.

She swung her legs down to the ground and leaned into kiss Ethan, but he instantly pulled away, as if she was on fire, and looked into her eyes.

"Don't" he said.

"What?" she said leaning towards him.

He accepted her advance, and Jezmeen was pleased. She kissed, but he drew back after a moment.

"Stop," he said, blowing out a breath.

"Why?" she said edging near again.

"It's your eyes," he said.

"What?"

Jezmeen sat back against the couch. The fire extinguished.

"How can I explain it?" Ethan asked, running his hand through his hair. "It's like it's not real to you. Like you're acting in a movie or something. This isn't a game to me, Jez."

She fiddled with a tasseled cord on the throw pillow next to her, and Ethan looked up at the ceiling.

"How many men have you been with, Jez?" Ethan grimaced.

"I never thought that mattered to you," she replied coolly.

"Just because we haven't talked about it doesn't mean it hasn't mattered."

"Well, it was about to go down in history as the perfect birthday," she sighed.

"You're right. Let's drop it."

"Fifteen. Twenty. Twenty-five?" she replied, nonchalantly.

Ethan forcefully exhaled.

"Not sure your God would like it? Need this back?" she asked, twisting the ring around her finger. This wasn't how she wanted the evening to end, but somehow the conversation had taken an ugly turn.

"To be honest, I wasn't thinking about God. I just want your affection to be honest, and I figured somewhere along the way you lost the ability to feel. Or trust."

"Maybe I never had it," Jez replied cold and hard.

Ethan stood up and started pacing. "I don't know what to say."

"Here," she said, taking off the ring and setting it on the coffee table. "You're free."

He stopped in his tracks and looked at Jezmeen. "That's *not* what I want. I'm in this. Please put it back on."

He crouched down next to her. "Please."

She reluctantly reached over and retrieved the ring.

"Thank you," he said with relief.

"I can't give you what you want," Jezmeen replied, like slate, not looking at him.

"But you are—you're giving me a child…and a wife."

Jezmeen laughed darkly. "I think I've had enough of being thirty for one day. I'm going to bed."

Chapter Nine

As Ethan pulled into the Thompson's driveway, he felt thankful. With sixty-degree weather and sunshine, working at Ariana's parents' home on a Friday morning was like playtime. Transcribing medical records had been just the opposite.

Two days passed since his conversation with Jezmeen, and he'd barely seen her. She'd spent the evenings in her room—complaining of headaches or stomach aches. Ethan was anxious for the appointment with Dr. Wallace. Maybe that would get them back on track. Things had been going so well until the night of her birthday.

Tuesday afternoon couldn't come quickly enough. He had so many questions to ask...including how to help Jez with her aches and pains. And he was bursting to share the news.

Perhaps it was because he was nearing thirty-five, but he found himself excited to become a father. When birthmarks covered half his face, he'd lost hope of ever having a wife or a child. But God had been filling him with hope for his future.

After Ethan stepped out of the truck, he grabbed a small chain saw. VJ and Mark hadn't arrived yet. Ethan liked to be early, and it wasn't even eight. As he headed to the overgrown mess of blue holly, he reasoned he'd be sufficiently sore and would likely need to take pain medicine to make it through Izzy's opening night.

By the time his two assistants arrived, he'd chopped all the hedges to nubs, so he could start digging out the root balls. One day he'd like to own a stump grinder, but until that day it was done by hand, or by truck. Five of the ten hedges V.J and Mark could rope and wrangle out of the ground using their truck. It went faster that way, but not all the bushes were in a location to employ that technique. And he figured the Thompsons wouldn't be pleased if they had skid marks in their grass.

"Hey, boss," V.J hollered out the driver's side window. "Should we back 'er up?"

"Yeah. I've got the ropes in my truck," he shouted.

VJ put the vehicle in reverse when Ethan bellowed, "Whoa! Whoa! Whoa!" VJ stopped in time to see a sporty blue car entering the driveway behind him. VJ pulled over to the left side of the driveway as the blue car maneuvered around until it reached the garage, and Ethan was surprised to see Ariana. She waved to him and then grabbed a laundry basket out of the back seat.

Noticing the raven-haired beauty, VJ slid out the driver's seat and onto the grass as Ariana approached. VJ ran to her side. "Let me help you with that," he said, taking the hamper from her arms.

"Thank you."

"Ariana, I didn't expect–"

"I took the day off of work. Doing laundry at the apartment complex is such a hassle, plus it's my grandma's birthday tonight, so I told my mom I'd bake a cake. Kind of always been my thing."

"Gonna have any leftovers for the hired hands?" VJ joked, his arms hugging her laundry.

She smiled. "I think I could work that out."

"Ariana," Ethan said, "this is VJ, and my other assistant, Mark, is..." Ethan looked around for Mark, only to find him rummaging through the back of Ethan's truck. "Over there," Ethan finished.

Barely acknowledging VJ, she returned her attention to Ethan. "So, you're taking out all these bushes and putting new ones in," she said.

"That's the plan," Ethan replied.

"How long will it take?" Ariana asked.

"Hope to have it done by three. We'll see how fast these guys work," Ethan joked, throwing his glance to VJ

"Hey," VJ retorted.

"He and Mark are actually fantastic," Ethan boasted. "Just giving them a hard time."

"Well, they've got a great boss," Ariana replied. "I better let you get back to it," she said. "Thanks for carrying–"

"I've got it," VJ interjected. "Just lead the way. And if you need any help tasting frosting or anything, let me know. I'm your man."

Ariana giggled and headed to the front door. Mark joined Ethan at his side. "Looks like VJ just found someone to help him get over Sydney" he said, referring to VJ's last girlfriend.

97

"Didn't take him long," Ethan replied.

"Never does," Mark said.

The three men swapped stories about sore shoulder blades as they sat on the grassy front lawn eating their lunches. VJ's truck was filled with the uprooted bushes, and Ethan's was holding the boxwoods and hydrangeas yet to be planted, so they couldn't tailgate, like they sometimes did at noon.

"Ice constricts the blood vessels and takes down the inflammation," Ethan said before taking a swig from his water bottle.

"Ice or heat?" VJ said, calling to Ariana. Ethan turned to face the house and saw Ariana walking down the front steps carrying a container of cupcakes.

"Ice or heat?" she repeated when she stopped in front of the group.

"Yeah. Dr. Ethan Adams here is telling us that we should use ice for sore muscles, but I thought it was heat."

"Umm?" Ariana muttered.

"Ethan told me you worked at a doctor's office," VJ said.

"I do, but I just answer phones," she laughed. "I'd be happy to type out that question and get it back to a doctor or nurse. That's really what I do."

"How many doctors do you work for?" VJ asked, wanting to keep the young lady engaged for as long as he could.

"There are five in the department where I work, and then there are two physician assistants and a nurse practitioner."

"Whoa. How do you handle all those calls?"

She giggled. "I'm not the only one answering the phone. There are five of us who work at the front desk."

"You work for Memorial Health Care, don't you?" Ethan interjected. Jezmeen told him Dr. Wallace was with Memorial, and not the other two medical practices in town.

"Yeah. Why?" Ariana asked.

"Oh nothing," Ethan said. "Just trying to figure out which location a certain doctor is at. I'll just look it up on my phone."

"I can try to help," she replied. "Which doctor?"

"Wallace," he said, hoping she wouldn't know he was an OBGYN.

"He moved," she replied.

"What do you mean? Moved buildings?"

"No. He moved away. I think he had family in Indiana and got a job there."

"When?" Ethan said, shocked.

"Like a year ago."

Ethan was dumbfounded. Who had Jezmeen been going to see if she hadn't been checking in with Dr. Wallace? And why would she lie about her doctor?

VJ noticed Ethan's silence and picked up the conversation.

"Do you like your job?" VJ asked.

"It's okay," she replied.

"Ethan told me you're a singer. I'm going to have to come check out your pipes."

"Nobody's ever told me that before," she laughed.

"Did you ever want to be a famous rock star?" VJ asked.

"Sure, but what kid doesn't want to be something unattainable...ball-player, actress, you know."

"She any good, Ethan?" VJ asked.

"Very good," Ethan said, in a trance.

"Well, that settles it. I'm going to church," VJ said, leaning his hands back into the grass. "I'll sit by you and Jez."

"Who's Jez?" Ariana asked curiously.

"He hasn't told you about his fiancé?" VJ interjected.

"Jezmeen doesn't go with me on Sundays," Ethan said flatly.

"Tell Jez if I'm going, she has to go," VJ said, completely missing the fallen look on Ariana's face.

"I just wanted to share these," Ariana said, extending the container towards the men. "I better get back to help my mom with the fruit salad." Ariana turned to go.

"Hey," VJ called.

Ariane pivoted. "Thanks," VJ said, "and see you Sunday."

Once she was back inside, VJ exploded. "She is so hot. Are all girls at church that good looking? And she makes cupcakes."

"She's not into you. She likes him," Mark said, throwing his glance at Ethan.

"What are you talking about? There's no contest," VJ said. "No offense, man," he said to Ethan.

"Okay. Whatever," Mark said, taking a cupcake and unwrapping it from the paper liner.

"He's engaged," VJ continued, defending his point. "Why didn't you tell her?"

"Never came up," Ethan said.

"You want to go to church with us, Mark?" VJ continued, still on a high from interacting with Ariana. "We could have a whole Adams Landscaping pew. They still have pews in church, right?"

"We sit in chairs," Ethan replied.

"Okay, well we could have our own row."

"Rows are like twenty chairs."

"Well, then our own section," VJ said, not giving up.

"There are three of us," Ethan said.

"We could invite the mowing guy and Claire."

"Claire goes to a different church."

"Can't three be a section?"

"Sure, VJ, we can have our own section," Ethan replied.

"You in, Mark?" VJ asked.

"Nah. I have a date with my pillow. Hey, Ethan, you okay?" Mark asked, noting Ethan's dazed stupor.

"Yeah. I just need to go make a call," he replied.

"This feels like a real date," Jez smiled, as Ethan opened the passenger door for her. Then he walked around and slid into the driver's seat.

"Hope it's clean enough in here," Jez said, taking the arm of her coat and wiping a light layer of dust off the dashboard.

"Thanks for letting us take your car," Ethan replied flatly. He'd asked days earlier if they could ride to the play in her car instead of his old work truck.

After confirming with Memorial that Dr. Wallace had indeed moved, he'd been in a foul mood, and going to Izzy's show was the last thing he wanted to do. But he couldn't disappoint his sister, and he didn't want to start the evening out with a confrontation, so he held his tongue.

"How was work?" Jez asked brightly.

Ethan noted she was in a good mood. Maybe it was because they were going out. She liked socializing exponentially more than he did. When they first moved into the new home, she hosted guests at least once a week—until she learned how much he loathed it.

"Tiring," Ethan replied. "How about you?"

"Same. Were you in Springfield today?"

"No, Staunton."

"That's quite far, isn't it?"

"An hour. I was helping out someone from church."

When Jezmeen recognized Ethan wasn't going to share anymore, she took over. "Well, in the morning, I hung artwork for the Noble project, and in the afternoon, I visited the Amanis to see how they're liking the nursery. Monica should be pleased. I followed her directions to a 'T,' with the Amanis."

Ethan gently pressed the brake as they reached a stop sign, and he signaled to go left. Everything inside him burned to find out the answers to his questions, but there hadn't been time before they left. Jezmeen had been getting ready—putting on her necklace and earrings…the beautiful diamond necklace she'd told him months earlier was from her grandma.

Jezmeen noticed Ethan's silence, so she continued to carry the conversation. "Monica's coming next Friday, and the flooring for the Noble project isn't getting finished until Monday, which means all the furniture *has* to be delivered on time next week."

"Hmmm," Ethan said softly, as they neared town. No words passed for a few minutes before Jezmeen broke the stillness.

"Is everything alright?" she asked.

"To be honest, I don't know," Ethan said.

"I'm wearing the ring."

"It's not that."

"Do I dare ask what's wrong?"

Ethan mentally calculated how far they were from Izzy's school. Two minutes. Should he even—

"Dr. Wallace," he burst, not able to contain it any longer.

"What about him?"

"Have you been driving to Indiana for appointments?"

104

"What do you mean?"

"He moved a year ago, Jez."

Chapter Ten

Jezmeen was silent as Ethan pulled into the school parking lot. He turned into a row with open spaces, only to see Wayne smoking a cigarette outside of his truck.

"I shouldn't have brought that up. Later would have been better."

Jez remained mute. Ethan sighed as he pulled into the spot next to his dad.

"Could you grab the flowers?" he asked, and then he zipped up his emotions and his coat as he got out of the car.

"Hey, dad," Ethan said, extending his hand.

Wayne put the cigarette next to his side and shook Ethan's hand.

"Evening, Wayne," Jez said, joining them.

"Like the earrings," he replied, taking one last drag of his cigarette before casting it to the ground and stomping the flame. "I don't want to be responsible for starting a forest fire," he joked.

"Yeah, I heard about the one that's going in California right now," Ethan said.

"Supposedly it got started from one of these things," Wayne said, grinding the toe of his boot into it.

"It's amazing how something so small can do so much damage," Ethan replied, as they started walking towards the entrance to the school. "I didn't think you could smoke on school grounds."

"I don't think I can. It's just that these things are so annoyingly addictive."

"How's Izzy doing?" Jezmeen asked.

"She's nervous."

"You, too?" Jez questioned.

"Can you tell," he laughed sheepishly.

"I just know if it was my daughter on opening night, I'd be nervous," Jez said, patting Wayne on the shoulder. "She'll be great."

Ethan was amazed at how well Jezmeen hid her thoughts, and he wondered how many people walked around carrying heavy loads but acting as if nothing was wrong.

"I thought you were bringing Izzy's grandma?" Ethan asked.

Wayne opened the school's front door and held it for them.

"Well, I tried to pick her up, but when I arrived, she wouldn't answer the door. I knocked and rang and knocked and rang. When she finally opened it, I could tell she had been sleeping. She was in her nightgown and her hair was a mess. I didn't have time to wait for her to get dressed, so I told her I'd bring her tomorrow."

"Are you going to all three shows this weekend?" Jez asked.

"That's the plan," he replied.

"I guess if Verna isn't ready again tomorrow, she'll have one more try," Wayne teased.

"It doesn't sound like Verna is doing too well," Ethan said.

They stepped into a short line, and Ethan grabbed the wallet out of his back pocket to retrieve the tickets.

"Izzy's been telling me that for weeks, but I guess I didn't believe her. She can be dramatic, you know," Wayne said.

Ethan handed the lady behind the table his tickets, and she ripped them apart before handing him the stubs with their seat numbers. The three made their way into the gym where they shuffled down a row of folding chairs to their spots. They made small talk until the curtain parted, and for the next ninety minutes they were entranced by the entertainment.

When Izzy took her bow, they clapped until their hands hurt. She was a star. After standing up and stretching his legs, Ethan asked if they wanted to wait in the hallway for Izzy to come out. Wayne declined, saying he needed a cigarette break, but told them to go on ahead.

Ethan picked up the bouquet of flowers, and Jezmeen grabbed her coat, throwing it over her arm. Ethan had gotten used to her oversized clothes, but he kept wondering when he'd see her baby bump. With the coat resting against her stomach there was no chance. If only he knew what she was hiding. Why lie about her doctor?

Without words, Ethan led the way towards the hallway near the stage. Once there, they found out they weren't the only ones to have the same idea. A row of people stood before them, waiting for their favorite performers. The man in front of them cast his glance backwards and then his eyes lit up.

"Jez," he said, drawing her into a hug, not noticing Ethan behind her. "I had no idea I'd see you here," he gushed. "You look great—as always. How long's it been? Two months? And you're still wearing the necklace," he smiled broadly.

Ethan didn't like the way the man was so friendly with Jezmeen, and he smugly wondered how long it would be before she introduced them.

"My sister's kid was one of the princesses, so I had to come see my niece. How 'bout you? Who were you here to see?" the man asked with energy.

"We're here to see my sister, Isabella Copeland," Ethan interjected. "I'm Ethan," he said, extending his hand.

"Nick," the man said, taking his grip.

"How do you two know each other?" Nick asked.

"She's my fiancée," Ethan replied.

"Oh, wow man. I didn't know," Nick replied apologetically. Then his eyebrows furrowed as a cloud of anger crossed his face.

"You're really something, Jez," Nick said. "I bet she told you that necklace was from her grandmother," he laughed cynically.

Just then the backstage doors burst open and a stream of colorfully costumed junior high students emerged like bees from a hive. As Izzy made her way towards them, Nick muttered to Ethan, "I'm glad she's with you and not me. Piece of trash."

"Ethan, Jezmeen," Izzy bubbled, hugging them both. Ethan glanced at Jez. She looked as if she had been stabbed.

"Hey, sis," Ethan replied, pulling it together for her. "You were amazing. Seriously. The best one up there—hands down, and I'm not just saying that because we're related."

She laughed. "Thanks. I was so nervous all day. I could barely concentrate at school. You think they'd give us the day off, but no, we had to come and learn about the periodic table and pronouns. Like I paid any attention. And then before the show, I felt like I was going to throw up. I didn't, but I could have. Hey, is Dad with Grandma?" Izzy asked, just realizing they were missing.

"Your grandma couldn't come tonight, and Wayne will be right back. He went outside for a second," Ethan replied.

"Oh," she replied. "Jez, did you like the show?" Izzy asked, pulling her out of her trance.

"Yeah, you were a real star, Isabella," she said, touching Izzy's blonde curls with her hand tenderly. "Watching you up there…I felt so proud," Jez continued with a catch in her voice.

110

Izzy hugged Jezmeen again. "Thanks, Jez, for coming," Izzy replied. "I'm so glad you could make it."

"It was such a thoughtful birthday gift," Jez replied. "And I'd like to return the favor." Jezmeen reached up and undid the back of one earring and then the other. Then she handed the pair of diamonds to Izzy.

"What?" Izzy exclaimed. "My dad said—"

"I'll talk to Wayne," Jez replied. "You don't need any help shining on stage, but I'll be really honored if I was up there with you in a small way."

"Thank you," Izzy replied. Then she shouted, "Hey, my dad's here," and she ran towards him.

After a few more minutes hearing about wardrobe malfunctions, missed lines, and microphone problems, they shared loving goodbyes, and Ethan and Jezmeen made their way silently to the parking lot. Ethan was still reeling. Who was Nick? Why had he seen Jezmeen two months earlier? Was the necklace from him? Had Jezmeen cheated on him?

He was so angry, he couldn't talk, and apparently neither could Jezmeen. So the fifteen-minute ride home was silent and tense. As soon as they entered the kitchen, Ethan went straight to the bathroom while Jezmeen headed upstairs.

As he dried his hands on a towel, he heard pounding on the steps. Out of concern, he ran to see what was going on only to find Jezmeen lugging a huge suitcase.

"What are you trying to do?" You could hurt the baby," he practically shouted.

"Give it a rest. I'm not pregnant," Jezmeen retorted.

Chapter Eleven

Jezmeen just kept hauling the suitcase through the house.

"What are you talking about?" Ethan asked, following her as she headed into the kitchen.

"Nick's right. I'm a piece of trash, and you deserve better. I'm done with the whole charade."

Jezmeen flipped the switch for the lights inside the garage.

"But what about the pregnancy test and all the headaches and stomach aches?"

"I saved the pregnancy test I took with Ace, and that's what I left on the counter two months ago."

"Don't those things go bad?"

"Obviously not."

She opened the garage door and headed to her car.

"Why in the world did you lie about being pregnant?" Ethan asked as he followed her.

"You wanted me gone, and I wanted to stay, so I helped you change your mind."

She heaved the heavy bag into her trunk and then turned to go back inside.

"Were all the aches and pains a lie, too?"

"I wish."

"Then what's wrong with you?"

"I don't know. Charles said it could be stress."

"Who's Charles? Another guy you're cheating on me with, just like Nick?"

"The Noble project—the counselor."

"So, are you sure you're *not* pregnant?"

Jez grabbed his hand and thrust it at her very flat stomach. "No limes, eggplants, coconuts…or whatever fruit or vegetable we're on this week are growing in there. There's no baby," she said firmly.

She strode swiftly back into the house.

"Hey, could you please stop?" Ethan exclaimed when she reached the kitchen island.

Her striking hazel eyes locked with his as her feet stilled their frantic pace.

"Thank you," he said, calming. "I think you owe me more than a honk and a wave as you drive away." Now that she was still, he didn't know what to ask. "Where are you going to go…Nick's?"

She laughed cynically. "I think that bridge has been burned."

"Did you cheat on me with him?" he asked, dreading the answer.

"Depends on how you look at it," she replied. "We were technically broken up at the time."

114

"Why?" he asked quietly.

"Why what? You kicked me out of the house. I had no place to go."

"But it didn't mean that…"

"Well, giving men what they want is what I do best," Jez replied with flint in her voice.

"Was I just some rich guy you could use for free room and board…in exchange–" he choked on his emotion.

"'Use 'em until you lose 'em, my mom used to say.' You're just a number in a long line of many, Ethan Adams," she said coldly.

"Did you ever see anything in me?"

"Besides your cheesy fedora, all those ridiculous blueberry marks after your laser surgery, or the way you can barely keep a conversation going…no."

Jezmeen twisted the ring off her finger and threw it at his chest. It bounced and hit the floor.

"You're free," she said, and then turned on her heel and continued to the stairs.

Ethan felt like he was drowning. He didn't know what to do, but he wanted to be as far away from Jezmeen as possible, so he grabbed the keys to his truck and took off.

By the time Jezmeen came down the stairs with her second suitcase, Ethan was nowhere to be seen. When she loaded it into her car, she noticed his truck was gone, so she took her time bringing down the last two. Before carrying out the final bag, she took a long look around the first floor.

From the curtains to the candle holders, everything was stamped with her touch. She was leaving the only home she'd ever loved, and yet she'd trained herself long ago to feel nothing when parting. So, in a zombie-like stupor, she scratched Chewy on the neck as he grazed her leg, then headed back to the kitchen.

Her engagement ring was still on the floor. She picked it up and put it in her coat pocket. After all, it was hers. But she only walked a few steps before she turned around and set it on the counter.

Once inside her car, she wondered where she could go. If she drove all night, she could make it to Georgia. Then she'd only be hours away from reaching a beach in North Carolina. What was stopping her? She'd always wanted to buy a small shack on the coast with her savings. That's why she'd lived off of men, so she could stop being like her mom one day.

As the car's motor hummed and warm air exhaled from the vents, Jezmeen wondered if she could leave Ace. Sure, he didn't even know she existed. But she felt like a better mother, rationalizing that she hadn't completely abandoned him, because of those weekly visits.

Then there was *Style Street.* For the first time in her life, she was doing something that made her want to get out of bed. And Charles was counting on her to finish the job. But Monica was a bear to work for, and Jez could be fired any minute.

Finally, there was Izzy. Jezmeen loved her, and now that she'd broken up with Ethan, she'd never see her again. Backing out of the driveway, she decided to make her way towards Centennial Park. It was after ten o'clock, and she trusted the little parking lot next to the walking path would be empty. Being on the far west side of Springfield, it seemed like a secluded spot to park for the night.

She didn't want to throw down some of her hard-earned cash for a few lousy hours of sleep at a hotel. When she and her mom were without a place to land, they slept in Sherry's car a night or two. Usually by night three, Sherry would have found them something. Jezmeen had learned to do the same, and it always worked out.

Within ten minutes, Jezmeen's car rested in the vacant lot. She wished she would have put the suitcase with her winter clothes in the backseat, but they were in the trunk. She'd need layers to make it through the night without running the heat. So, she popped the trunk and stepped out.

After unzipping the case, she began rummaging for a sweatshirt and sweatpants by the light of the trunk's tiny bulb. An icy wind blew, and she shivered—from cold or fear she knew not. As soon as she found what she needed, she hurried back into the car, hoping sleep would come so she could forget the present for a few hours.

But the night was long. After she bundled on the layers and balled up an extra sweatshirt to act as a pillow, she leaned against the driver's side window, but frigid air leaked through the crack, and it was too cold. There were only so many positions to lay, and nothing felt comfortable. An occasional vehicle would whiz past on the road behind the parking lot, and Jezmeen wondered if she'd get caught or someone would try to break into her car.

By midnight, she felt wide awake instead of terribly tired, and her throat burned. She thought it was from the icy air, but after drifting off to sleep for a few hours, she awoke to a congested nose and achy lungs. She felt miserable, and it was only 4:00 AM.

Jez had two potential client meetings at *Style Street,* and if she had been thinking more clearly the night before, she would have realized that the office would be more comfortable. It was in that early hour, she realized if she grabbed a throw blanket and a pillow from the store, she could crash there.

Unfortunately, there wasn't a couch, unless she slept on one in the showroom, but the floor was better than her cold car. She knew it was unprofessional, but she couldn't think of any other options, and her body was too fatigued to argue.

The chairs in the classroom weren't designed for men with long limbs, Ethan thought as he stretched his legs underneath the table. Two nights had passed since Jezmeen left, and he hadn't found the courage to tell anyone she'd gone. With Sunday's lunch canceled because of Izzy's show, he'd have a whole week to figure out how to explain it to them. And he was still trying to comprehend it himself.

Pastor David was in the front, teaching about Abraham, Sarah and Isaac. Pastor David said Abraham was a man of great faith, and Ethan wondered why God didn't honor his own. The day before, while laying a brick walkway at a new client's home, he wrestled with doubt.

If God was good, and Ethan was now in His fold, shouldn't blessings come? Didn't God tell him to love Jezmeen? He thought he had been listening and honoring God's plan when he proposed. Now the engagement ring was tucked away in a drawer in his bedroom. He was surprised Jezmeen hadn't taken it when she left. Actually, he was shocked everything was still in place when he'd gotten home late Friday evening.

Leaving her alone, with free reign of the house, had been dangerous, but he hadn't been thinking clearly. Obviously, Jezmeen could exercise integrity when she wanted to, which was why he was seriously troubled. Surely someone who could love his sister, her adopted son, and not steal when everything was unguarded, had a spark of light.

Ethan stopped his inner musing when David posed a question to the class. "Why were God's promises hard for Abraham and Sarah to believe?"

One man answered, "Because having a baby at their ages seemed impossible."

Ariana chimed in, "Maybe because they lacked trust?"

Ethan didn't dare raise his hand, but he answered inwardly, *"Because the promises were unfulfilled."*

Pastor David responded to someone else's comment, and Ethan sat with his unfulfilled hopes. He wanted to be married. He desired children. The first woman he loved, his old neighbor, Danielle, didn't return his love. And the second woman he pledged his loyalty to, Jezmeen, reaffirmed what he believed about himself…he was undesirable.

Ariana's voice pulled him back into the classroom conversation, as she read a passage from Genesis aloud. Ethan noticed she hadn't taken the seat next to him, as she always had before. When she arrived, she strode to an open seat near the front. Now from where he sat, he had a view of her thick, shiny black hair that always looked perfectly styled.

Maybe he'd ask Pastor David what to do about Jezmeen, he thought, sinking back into his mind. Not that there was anything he could do. He didn't know where she went, and he didn't know why he'd chase her. She'd made it clear she loved his money—not him. Jez said he deserved more. Maybe the better path was right in front of him.

Chapter Twelve

Jezmeen was thankful that *Style Street* was closed on Sundays. Her whole body ached, and the heat radiating from her forehead told her she was running a temperature. She felt too sick to go see Ace, which was a first. Pain reliever might help, but she was too lethargic to go get some, so she slept until her phone meeting with Monica.

She'd managed to work the day before, even meeting with two potential clients, faking energy and suppressing her cough as much as she could. But by Saturday night she was exhausted. Today, Monica had two client presentations to go over, and Jez dreaded the call. She considered canceling but knew Monica would be less than understanding.

At precisely two o'clock, Monica's number appeared on Jezmeen's cell phone, and with a froggy throat she answered.

"How's my favorite worker bee?" Monica asked cheerfully.

Not waiting for Jezmeen to respond, Monica charged ahead. "So, the amazing lake house project. Wow. That thing will bring in revenue. I almost considered coming to Springfield mid-week, so I could give the presentation. But, as you know, my clients here can't do without me. You need to nail it, Marie."

She agreed. The Turners were in the process of buying a house on Lake Springfield. They'd met with Jezmeen to do a walk-through of the property, and the remodel would generate a sizable income for *Style Street.*

"Everything needs to be redone. It's going to be a major undertaking," Monica began.

She then proceeded to spend the next half-hour intricately explaining everything she wanted Jezmeen to say at the upcoming presentation. Too fatigued to put up a fight about some of Monica's design choices, Jezmeen figured she would offer the Turners some alternate suggestions…if she felt well enough to meet with them on Wednesday.

"Well, Marie, we're about to see if you're ready for the big league," Monica said. "And you need to be." She paused, creating silence on the line. "All my pathetic assistants before you have run the Springfield franchise into the ground. If I had been running the store *personally* this never would have happened. Everybody loves my work here in Schaumburg. But anyhow…let's just say we need this account."

Monica cleared her throat.

"Now, let's move on to the potential dentist office remodel," she continued. "Did Dr. Slotter hear about me through Dr. Lapinkski?"

"Who's Dr. Lapinkski?" Jezmeen muttered.

"I did his office a few years ago up here. Thought maybe they were friends."

"Richard—Dr. Slotter—was a customer of mine at Finnegan's. Guess he heard about my new job," Jezmeen croaked and then coughed.

"Oh," Monica replied. "Everybody talks about me up here. I just figured the word spread. Dr. Lapinski loved what I did for him."

Jezmeen heard Monica shifting papers through the phone line.

"Just a little piece of advice, Marie, stroke their ego. Doctors need that."

After Monica finished going over her choices for Dr. Slotter's office make-over, she reminded Jezmeen that she was coming to Springfield on Friday afternoon.

"I trust everything is done at the Amani's, and that the Noble project will be complete by then. I'll meet you at *Style Street* at two."

Without a goodbye, Monica hung up. Jezmeen sighed and moved down from the desk to her makeshift bed. She had no idea how she'd muster the energy to make it through a major presentation, finish Charles' office, and meet with Monica at the end of the week. Chills came over her body, and she pulled the throw blankets over her shoulders wishing the ground was softer.

The only good thing about being sick was that she didn't have the mental energy to think about Ethan, her web of lies, or all that she'd lost, but reality was crouched, ready to spring like a panther when the time was right.

On Monday morning, the two throw blankets were covered in sweat when Jezmeen woke to the electronic bells of the alarm on her cell phone. With stiffness, she stood up slowly, nearly falling over before righting her balance using the shelves next to her.

She felt bad putting the blankets back in the storefront, but she had no other choice. Any traces of her "nest" had to be removed. She wasn't hungry enough to eat breakfast, but she knew she needed to stop to get cough medicine. More than half of the night was spent hacking until her lungs felt like they'd collapse.

All her clothes were still in the trunk, so when she arrived at the drugstore, she rolled up one of her non-wrinkled shirts and a pair of pants, so she could change in the restroom. After getting dressed, she shakily applied make-up, and wrapped her hair into a bun. Getting to Charles' office was a priority, even if she felt miserable.

When she arrived, Charles was talking on his cell phone in the reception area. To allow him privacy while he finished, Jezmeen went into the spare office where she'd been storing her purchases. The two fiddle figs she'd bought were near the window, and she walked over to see if they needed to be watered.

She bent down to touch the soil, but felt faint, so she leaned against the wall.

"Morning, Mar-"

Charles strode to her side. "What's wrong?"

"Just a little cold," she replied.

"You don't look well," he said.

"That bad, huh?" she laughed which brought up a cough.

"Here," he said, pulling over one of the chairs being stored in the room.

"Thank you," she replied, as she sat down.

"I don't think you should be here today," he said, resting his hand on her forehead. "You're running a fever."

"But the desks, bookshelves, and filing cabinets are coming today. I nee-"

"What you need is a bed."

If only Charles knew she didn't even possess that at the moment.

"But how will the workers know where to put them?"

"I'll stay. I can follow your floor plan."

"I can't ask you to do my job," she sighed and coughed again.

"I have to lock the place up after they leave anyway."

"But it could be anywhere between now and eleven. The company gave me a two-hour window."

"I've got my laptop out front. It's really no problem."

"You're wonderful," Jezmeen replied.

Charles countenance reflected pleasure in her words.

"Go rest," he said softly. "I'll text you when they're done."

"Can you send pictures, too?" she asked.

"Sure, pictures, too."

When Jezmeen got back to *Style Street,* it was only nine-thirty, and Gabrielle wasn't scheduled to arrive until shortly before ten. So, she left her a handwritten note on the counter, explaining she was working on the upcoming Turner project in the office and wanted to be left alone all day. Then she grabbed the two throw blankets and a fluffy pillow and headed back to the office. Within minutes of shutting the door, she fell asleep, even with the light on. She didn't want Gabrielle to be suspicious.

With cough medicine quieting her lungs, Jezmeen slept hard and long. She wouldn't have woken, except the door swung open, awakening her into a daze of confusion.

"Oh, sorry," Gabrielle murmured, spotting her curled up on the floor in the store's wares. "It's five. I was just going to let you know I was-"

"I'm not feeling well today. Just thought I'd take a little nap before I got back to it," Jezmeen said as convincingly as she could.

"Do you want me to get you anything?" Gabrielle asked politely.

"Nah. It's just a little cold. Plus, I'll be going home soon," she lied.

"Okay," Gabrielle replied. "If you need me to cancel any appointments this week, let me know. Monica can be a pain, but you do get sick time."

"Thanks," Jezmeen said.

"Night,'" Gabrielle replied, as she closed the door behind her, and Jezmeen breathed a sigh of relief and then let out another cough.

Izzy opened the door, and a strong gust of wind threw it back against the truck with force.

"Whoa!" she exclaimed, as she set her backpack onto the floor of her dad's truck before hopping into the passenger seat after school on Monday afternoon.

"Sorry you have to pick me up every day," Izzy said as her dad pulled forward out of the pick-up line.

He took a long drag of his cigarette and blew the smoke out the crack of his window. "Who else is gonna do it?" he said moodily.

"Good point. I guess Grandma isn't sharp enough these days."

"I'm not sure you should even be living there."

"But she needs me," Izzy exclaimed, putting her hands in front of the vent to capture the warm air.

"Taking care of her is not your job."

"If not me, then who?"

Wayne ignored the question and pulled onto the busy road in front of the school.

"Hey Dad, can we swing by Ethan's? I want to give the earrings back to Jezmeen before I forget."

"What if they're not home? It's not even 3:30."

"Claire works till four. I could always ask her to put them in the cash register. You know Ethan picks it up every night."

"Okay, I guess we better get it over with."

"Long day, Dad? You seem grumpy."

When he didn't answer, Izzy continued. "You're probably tired out from the weekend. I know I am. I could barely stay awake first hour. Of course, Mr. Poppelwell droned on and on about the angles of triangles, and that didn't help. Connor Renquist actually did fall asleep…"

Izzy rambled for the rest of the fifteen-minute drive to Ethan's, while Wayne finished one cigarette and started another. When they got to Ethan's house, Wayne curved around the circular drive, and Izzy ran to the door, earrings in hand. When no one answered, Izzy asked her dad to take her back to the storefront they passed on their way. No cars were in the lot, but Izzy knew Claire usually walked the two-hundred feet from her house to the store.

"I'll just give these to Claire," Izzy said.

Wayne put the truck into park. "Okay. While we're here, I might as well check the corner where Ethan said rain was getting in a few weeks ago."

They hopped out, and Izzy asked, "Can I walk on this stuff?" The ground around the store was covered with hay where Ethan was trying to grow grass.

"Probably should go around those patches," he replied.

Cigarette in hand, Wayne headed around to the side of the building. Only months earlier, he and his buddies had finished constructing the wooden storefront, just in time for the annual fall mum sale. Taking another drag, he looked up and saw a tiny gap in the corner. When he had more time, he'd have to get up on a ladder and fix it.

The last thing he needed was more on his to-do list. Izzy was requiring full-time care, and he was used to sharing the load with Izzy's maternal grandma. He needed to address the situation with Verna, but he didn't know how. And he was still running his own electrician business to pay the bills. Plus, he didn't have an assistant like Claire to help him write his invoices or schedule his appointments. Stuck in his own anxious thoughts, he cast the butt of his cigarette into the grass covered with hay by the corner of the building and got back into the truck.

Claire was locking the door as she and Izzy walked out.

"Night, Wayne. Night Izzy," Claire called, as she passed the truck.

"Claire's leaving for the night?" Wayne asked, as Claire strode by.

"Yeah. I guess her parents are out of town, so she's going to the grocery store to get a few things," Izzy replied, sliding into the passenger seat.

"What'd she do with the earrings?"

"Put them in the cash register. I told her I'd text Ethan to let him know. I'll do that now."

Izzy bent over and unzipped the front pocket of her bag to retrieve her cell phone while another gust of wind jarred the truck as it journeyed onto the two-lane road, heading home.

Chapter Thirteen

Ethan had to pull over twice to let firetrucks pass him on his way home from work, but he didn't think much of it until he turned onto Farmingdale Road and noticed billows of gray smoke clouding the horizon ahead. He said a quick prayer for whoever was in trouble and searched for clues for the next three miles.

When he was within eyeshot of his property, he knew the prayer he'd just muttered was for himself. The roof of the storefront was belching out orange blazes like an angry dragon, and all five of his greenhouses were in flames.

"Oh God," he whispered, as the smell of burning plastic overtook his senses. No other words would form. A police vehicle was parked in the middle of the road with its lights flashing. He put his truck into park and hopped out as a burst of wind slammed his body. All day long he'd battled the gusts as he attempted to do leaf clean-ups with his crew.

A female officer approached him. "Sorry, can't go this way right now. Soon as the fire's out you'll be able to get going, or you can turn around."

"But those are my greenhouses. My store," Ethan protested.

"Name?" the officer asked.

"Ethan Adams with Adams Landscaping."

"Let me get you to someone who you can talk with," she responded.

"What should I do with my truck?"

"Why don't you just park it in the grass."

After moving his vehicle, he followed the officer closer towards the sound of the alarm that was still going off inside his building. Three men in puffy light brown suits with yellow and gray reflective tape around their arms, legs and torso, and breathing apparatuses on their faces, held a hose that was forcefully projecting water to the roof of the store. To the left, more men doused the melting tarps, and he'd already calculated that at least four fire engines encircled the scene.

As they neared a fireman speaking into a walkie-talkie, the police officer waited for the fireman to finish before introducing them.

"Battalion Chief McCulley, this is the owner of the property," she said.

"Ethan. Ethan Adams," he interjected.

"Would anyone have been inside Ethan?" Chief McCulley asked. "We used an infrared camera and didn't locate anything, but we have to wait until this thing is under control to send in our crew."

Ethan looked at his watch. 4:33 p.m. Claire would have finished by four. He was sorry that hadn't been his first concern as he approached the scene, but he was too shocked to think clearly.

"I hope not. The store closes at four on Mondays, and my office manager, Claire, locks up then. Was she the one that called you to come?"

"No. It wasn't a woman. I believe it was someone driving down Farmingdale Road. Could you call Claire to make sure she's safe?"

"Oh, yeah. Good idea," Ethan mumbled. He put his hand into his back pocket and realized his cell phone was in the truck.

There was static over the walkie-talkie and a voice could be heard.

"Gonna need another redline on the A-side," Chief McCulley said into the device.

"I've gotta go get it," Ethan said to the preoccupied man.

The fireman nodded an okay, and Ethan sprinted to his vehicle. Claire lived right next door. If she'd been home, no doubt she would've spotted the fire. He didn't even want to think…

As soon as he got inside the truck's cab, Ethan pulled up Claire's number and hit the call button. One ring. Two. Three. Four. Five. No Ethan muttered. No…

"Hey boss," she said breathlessly on ring six.

"Oh, thank God," he said, nearly crying.

"What's wrong?" she asked in alarm.

"The store's on fire. The greenhouses, too," he said anxiously.

"Oh my…"

"I know. I'm just so glad you're okay."

"I'm fine. I'm at the grocery store. Your sister came by the shop with your dad a little before four, and I locked up then."

"My sister and my dad were here?"

"Yeah. She was dropping off the earrings Jezmeen let her borrow for her play. She was going to text you. They're in the cash register…" Claire said haltingly. "They left when I did. Look, Ethan, I'm so sorry. I'll be done here in less than five minutes, and I'll be over as soon as I get back."

"They may not let you through. They're blocking traffic."

"But I live right next door."

"I know. You can ask."

"Okay, I will. And Ethan, I'll be praying for you."

"Thanks," he mumbled.

Jumping out of the truck, he stuffed his phone into his pocket, and ran back to the Battalion Chief.

"She okay?" asked Chief McCulley.

"Yeah," Ethan replied.

"Anything explosive in the building?"

Ethan tried to remember. His new mowing guy had the rider. VJ and Mark each had a blower and hedge trimmer on their truck, as did he.

"Nothing I can think of," he said. "It mostly held plants. Bags of mulch. Potting mix. Planters. Garden tools. That kind of thing."

"No wonder it's burning the way it is," the chief said. "The fuel load is causing it to burn faster and hotter."

The smoke shifted in their direction, and Ethan coughed.

"Why don't you take him to your squad car until this thing is extinguished," Chief McCulley said to the officer.

Sometime in the middle of the night, the blazing heat radiating from Jezmeen's body cooled. And she was able to sleep peacefully for the first time in days, waking at seven with a burst of renewed energy. With the fever gone, Jez noticed her appetite return, and she realized it had been over twenty-four hours since she'd eaten.

She stretched, feeling tightness in her back. The combination of sleeping on the floor and being achy was a miserable one. Her mouth felt dry, and she reached for the water bottle by her pillow. After she took a sip, she ran her hands through her brown, naturally wavy hair.

How many days had it been since she'd taken a shower? Four, Jez calculated. The Thursday before she left Ethan's had been the last time she felt hot water, and after sweating through a few nights, she felt grimy.

Staying in the office had seemed like a great solution at the time, but she needed a bathroom with more than just a sink and toilet. Maybe she could get a gym membership. Workout facilities had showers, she reasoned.

Needing fuel, she thought about where she could get breakfast. Although there were a few places within walking distance, she felt too weak to do anything but get in the car and hit a drive-through. So, after bundling in her coat and locking *Style Street*'s back door, she headed to the golden arches.

As she sat in the line at McDonald s waiting for a sausage biscuit, hash browns, and a coffee, she blew her nose while she thought about her shower dilemma. Why couldn't she bring herself to invest in a small place of her own or rent something, she mused, as she pulled up to the window.

"That will be $5.16," a young lady in uniform said.

Jezmeen handed her a ten and received her change. Inching up to the next window, Jezmeen wondered if Charles would let her stay with him. Of all the skills she possessed, reading men was one of her finest, and she could tell he found her attractive.

But he was an honorable man, he'd never let her stay...would he? It was so unprofessional to ask, but she could spin a good tale. Then Nick's words popped into her mind. *"She's a piece of trash."* No, Charles didn't need her to drag him down, like she had Ethan.

Ethan. She'd dreamed about him in her fitful sleep. He was holding a glass of ice water in his hands. Condensation covered the glass. She was so thirsty, if only she could reach him. But there was a fence in the way. She threw her suitcases at it, but it wouldn't fall down. She ran into it. Kicked it. But it wouldn't budge. Then Charles came and opened a gate that didn't appear before. That's when she woke up.

The car in front of her pulled away, and she crept to the next window. A man leaned out and handed her a brown bag with a grease stain on the bottom and a cup of coffee. She muttered a thank you. It was time to get back to *Style Street.* Gabrielle arrived at ten, and the night before was already a close call.

She had two-and-a-half hours to get the office and herself ready before Gabrielle arrived. So, she didn't feel rushed, but she hoped the coffee would help her muster the energy she needed to do her *own* work on the Turner project and meet Charles at his office in the afternoon. The couches were set to be delivered. If they didn't come, it wouldn't look finished, and that was the last thing Jezmeen needed with Monica's upcoming inspection.

It was completely dark by the time the fires were fully extinguished. Ethan was thankful for the warmth of the squad car, as he sat alone in the passenger seat watching all that he'd worked for over the past three years collapse before his eyes. The female officer continued to direct traffic outside the car, although Ethan paid little attention, too consumed in shock and grief.

A knock on the window brought him out of his trance, and he looked out the passenger side window to see Claire. Stepping out, Claire enveloped him in a hug, and Ethan felt his defenses slide at the first warm touch of empathy. Tears slid down his cheeks as he pulled away, wiping them with the back of his hand.

"Oh Ethan," she sighed. "I'm so sorry."

They stood side by side, watching the firefighters reel in their hoses, while the red and white lights from the trucks lit the scene.

"Claire, if anything would have happened to you, I don't think I could have-"

"But I'm right here," she said, rubbing his back gently.

"Do you remember when the tornado hit three months ago?"

"Of course."

"Do you remember what I found outside the greenhouses?" Ethan asked.

"You mean my Bible?" she replied.

"I know I told you I became a Christ follower that day because God passed over my business. But I never told you the other part of it."

A small cloud of smoke gusted in the air towards them, and Claire instinctively put her hand over her nose.

"Your Bible was open to Isaiah 31:3. I've memorized it now. *I've loved you with an everlasting love. I've drawn you with unfailing kindness.*'"

Ethan choked back a sob.

"Jezmeen left me on Friday night. Gave back the engagement ring. And now this..." he continued.

Claire continued to rub his back.

"I'm so, so sorry," she said softly.

"The circumstances of your life have changed, but God never changes. He will work this out, I promise," she said.

Chief Battalion McCulley was headed their way, so they paused their conversation, awaiting his arrival.

"Chief McCulley," Ethan said as he approached. "This is Claire, my office manager and neighbor. She lives right over there," he said, pointing to her farmhouse on the left.

"Nice to meet you, Claire. Sorry it's under these circumstances. I'm glad you're both okay," he replied.

Chief McCulley moved to stand next to Ethan, so he could continue to watch his crew put out the hot spots so they wouldn't rekindle. "The fires are all out, although I wouldn't recommend walking around the grounds until tomorrow morning."

Voices crackled over his walkie-talkie, but he ignored them.

"We don't know what caused the fire to start, but a fire investigator should be here sometime tomorrow to check it out. The Bravo corner-the back left side, next to greenhouses, seemed to be the origin of the fire. Did you store anything flammable in that area?"

Ethan tried to remember what was in that back corner.

"That's where we kept the potting mixes, mulch, and bags of peat moss for sale," Claire interjected.

"Do you burn candles or anything inside the store? Were there any radiant heating units going?"

"No," Ethan replied.

"Did you allow smokers on the premises?"

"There was a 'no smoking' decal on the door," Claire replied.

"Well, I know the investigator will have more questions for you both tomorrow. I'm sorry this happened to your business, Ethan. If you decide to rebuild, you might want to consider putting in a sprinkler system. I know it's an expense, but it's something to think about," Chief McCulley said.

"Thank you for everything," Ethan replied.

"Yes, thank you," Claire chimed in.

"Just doing our job," Chief McCulley said with a small smile.

After Chief McCulley was out of earshot, Ethan sighed. "Sorry to rope you into talking to an investigator tomorrow."

"It's no problem," Claire replied.

"I'll pay you, of course, for your time."

"Oh, Ethan, you don't have to."

"But you still had a whole month and a half left to work before Christmas, and now you don't have a job."

"I can still do the invoices for you. And you don't need to pay me for them. There are only a handful left to do."

"Thanks," Ethan said softly. He didn't want to take her charity, but he was too overwhelmed to argue.

Ethan wanted to hug Claire, but he felt awkward initiating it. If Izzy was here, she would have handled it for him. "Claire, I just remembered you said Izzy and Wayne were here. I need to call them and make sure they're okay."

Chapter Fourteen

"You drivin' somewhere?" Ethan asked his dad over the cellphone. He'd just stepped into the mudroom, and the connection over their lines made Wayne sound far away.

"Izzy forgot her compass at school, and she needs it for a math assignment," Wayne muttered moodily. "So, I'm headed to Walmart to get her a new one, since the school building is locked up for the night. She also told me her dress shoes are too tight, and there's a dance on Friday, so I need to take her shopping before then. Please don't tell me you need something, too."

"I'm just glad to hear your voice," Ethan said, while sitting at the island in the kitchen. He stared at the spot where he'd laid the engagement ring days earlier. He half thought Jezmeen would've returned by now.

"Everything okay, Ethan?" Wayne asked, concern entering his voice.

"Claire told me you and Izzy stopped by the store this afternoon."

"Another of Izzy's errands. We were dropping off Jezmeen's earrings. Izzy was supposed to text you."

"Yeah, she did. I just forgot to text her back. When you left the store, did you see anything out of the ordinary? Anybody lurking around?"

"No, why?"

"Well, when I got home around 4:30, everything was on fire…It's all gone, Dad," Ethan said, choking back a sob. He knew how hard Wayne had worked to help him build the storefront.

"You can't be serious."

"The firefighters just left. Crews from Springfield and Pleasant Plains had to come and put it out."

"Wow. I'm shocked. I don't know what to say."

"I feel the same way."

"Do you want me to come over?"

"No, it sounds like you have your hands full," Ethan smiled for the first time in hours. Thinking of Izzy had that effect on him.

"Well, we can rebuild. Not this winter but–"

"I don't know if I'll have the finances to do that, but thanks for the offer."

"You didn't have insurance on the store? Or the greenhouses?"

"Just worker's compensation, which I carry for all my employees. That's all the state requires. I'm kicking myself that I thought it was more important to invest in equipment for the business this fall. I didn't think I had it in the budget to get a general liability plan."

"Do the firefighters have any idea what caused it?"

"No. They think they know where it started but not why. A fire investigator is coming in the morning."

"I can't believe it," Wayne repeated. Ethan could almost hear him shaking his head in disbelief. Wayne was silent for a few moments before he uttered, "I'm so sorry about this, son."

"Thanks, Dad," Ethan replied softly.

Jezmeen stared at the computer screen and blew her nose with a tissue. She felt it was high school finals week, and there just wasn't enough time to get it all done. All day she'd been working on an alternate plan—her own design—for the Turner presentation, only stopping to pick up dinner after Gabrielle left for the night.

When Jezmeen had walked through the Turners' estate, she felt like she'd gotten a hundred-dollar tip from a ten-dollar order. The Turners were one of the nicest couples she'd met...kind to each other and her. Even though they both had lucrative careers—Tom was a dermatologist, and Denise was a computer programmer— they didn't act pretentious.

The remodel budget was $300,000, and *Style Street* would pocket ten percent, if they won the job. The Turners said they wanted their home to feel like a coastal retreat every time they walked in. Denise said she wanted "classy," but she didn't say "classic," as in antique. However, Monica chose brass fixtures, chandeliers, and wallpaper for the first floor.

Sure, she'd incorporated more of what they'd asked for in the walkout lower level, but Monica mentioned the Turners were moving into a lucrative area in Springfield, and they'd want the house to reflect that with a classic style not a beach vibe. As always, Monica felt certain that the Turners would love her choices, because "everyone did." But Jezmeen felt she was being set up for failure with something that Monica told her to "knock out of the park."

While Jez worked, her mind wavered between confidence and concern. Half the time she thought her design was exactly what they wanted, and the other half she wondered what she was thinking. Afterall, she'd never been to school for design. The only real practice she had was with Ethan's home, until Monica hired her. Could she really trust her instinct?

Denise and Tom had a 7:00 PM appointment tomorrow evening to go over the plans. For a brief second, she thought about calling Monica to express her concerns. But Jez had heard Monica's retort enough times to know what she'd hear, "You're paid to implement and communicate—not create."

Jezmeen felt unpleasantly rebellious as she worked to come up with alternate choices. She truly wanted them to be satisfied, and she wouldn't completely disregard Monica's work. She'd just present them both. The Turners had been upfront that they were seeking plans from one other local designer and a firm they'd found over the internet. There was a strong possibility neither of the plans from *Style Street* would be chosen, but she had to give it a shot—even if she was recovering from a virus.

Jez had managed to stay upright all day, even getting to Charles' office, only to wait an hour for couches that never arrived. The store called, saying the truck had gotten a flat tire, and her shipment was being postponed to the next day. She trusted she'd feel well enough to present the plans.

Now, if only she could find a place to shower…

The high, shrill sound of a fire alarm made Ethan bolt upright in bed, heart racing. He looked around for flames, but it was pitch black. When the bell sounded again, he realized he'd been dreaming, and what he heard was his cell phone ringing. Who would be calling him at home at midnight, he wondered, glancing at the neon numbers on the bedside clock.

"Hello," he answered.

Sobbing filled the air waves.

"Jezmeen?" he questioned.

"No, it's Izzy," she said between hiccups of sadness.

"What's wrong?"

"It's Dad."

Not able to control her grief, she cried until she was able to take a breath and string words together again.

"He's passed out in his recliner."

"Do I need to call an ambulance?"

"No. He's been drinking. I found eight empty beer cans in the garbage, and there are two here by his chair."

"I'm so sorry, Iz."

"I should've known. He seemed way too happy when I said goodnight. I got up to go to the bathroom, and the tv in the living room was still on."

"Does he usually just sleep it off?" Ethan asked, unsure of what to do.

"Yeah, but I don't want him driving me to school in the morning," she cried.

"Do you want me to come get you?"

"Yes, please," she said gratefully.

Within minutes, Ethan was driving through the nearly deserted Springfield streets in his cold truck. He felt partially to blame for his dad's slip. Maybe if he hadn't told him about the fire...but he would've found out eventually. The burned-out structures weren't something he could hide.

As if meeting with the inspector in the morning wasn't enough, now he had to get Izzy to school and check on his dad. He wasn't even sure if it was safe to leave him alone in the house. Ethan waited at a four-way intersection for the light to turn green. There were no cars coming from any direction, and he felt like running the light. His left leg bobbed up and down with nervous energy.

God it feels like everything around me is falling apart. I don't think I'm strong enough to handle all of this. Give me strength. Show me You're still with me.

The L.A. Fitness Center's one-week trial membership had already proven its worth, and Jezmeen's clean hair and skin agreed. For the second day in a row, she'd taken a shower and curled her hair—thanks to the use of the women's locker room. Her stuffy nose, occasional cough, and mid-afternoon fatigue revealed that she wasn't completely recovered from her illness, but things had gone so well the day before she barely noticed.

Denise and Tom Turner had shown no interest in Monica's plan, but asked at least twenty questions about hers. And while they didn't hand her the job, Denise hung back when Tom walked out of the store, and said the "Coastal Retreat" layout, as Jez had called it, was everything she was looking for.

Just hearing those words validated all the time Jezmeen had poured into the project and reaffirmed how much she loved her job. That news, coupled with the delivery of the couches to Charles' office, numbed the nagging worry about being homeless. She figured after Monica's inspection, she'd spend time problem-solving her living situation.

As she pulled into the parking lot at Charles' office, she was overcome with sadness, and for a second, she couldn't figure out why. Then she knew. It was because her time with Charles was coming to an end, and he was the best first client she could have asked for. The Amani's had been nice, and working for the bank was okay, but Charles was special.

He'd gotten her a cake, sent her home when she was sick, and listened to the little bits about her past without judgment, only compassion and understanding. She felt safe around him and wished this wasn't the end.

Jezmeen recognized Charles' car, and she was thankful he agreed to meet her a half-hour early. She had a few loose ends to finish—mugs for the coffee station, book holders for the shelves, and light bulbs for two lamps all needed to be put in place. She'd taken a dose of cough suppressant which made her jittery and amplified any normal anxiety over the situation. The rapid-fire of her words, as she conversed with Charles upon entry, only confirmed it.

"Hey, Charles! Well today's the day you'll get to meet *thee* Monica Taylor from *Style Street,*" she said, setting down her bag onto one of the chairs in the reception area.

"What's she famous for again?" Charles asked.

Jezmeen lifted out the box of light bulbs and moved to the standing lamp in the corner.

"Well, she went to a fancy, expensive school for design. Then she opened the Springfield store, and now she owns a store in Schaumburg, too. She's got a lot of experience."

Jezmeen tried to portray Monica's luster with bravado, even if she'd yet to win the woman over. Jez took off the shade and screwed in the bulb.

"What do you think of her?"

"Monica? She's great. Really great. Since she's going to be here any minute, I better give off some positive vibes about her, right?

Charles raised an eyebrow.

"Okay, truthfully, she's really into herself, and I don't think she likes me much, but I love my job despite that."

"Well, I think you did fantastic work, and I can't wait to tell her so."

"Thank you," Jez said, looking up from tightening the finial on the lamp shade. "It's been a pleasure to work with you. And to be honest, I am pretty sad this is coming to a close."

"I was going to wait and tell you and Monica at the same time," Charles said with a twinkle in his eye, "but since you brought it up...I loved what you did here so much that I'd like to hire you to decorate my family room. It's the only room in the house I haven't touched because I want to make it a nice space for entertaining but can't figure out how."

"Charles, that's wonderful. It would be my privilege."

"What would be your privilege?" Monica smiled, as she pulled open the glass door to the office.

Chapter Fifteen

"Monica! You're early!" Jezmeen sputtered.

"Charles Noble, I presume," Monica said, ignoring Jezmeen and striding in wearing an emerald green blazer with matching emerald green rimmed glasses.

Charles shook Monica's outstretched hand.

"Nice to meet you," Charles said.

"You as well," she said with charm. "I'm sorry to surprise you both. I happened to make good time, and when I stopped by *Style Street*, Gabrielle told me Marie was already here, so I thought I'd head over. I see you're doing some things last-minute, Marie."

Monica glanced at the bag on the chair.

"So many young designers want to come work for me," Monica told Charles. "And I take them on to help them learn. This is Marie's first decorating job, you know?"

"No, I didn't know that," Charles said, maintaining eye contact with Monica. "I never would have known. Marie has been a joy to work with. Actually, that's what you overheard as you walked in. I'd like to hire Marie to decorate a room in my house."

Charles smiled at Jezmeen.

"Wonderful," Monica gushed. "People always tell me I know how to pick 'em. I've got an eye for good assistants."

Jezmeen grabbed the bag and started rummaging for the book ends.

"Don't worry about that, Marie. You can finish when we're done with the walk-through. And just a little piece of advice, always act like the walk-through is a day earlier than it actually is, then you will always be ready."

Monica grinned at Charles. "See, I'm constantly teaching." Monica glanced at her watch. "Well, why don't we begin?"

For the next fifteen minutes, they spent time in each space of the office complex, looking at the final results and getting Charles' feedback. Charles was pleased with everything, and the only time Monica paused was when they got to the counselor chair.

"I thought we went with something a bit more sophisticated," Monica pondered, running her hand over the black fabric of the chair in Charles' office.

"Marie gave me a few choices. Since I sit so much, it's really important to have a chair with good back support. I was thankful Marie was willing to include it in the design, even if it wasn't the best-looking choice. Kind of like me," he joked.

"Of course we do all we can to make the client happy," Monica replied, covering her tracks.

After they finished the walk-through and Charles confirmed he was completely satisfied with the end result, Monica thanked him for his business and

153

told Jezmeen she'd meet her back at *Style Street* when Jez finished the odds and ends.

Once they watched Monica leave the building, Charles said, "No wonder you thought Monica was really into herself. She has all the signs of narcissistic personality disorder."

"What's that?" Jezmeen asked, picking up the bag and slinging it over her shoulder.

"It's when a person has an inflated sense of self-worth. A strong need for praise and admiration. Inability to feel for others."

"Wow. That describes Monica so accurately."

"I imagine it's been hard to work for her."

"That's an understatement, but I thought it was just me. Because I was new to all of this."

"I've counseled quite a few clients who needed help dealing with a narcissistic family member. The narcissist can really do a number on the mind—so much so that people can't always tell what's the truth and what's not."

Jezmeen plopped down into a chair in the reception area, setting the bag into her lap.

"You are amazing," she said sincerely with a sigh. "Not only did you make me look good in front of my boss, you've lifted a huge weight off my shoulders. All this time, I thought all the problems with the job were just me."

He sat down beside her and patted her on the shoulder. "Happy to help." As he patted her shoulder, he realized her hair was caught in the strap of the bag. He reached to untangle it for her.

"Thanks," she said softly, locking eyes with him.

"You're welcome," he replied quickly, standing up.

"I unloaded the dishwasher and fed Chewy," Izzy said as Ethan entered the kitchen in his work uniform. "Oh, and I made you a lunch when I made mine."

Izzy wiped the counter where breadcrumbs remained.

"You're doing too much," Ethan said as he put his arm around his sister's shoulder and squeezed it. "Why don't you come eat breakfast with me," he said.

Ethan took two bowls out of the cabinet and handed one to her. "You haven't eaten, have you?" She shook her head no.

They each chose a box of cereal, and after pouring flaky grains and oatmeal squares, Izzy and Ethan sat side by side at the kitchen counter.

"You doin' okay, Iz?" Ethan asked, between bites.

"You mean besides the fact that my brother's business burned down, my dad's going to a 28-day rehab program, my grandma's moving in with her sister, and I'm no longer the maid of honor at your wedding, because there is no wedding," Izzy said dramatically.

"Yeah, besides all that," Ethan joked. "Just another normal day, right?"

"You could be the coolest brother and call me out of school today," she said. "I haven't missed one day this week, and it's the last place I want to be."

"But what about the second hour science test? And the dance tonight?"

"Oh right, the dance. But if I stay here, I could help find more stuff in the rubble."

"I still can't believe you found the diamond earrings."

"I read online that if you take them to a jeweler you can get them restored."

"Is that right?" Ethan said, crunching a bite of flakes.

"Maybe she'll come back," Izzy said, pouring herself a second helping.

"Possibly. But what if her leaving was part of God's plan?"

"Only to bring her back restored," Izzy interjected.

"Huh?" Ethan asked.

"Maybe God's plan is to take her from broken to beautiful, and He can't do that with her here."

Ethan just stared at Izzy.

"What?" Izzy retorted. "When you grow up with a mom in jail and a dad who's an alcoholic, you go deep or you do drugs," she joked.

"Well, I'm glad you went deep because I don't want to take another family member to a rehab program anytime soon."

"I still can't believe Dad slipped. He's been sober for two years. Two years! Why now?"

Ethan shrugged, not wanting to share his internal dialogue.

"Do you think I'm too much for him?" Do you think I wore him out?"

Ethan rubbed Izzy's back.

"Isabella Copeland, you make the world a better place. We all need you in this family. No, I do not think *you* wore him out. I think Wayne just has to learn some new skills with how to cope with stress. Life. He's committed to you. That's why he wanted to go."

"I thought his buddy from A.A. talked him into it."

"His buddy gave him the information. Dad knew it was the right thing to do."

"But now you have to take care of me," Izzy sighed.

157

"I missed out on the first twelve years with you. Spending time with you is a gift not a chore."

Izzy hopped off the bar stool and encircled Ethan's waist in a hug. "I hope you feel the same way when you take me shopping after school for shoes."

Jezmeen's left temple pounded as she maneuvered the downtown traffic back to *Style Street*. She hoped her headaches would've gone away after she stopped carrying around the burden of the lie. Maybe this was just leftover sinus pressure from her cold, she reasoned.

She signaled to move over a lane, and the car in front of her let her in. Monica would be waiting for her at the office. Then they'd head to the Amani's together, since the Amani's wouldn't be home from work until later. Jezmeen imagined Monica would spend the hour in between appointments praising herself about something—or everything. But now Jezmeen knew why.

Monica was a narcissist. Jez was thankful she'd never had to work with one before. She was insecure enough about this new career, and Monica certainly didn't help. But Charles had made her day with the rehire and his kind words. And when he brushed her hair away, she knew something had happened to him. She felt it and hoped things wouldn't get awkward between them. Jezmeen couldn't remember if she'd ever had a male friend.

As she pulled into the alley that led to *Style Street's* back parking lot, she thought about Ethan. Months earlier, he called himself her friend. That was when she knew something had to change, so she conveniently became "pregnant." Being "just friends" with Ethan hadn't been enough.

It was cold when she stepped out of her car, and the heel of her leopard print shoe almost got stuck in a crack in the blacktop. After wiggling it out, she made her way to the back entrance, opened the door with her key, and strode down the hallway.

Monica was on the phone when she popped her head into the office. She started to leave so Monica could have privacy, but Monica gestured for her to stay. As she waited for the call to end, Jez glanced around the room, double-checking that her clean-up efforts were satisfactory.

She'd put her pajamas, make-up bag, curling iron, and deodorant in the trunk of her car. The blankets and throw pillows were back on display—fluffed up for good measure. And she'd even dumped the trash in the parking lot's big receptacle, so there'd be no evidence of her fast-food wrappers. As long as Gabrielle hadn't blabbed about what she'd seen, everything would be fine, Jezmeen silently mused, reassuring herself.

"Well, I'm sorry to hear that," Monica said, which caught Jezmeen's ear. "If you change your mind let me know."

Monica sighed as she laid the phone back into its cradle on her desk.

"A little piece of advice, Marie," Monica began. "Never present two different plans for one job. It confuses the customer."

Jezmeen's face clouded.

"Yes, Marie. I know you made your own little layout for the Turners. That was them on the phone. And no, they didn't tell me. Free tip," Monica continued angrily. "When you're using the software on my computer, I can see it."

Jezmeen wondered how that was possible. She made sure to save it under a very general name, "Design Ideas," and it was in her own personal folder.

"The program is set up for collaboration. I can hop on to your work anytime. Had I seen it before you presented, I would've contacted you. However, I didn't see it until today when I was on the computer here in the office."

"I thought that two options would be a benefit to the client," Jezmeen interjected.

"Whatever your intention was, it didn't work. That was the Turners on the phone, and they are going with the firm they found online."

"I thought they loved–"

"Had you spent more time getting *my* design ready for the presentation, they might have chosen *Style Street,*" Monica cut in. "But now we've lost a very sizable project," she sighed loudly.

"I'm sorry," Jezmeen said sincerely.

"A little too late," Monica said. "Sadly, you're just like all the others. Unable to follow directions. I'm afraid I have to let you go."

"Just for that?"

"No. You also didn't implement the plan I gave you for Mr. Noble."

"I did everything you asked!"

"The counselor's chairs?" Monica questioned with raised eyebrows.

"But you heard Charles say that's what he wanted."

"And I've told you before, the client doesn't always know what looks best."

"Don't you think he'll be happier having a chair that really works for him in the long run?"

"Marie, I don't care–"

"That's another thing," Jezmeen interjected. "My name is Jezmeen," she said, grabbing her purse and standing up.

Jezmeen walked to the door, and Monica called to her.

"Gabrielle will send your last paycheck to the address we have on file."

"Don't bother. I'll pick it up," she bellowed back from the hall.

Chapter Sixteen

"Now where to?" Ethan asked Izzy as she slid into the passenger seat after school. He knew she needed shoes for the dance but had no clue where a teenage girl would want to shop.

"Would the mall put you over the edge?" Izzy asked.

Ethan laughed. "I'll be okay. Spending time with you makes it worth it."

"Umm. That's really sweet of you to say, but I better tell you one more thing before you totally commit. All of my money is at dad's house. I can pay you back, but I don't have any on me."

"I was planning on buying your shoes," Ethan said, pulling up to the stop sign and looking both ways. "And you don't have to pay me back."

"But the fire. Your business. Aren't you broke?" Izzy groaned. "Too personal. Strike that."

"It's okay, Iz. I'm not broke. Remember my pergola invention? Tryton pays me royalty checks every three months. So there's that. And I still have the mower and the blowers and stuff like that. In fact, VJ, Mark, and I did three yard clean-ups today."

"But all your plants…"

"I know. I'm disappointed about them too. Maybe someday I'll rebuild."

"Why not right away?"

Izzy pulled down the passenger side mirror, took the hair tie off her wrist and pulled her blonde locks into a ponytail.

"Well, winter is coming."

"How 'bout in the spring?"

"Maybe" Ethan said, not wanting to reveal he didn't have the finances to start over just yet. But he planned to start some cuttings in his garage over the winter.

"Did you get any word from the fire inspector today?" Izzy asked, sitting back against the seat.

"The guy said it could take a week, remember?"

"Yeah. I just hoped we'd find out what caused it."

"What good will just knowing do?" Ethan asked.

"Can't you sue someone or something?"

Ethan smiled at her logic. "Myself? For faulty wiring?"

"Is that a thing?"

"Yeah, but the chief on the scene didn't think that was it."

"What do you think started it?"

Ethan bit his bottom lip. "Probably some natural cause. Maybe we'll never find out."

Jezmeen didn't want to be anywhere near Monica or *Style Street,* so she sped off without a plan. For the second time in a little over a week, she was homeless—this time completely. She considered stopping by Finnegan's Taphouse, her old workplace, but she wasn't friends with any of her co-workers. While the regulars might be happy to see her, it would be weird to sit on a barstool next to them as a customer.

Thoughts of Izzy crossed her mind. She missed her so much. Maybe she could stop by her house. She'd dropped her off once at Wayne's, so she knew the way. But if she went to see Izzy then Ethan would find out, and he'd think she was trying to weasel her way back into the family.

A week ago she could have been Mrs. Adams. She couldn't believe she told him the truth. The truth was awful. Embarrassing. She'd planned to say she'd miscarried. Then he would have been sympathetic. Compassionate. If she'd done that she would still be living there.

But he'd found out Dr. Wallace wasn't practicing in Springfield anymore. Why hadn't she done her homework? Because she was a piece of trash, just like Nick said. She'd invented a pregnancy so Ethan wouldn't kick her out. Certainly someone like him wouldn't love someone like her.

When she met Ethan, he hadn't been her "type." He was too shy, insecure, and introverted. But kindness had overtaken him. He'd become attentive and caring. And when he kissed her two weeks ago, on the couch, something inside her stirred. Sadly, she'd thrown it all away.

Charles popped into her head. Yes, she could go see Charles. Making up a fake errand—like needing to see the dimensions of his family room for the next project would be easy. And he might be able to help her...take her in. But she didn't know where he lived, and she wasn't about to go back to *Style Street* and ask Gabrielle for his address.

How could she find him? Jezmeen wondered as she waited at a red light in downtown traffic. Then she remembered he'd once mentioned the name of the neighborhood he lived in. What was it again? If she could recall the name, she knew what his car looked like...if it was parked outside.

As she turned left, headed towards the mall, she realized she could always go to L.A. Fitness which was a part of the huge shopping complex. The club was the one place she actually belonged—at least for a few more days. "The club," she said to herself. Country Club. Country Club Estates. That was where Charles lived. With renewed hope, she drove on.

Only fifteen minutes into house hunting, Jezmeen realized how ridiculous her plan was. She'd driven down seven streets...slowly. Half the houses had cars sitting outside, the other half had closed garage doors. What if he lived in one of those? After searching Lost Tree, Seminole, and Glen Eagle, she only had Pinehurst and Oakmont left to cover.

What would she do if his gold-colored Toyota Camry wasn't anywhere to be seen? She was only a mile from his office. Maybe she should've tried there first. But he didn't have any clients until Monday. However, she only left an hour earlier. Maybe he'd still be there. At the next stop sign, Jezmeen decided to abandon the last two streets and try the office.

Within minutes, Jezmeen pulled into the parking lot, spied the Camry, and exhaled a sigh of relief. She'd spent so much time worrying if she'd find him, she didn't think about what she would say now that she had. What could she have "forgotten" that she'd have to retrieve?

Her color wheel. She carried it everywhere. That would be believable. Actually, it was in her glove compartment, but Charles didn't need to know that.

She felt shaky as she walked inside. Maybe it was the cough medicine or maybe it was her nerves. Jezmeen was tired of all the acting, and she wondered how her mom had done it for so many years.

The door to the reception area was unlocked.

"Charles," she called out after she entered. But there was no answer. She said his name again a bit louder. With no response, she headed to his office. The door was partially closed, and she could hear him talking. Maybe she misunderstood, and he did have a client.

But when she peered through the crack, she saw that his face was buried in the cushion of the couch, and she got concerned.

"Charles," she said, bursting inside. "Are you okay?"

He looked up, startled. She'd never seen him without his glasses, and his blue-gray eyes were filled with tears. He quickly retrieved his glasses from the coffee table and put them back on.

"Marie. I didn't expect to see you again today," he replied standing up. He looked nervous to see her, and Jez remembered how he'd held her gaze just an hour earlier.

He ran his hand through the thin strands of hair that lightly covered his balding head. "I was just praying."

"Oh. I'm so sorry to interrupt. I didn't know…"

"It's alright."

"Are you okay?" she asked.

"Sure," he said, trying to sound reassuring. "I just have a lot on my mind."

"I think I may have left my color wheel here," she said, forging ahead with her plan.

"Hmmm. I haven't seen it, but I can help you look."

After they'd scoured all three spaces, they returned to his office to check it one more time.

"Maybe you left it at *Style Street*," Charles said as he scanned the bookshelf.

"Maybe," Jezmeen replied.

"How'd things go with Monica?" he asked, pushing aside one of the bookends to look behind it.

"Actually, not so well," she said, lifting up a throw pillow and searching underneath it for the "missing" color wheel.

He turned to face her. "How come? You didn't call her a narcissist, did you?"

Jezmeen laughed and a little cough erupted. "No, but after she fired me, maybe I should have."

"She fired you?"

"The chairs," she said pointing to his counselor chair in the room.

"For not going with her chair choice?" he asked exasperated.

"That, and I presented an extra design plan to some big clients this week."

"She didn't like that you offered clients *extra* options?"

"Not when they were designed by me."

"Oh. She only wants *her* work featured."

"Right."

"I'm so sorry."

"Thanks," she said sincerely.

Now was the time to start weaving a story about how she needed a place to stay until she landed a new job. But as she looked at him standing by the bookshelf dressed in his usual khaki pants and a striped dress shirt, his eyes still red with tears, she

168

couldn't bring herself to do it. She didn't want to take advantage of him, sell her body for a place to sleep, or pretend. And all of a sudden, she felt scared.

Chapter Seventeen

"What's wrong?" Charles asked, as if he was able to read her thoughts.

She sat down on the couch. "Everything actually."

Charles found his way to his chair and took a seat.

"I'm kind of in a bad place right now. My fiancé and I broke up last week. We'd been living together, and I left him. Since then, I've been staying at *Style Street*. Now I don't have a job or a place to crash."

"Do you have any friends or family in the area?" Charles asked.

"No...unless you count my fiancé's thirteen-year-old half-sister," Jezmeen replied. "Sad, isn't it?" she said, pressing her lips together to keep from crying.

"Sounds lonely."

Jezmeen didn't respond.

"How's your financial situation?"

Jezmeen paused, not knowing how to answer. How truthful was she willing to be with Charles? His blue-gray eyes searched her face.

"Are you uncomfortable talking about money?" he asked.

"No. I'm not scared to talk about it. I'm terrified to spend it." Her leg began tapping up and down, and her breathing became shallow.

"Are you concerned you'll run out?"

"Yes."

"Does holding on to your money make you feel safe?"

She shook her head in affirmation.

"How would it feel if you spent some of your money on a place to stay tonight?"

"Frightening. Like I'd be turning the handle on a faucet that would just keep running."

"So, you're afraid that if you start spending, you won't be able to stop. Then all your resources will run out, and you'll be truly homeless."

"Yes," she said, awed that he understood her so well.

"Being homeless—even for a short period of time—can be hard mentally. Have you run into this problem before?"

"A handful of times as a kid."

"I'm sorry. That had to be hard."

"I guess I didn't realize how much it affected me."

"Early memories are stored in our hippocampus. But you can learn some new habits and

171

thought patterns that will help you have more freedom. Are you open to that?"

Jezmeen wanted to say "yes" but wasn't sure she was strong enough to face her fears. It seemed easier to do what she knew. Plus, sleeping in her car wasn't so bad.

"I don't know," she said breathlessly, experiencing an overwhelming wave of anxiety. She hadn't felt this way since she was ten, packing up her bag because she and her mom were leaving another man's apartment.

"You could try staying in a hotel tonight. That would be a small start as a way to begin pushing into your fear. But even if you choose not to, I believe you are a very resourceful woman, and you will be okay. Either way, I'd like to see you again soon—Sunday afternoon okay? I have plans tomorrow with my parents, otherwise I would've asked to meet then."

"You mean for a therapy appointment?"

"Whatever you call it is fine with me, but I think of you as a friend, and I want to help."

"Are you going to psychoanalyze me?"

"Isn't that what counselors do?" he teased.

"What time?" she asked, trying to act aloof, but secretly grateful for his concern.

"How about one? That'll give me time to go to church and have lunch."

Jezmeen stood up to go, and he followed suit. Even if she didn't know what she'd do about the night, she felt better because she had someone to talk to. Someone who was watching out for her.

"I can't believe I just told you all that. We barely know each other."

"I'm glad you felt safe enough."

"I guess I've hit rock bottom."

"Well then there's only one way to go from here...up."

The Sunday School room filled slowly, as the regulars came in carrying Bibles and conversations. Ethan was glad Izzy agreed to attend Sunday School with him, since he hated to miss it. After two months, the class had become a highlight of his week.

While Izzy happily made conversation with the married couple sitting next to them, Ethan thought about Wayne. They both talked with him the night before. Although they weren't allowed to see him until the program was over, Wayne had phone privileges.

Over the past week, Ethan noticed Izzy waffled between anger and compassion for her dad, and he felt sorry for his sister. She'd experienced so much turmoil in her short life—with a mom in jail, a grandma dealing with dementia, and a dad battling for sobriety. He was thankful to play a role in her life. Hopefully a healthy one. But he wished Jezmeen was still around.

She'd have been the one to really connect with Izzy, and even though Izzy could talk circles around him, he wondered if all the noise was because she hurt in the silence. It had only been a week since Jez left, but it felt like a year. He wondered if she'd call or come back, but she hadn't, and Ethan felt the sting of being discarded. He knew she could be with any man she wanted to be with, and it was easy to see she no longer wanted him.

Everything in his home reminded Ethan of her. Doing laundry was the worst. The clear jar holding powdered detergent, the fake green plant on a shelf above the washing machine, and the basket of paper towels all held her touch. He hadn't really appreciated her ability to make a space beautiful until she was gone.

"Good morning," Pastor David said from the front, garnering the attention of the class. "As you know, the last two weeks we talked about Jesus' life, death and resurrection. Today we're going to talk about the third person of the trinity—and yes I said person—the Holy Spirit."

Ethan kept glancing at Izzy for the first few minutes of David's lesson, seeing if she was enjoying it or even listening. And on one of his glances, he locked eyes with Ariane, as she took the empty seat at the end of the row. He smiled, and she politely smiled back.

The hour went by quickly, and by 11:15 class members were shuffling out of their seats. The couple next to Izzy said their goodbyes, and as they left Izzy noticed Ariana talking with another class member at the end of the row.

174

"Isn't that one of the worship leaders?" she whispered to Ethan.

Ethan nodded in affirmation. Then he grabbed his Bible, and they walked behind Ariana.

"You were great this morning," Izzy said, causing Ariana to turn her head in their direction.

"Thank you," Ariana said in her sweet, high voice.

"I think singing on stage would be awesome," Izzy said.

"They have a student-led worship team for youth services. I could get you more information, if you'd like," Ariana replied, reaching for her bracelet and rolling it around her fingers.

"I don't think I'm good enough for that. And I'm not sure how long I'll be going to church here. It's kind of a temporary arrangement."

"Ariana, this is my sister Isabella," Ethan cut in.

"Everyone calls me Izzy," she interjected.

"Nice to have you with us today, Izzy," Ariana replied.

"Thanks. I usually go to my dad's church, but well—" Izzy stopped herself, unsure of what to say.

"He's out of town for a few weeks," Ethan added.

"So, you're staying with your big brother?" Ariana asked.

"Hey," Pastor David interrupted as he walked up to their table. "I just came to say hello to our youngest guest today. How would you two like to join Ariana, my wife and me for lunch?"

Ethan started to politely decline while Izzy enthusiastically accepted. Ariana and David laughed at the apparent mix-up, and Ethan's cheeks grew red.

"We've tried to get your brother to have lunch with us for months. I guess you're our secret weapon for success," David said.

"We don't have to," Izzy said. "It's been kind of a rough week for Ethan. His business burned down. When you were taking prayer requests, I thought Ethan would say something. And I didn't want to embarrass him. Although I guess I'm doing that now."

"What?" Ariana gasped.

"Oh, Ethan, I had no idea," Pastor David said. "I'm so sorry. Is there anything I can do?"

"I don't think so, but thank you for asking," Ethan replied.

Ethan didn't like to be the center of attention and raising his hand in class to offer a prayer request was outside his comfort-zone. But he was glad they knew, so they could pray for him. He needed all the help he could get.

"Well, lunch is my treat," Pastor David said.

A half an hour later at Joe's Italian Pizza, they were seated on black vinyl chairs, with a football game playing on the flat-screen television mounted in the corner of the room. Their two extra-large pizzas had just been delivered, and Pastor David had prayed words of thanks for their food, direction for Ethan, and restoration of what had been lost.

Ethan had already filled them in on the details of the fire—at least what he knew, and Izzy shared the spotlight by talking about her recent role in the fall play.

After the prayer, Laurie, David's wife, took a slice of pizza from the pan in the middle of the table, and said, "Izzy, you and Ariana seem to have a love for the stage. Ariana did a lot of shows when she was younger."

Ariana shook her head affirmatively while she finished chewing her bite of pizza. "I was in a few musicals in junior high and high school."

"What else did you like to do when you were my age?" Izzy asked, shaking some parmesan cheese onto the top of her slice.

"Well, I was a cheerleader. And I was really involved with my church—youth group, worship team, church choir, children's Sunday School teacher. All that stuff."

"How did you two become friends?" Izzy asked Laurie and Ariana.

They looked at each other and laughed.

"My sister would make a great reporter," Ethan said, not sure if he should be embarrassed or proud of her conversational skills.

"Church," said Laurie.

"When I first came to Springfield, Izzy, I had just gotten a divorce, and I was having a really tough time. David and Laurie have been really, really good friends," said Ariana.

"Ethan just broke up with his fiancé, so I bet he relates, don't you Ethan?" Izzy asked.

Ethan no longer felt any sense of pride in Izzy's skills, only self-consciousness.

"Oh sorry," Izzy said, noticing Ethan's pained face. "At least I didn't say anything about Dad–"

Izzy's hand flew to her mouth. "Whoops. I think now would be a perfect time for me to go to the bathroom," she said before getting up and scurrying away.

After a moment of silence, David said, "seems like you've had quite the week."

"If Izzy was still here, I'm sure she'd be happy to fill you in," Ethan replied, half angry at her words, and half thankful for her outgoing personality that shielded him from having to carry the conversation for the majority of the lunch.

"She's really sweet," Laurie said, defending the girl.

"She is," Ethan replied honestly. "And David's right. This week has been rough."

"If you ever want to talk, let me know," Ariana said. "When you're committed to someone and they leave, it's really devastating."

"Thanks for the offer. I might take you up on that sometime," Ethan replied.

Chapter Eighteen

"I was beginning to think you weren't coming," Charles said when Jezmeen walked into his office on Sunday afternoon, ten minutes late.

"Sorry. There was a car in the ditch on the interstate, and I got stuck in traffic."

"It's icy out there. I'm glad you're okay."

As Jezmeen took off her coat, she reached into the pocket and pulled out a package wrapped in tissue paper.

"What's this?" he asked.

"Just something small for that hole on your bookshelf." Jezmeen pointed to the empty space between a miniature fake plant and a stack of books angled for aesthetics.

"A candle," he said, after unwrapping the tissue paper. He turned the light purple jar around to look at the label. "Lavender thyme."

"I read an article somewhere that said Christian counselors sometimes light a candle at each session to remind them the Holy Spirit is present. And lavender is calming," Jezmeen responded.

"You seem upbeat this afternoon. Does that mean you got a good night's sleep at a hotel last night?" Charles asked, leaning back into the chair.

"I've been looking forward to seeing you," Jez said with a smile.

"Well, the feeling is mutual," Charles replied looking into her eyes and then quickly down at the notepad he held in his hand. "I take it from the way you avoided the question that maybe you slept in your car?"

Jezmeen nodded her head sheepishly.

"I figure you'll fix all my problems. I guess I'm hopeful this therapy stuff will work."

"Well, Marie, I'm afraid you have your hopes pinned to the wrong person."

Jezmeen looked at him with concern.

"There's only One who can change everything for you. Thankfully He's with us now," Charles glanced at the candle. "But I'm going to do my best to listen and guide you with His help." He leaned forward. "Do you mind if I pray?"

"Sure," she replied.

After Charles asked God for wisdom, peace and direction for Jezmeen, he jumped right in. "Tell me about your mom. I know you told me a little about her, but I'd like to hear more," he said.

"No offense, but how does knowing about Sherry help me be less scared to part with my money?"

"Everything you're experiencing and feeling is connected to your thoughts and memories. If I can show you some of your false narratives, then I can help you learn to speak the truth."

"Okay," Jezmeen said with reservation. "I know I need help, so if you think this is the way to go, I'm game. Let's see, Sherry had me when she was nineteen. I guess we lived with her mom when I was one or two, but I don't remember that far back. Mostly I just remember her bouncing from one relationship to another."

"And she was a hairdresser?"

"Yes, but not a very good one, to be honest. She got fired from at least two salons."

"Was that because she didn't show up?"

"I don't think so. I think it was because she worked slowly."

"Did she ever leave you home alone when you were young or neglect to feed you, take care of your basic needs?"

Jezmeen laughed. "When I was young, all those questions would've gotten me placed in foster care."

"Would you have preferred that?"

"Quite possibly."

"So, she was neglectful?"

"In every way," Jezmeen said looking down.

"Did anyone ever see that and try to help you?"

"My second-grade teacher, Miss March, tried. One day I came to school with a feminine product on my knee. You know why it was there?"

"Why?"

"I scraped it playing outside, and we didn't have any band-aids. Of course, my mom wasn't around. She was out. Didn't get in until four in the morning. So, she didn't know about it. So I found a feminine product in the bathroom and taped it on my leg. Maybe that gave it away to Miss March, or maybe it was because most of my lunches consisted of a bag of cereal. And when I say bag, I mean the inner plastic lining part, curled up and rubber-banded or taped shut.

"What did your teacher do to help?"

"Well, she called my mom in for a conference. Of course, my mom didn't go, and she thought I had been saying bad things about her. So, Sherry threatened to give me away. I don't know who she thought she'd give me to, but when you're seven, you take your mom at her word. Shortly after that we moved apartments, which meant I moved schools."

"I take it you lived in many places when you were growing up?"

"I lost count. That's why I keep the list," Jezmeen said, oddly aware that she felt proud because she wasn't exactly like her mother.

"How many people have you lived with?"

"Ethan made 16."

"You must get tired of constantly trying to stay a step ahead of your situation."

"I guess I've gotten used to it," Jez lied.

"Would you like to try a different way of life? One that could be more peaceful?"

"You want to take me in?" Jez asked only half-joking, knowing she'd jump at the chance to move in with Charles.

"You assume living with me would be peaceful," he said, with a teasing twinkle in his eye. "Seriously, staying with me won't solve your problems. It would just enable you to continue in this cycle."

"I know it seems like I am following in my mom's footsteps, but I'm not. Really. I'm saving up. She never did."

"And the more you save up, the less you're like her?"

"I plan to move near the ocean. One day I won't have to live like her. I won't have to depend on anyone. But if I spend it all now, I'll never have freedom."

"If you don't feel comfortable answering this, you don't have to, but in order to understand your situation, I'm wondering if you could give me a ballpark figure of how much you have saved?"

Jezmeen sighed. How much did she trust Charles? She'd never revealed this information to anyone. Someone could try to steal from her.

"Over a quarter of a million dollars," she replied easily, realizing she trusted him. After saving for so long, without telling a soul, she felt a sense of pride at how much she'd acquired.

"Wow," Charles said, shaking his head. "You have been really disciplined with your finances." He paused, thinking. "Have you *ever* had to pay for housing?"

"Well, it's not like I wasn't paying 'rent,' if you know what I mean," she looked down, embarrassed that she admitted this to him. Jez respected Charles and wondered if he would look at her with judgment. But his gaze was filled with compassion. "My mom always said, 'Nothing in life is free,'" Jezmeen continued.

Charles sat quietly for a moment, as if contemplating which direction to take the conversation. "Have you ever calculated when you get to 'retire?'"

"All the time. If I buy a small place, I think I could get by for about eight years."

"And you just turned thirty," Charles said, remembering the cake he gave her. "So, you still have quite a while to save for retirement?"

"Unfortunately. Now you can see why I *have* to sleep in my car until I find a new place. And I've been thinking, if I go back to bartending, I'll have the best opportunity to find someone to stay with for free."

"Did you enjoy interior decorating?"

"It was the best job I ever had."

Again, Charles paused and then rerouted the conversation again.

"Have you ever thought about how your mom felt giving herself away?" Charles asked gently.

185

"Huh?" Jez asked.

"Your mom modeled many things for you, and one of them was low self-worth. She valued herself so little that she willingly let anyone take a part of her."

"Yeah, but that was Sherry. I already told you, I'm not like her," Jez said with slight disgust at being compared to her mom. "Sherry is *still* being played. She's never been in control a day in her life. I'm in complete control," she argued.

"So, if you're in complete control, you could change direction today, right?"

"Sure, but you know I'm not prepared yet financially," Jezmeen said, beginning to get upset. These questions seemed to be circling into a pointless abyss.

"Then you *want* to keep living this way?"

"No, but what other choice do I have?"

"You don't have to wait ten, twenty more years to be free. You can decide you want your body. Your mind. Your soul. You can choose to do things differently. Starting today...if you want."

Ethan should've known he controlled very little. Working at the command of the weather had been his life the last three years, but he still wished it was more dependable. He shifted a lever and released the bucket on the track loader he'd rented for the day.

He'd planned to start cleaning up the debris left from the fire the Saturday before, but it had rained...finally. The land had been dry for so long...which the fire inspector said helped fuel the conditions for the blaze.

Ethan also rented a dumpster, and he emptied the charred debris into the big, brown trash receptacle. Izzy had wanted to help, but he assured her it was a one-person job. Plus, after two weeks of living with her full-time, and without Jezmeen to absorb some of her words, he was worn out. She was a wonderful younger sister, but she wanted to be near him whenever he was home. And he was used to personal space...and time.

Together they had walked through the rubble weeks earlier, seeking any surviving treasures the fire left behind. Besides some plastic pots that melted into an enormous, odd octopus-shape, they'd only found a few metal strips from the greenhouses and some blackened boards.

Until Izzy found the earrings. She hunted for them with an eagle's eye. The cash box was still intact, but the paper money inside was burned. But the pennies, dimes, nickels, quarters...and the earrings endured. Black soot covered them all.

Ethan pushed another load of ashes into the bucket and headed to the dumpster again. The clean-up project was monotonous, but many jobs as a landscaper were repetitive, and that didn't bother him. However, the continued dumping of waste did. It was as if he was slowly saying goodbye to his dreams one pile at a time.

The fire inspector had told him that the blaze was caused by environmental factors—not faulty electrical wiring or arson. A cigarette butt was mentioned again, and Ethan couldn't help but strongly suspect his dad. Afterall, the inspector was certain it had started in the back left corner of the building. At first, Ethan wondered what his dad would have been doing in that area, but then he realized it was the exact location of the leak in the roof. He had talked to Wayne weeks earlier about checking it out.

If Wayne knew the fault was his, the guilt could've led Wayne to his relapse, but Ethan wasn't about to ask. During their brief five-minute phone conversation the day before, Wayne sounded more upbeat and hopeful than he had two weeks earlier when Ethan dropped him off.

When Ethan first met Wayne, he seemed so strong and full of faith. Wayne had shared that he was a recovering alcoholic, but he'd been sober for two years. So Ethan was shocked by what seemed like a sudden downfall, and he wondered why Wayne's relationship with God didn't keep him from backsliding. Then again, since Ethan had become a Christian, his business had gone up in flames, and his fiancé left him. Didn't God protect His children?

With another load in the bucket, the track loader rumbled over the littered ground, and Ethan thought about the earrings. Amazingly, the diamonds were just fine. All that needed replacing were the stainless-steel wires. With the earrings and the engagement ring, he was gathering a little collection of jewelry, thanks to Jezmeen's cast-offs.

Jezmeen had walked out two days before their one-year anniversary. After reciting "love is a choice" so many times before the marriage proposal, he wondered why he still didn't feel a sense of relief. After all, he was no longer bound by commitment. There was no baby. He wasn't going to be a father. She wasn't a woman of good character. And she clearly didn't need him. He was free.

He could date anyone he wanted, but there was no one he desired. Not even Ariana. Once she found out about his break-up with Jezmeen, Ariana had become suddenly friendly again. After church the day before, she'd rested her hand on his bicep while she visited with him and Izzy. And when he said something that wasn't even funny, but could've seemed like a joke, she laughed far too excitedly.

Maybe it was because his co-worker Mark had told him Ariana liked him, but he sensed her affection was angled at him. Which was ironic because his assistant VJ couldn't stop talking about her, even though he never showed up at church, as he'd promised. With her beautiful voice, angelic face, shiny black hair and a desire to please God, Ariana seemed like a perfect match. Could it be God's leading?

Chapter Nineteen

Jezmeen fanned out the paint swatch book and held up a line of neutrals against Charles' family room wall. Instead of meeting at his office, Charles said that they could talk and work at his house because he still wanted to hire her to decorate his family room. So, a week later she was at his cozy ranch assessing the space.

"Can you believe that?" she asked Charles, who sat at the kitchen table while she worked.

"It's a great story," he replied. Jezmeen had just finished telling Charles about her first night's stay at a hotel. She was very proud of herself for being brave enough to part with $68, but she was more pleased with what happened while she was there.

"And to think of all the rooms I could have stayed in, mine would have a Bible?" Jezmeen said, flipping to another row of colors.

"Have you ever stayed at a hotel before?" Charles asked skeptically.

"No, why."

"It's the Gideons."

"Huh?"

"Gideons International is a Christian group that puts Bibles in hotel rooms all over the world."

"Oh," Jez said deflated.

"But still," Charles replied, "You turned to the scripture, '*The Lord will provide,*' and right afterwards you got that call."

"I was shocked to hear from the Turners," Jezmeen exclaimed.

"They know you're a great decorator. Just like I do," Charles said, taking a sip of his coffee.

"Well, if they really knew that they wouldn't have turned me down while I was at *Style Street.*"

"Don't you think that God may have wanted you to get the job when you were free from Monica's control? Instead of sharing the profit with her, while doing all the work, you're getting enough to live on for the rest of the year," Charles replied.

"I hadn't thought about it like that," Jez said, turning to look at Charles.

"And did you notice that when you took a step out in faith, doing something brand new—parting with some of your money and finding a place to stay—God blessed you," Charles continued.

"The Turners said the online company they hired had too many hidden costs, and they loved everything about my plan but the kitchen. They asked if I could tweak it a bit."

"Are you okay with that?"

"Of course. I don't cook, so maybe that's why I didn't do so well with that space."

"It's a good thing I didn't ask you to redo mine then," Charles teased.

"Are you hosting Thanksgiving?" she asked nonchalantly, while holding up another small tan square against the wall.

"No. I'm just picking up the pies. My sister's doing all the hard work, and we're going to my parents. Maybe you would like to–" Charles stopped himself. Pausing a second, he continued, "–would like to show me what color you're thinking of using?"

"Well, it's your choice. But I like white sand or golden ecru," Jezmeen said. She walked over the two strips and put them on the table in front of Charles.

"Both are nice," he said.

She headed into the family room, which was empty except for a navy blue couch, flat screen television and an oval-shaped coffee table. Charles followed.

"So, you'd like a couple of chairs. Side tables. Plants. Lamps. Maybe a picture or two. What's your budget?" she asked.

"After furnishing a whole office, it's limited. And I'll paint the walls myself."

Jezmeen wondered if Charles had hired her because he felt sorry for her, but then she remembered he offered the job before she'd been fired or knew she was homeless.

When she learned he lived in Country Club Estates, she thought he was rich. But the houses in the neighborhood were primarily built in the 1970's and weren't as upscale as the title made them sound. Starting a new practice had to be financially risky, and while she didn't know what counselors made, she figured it wasn't as lucrative as some careers.

"How was your first week with clients?" she asked, making small talk as she measured the walls with a laser measuring device.

"Good. After four months off, I was ready to begin again. And being here is a completely fresh start," he said with intention.

"Well, you haven't had a complete four months off, you've been counseling me," she said, sending a smile his way.

"You're different," he said sincerely.

"How so?"

"You're not a client. I care about you," his voice was warm and rich.

Jezmeen laughed. "That makes it sound like you don't care about all the others."

"True," he chuckled. "I guess that didn't come out right. I care about *all* my clients, but a client would never come to my house. There are professional boundaries. And I certainly wouldn't be going with a client to look at rental houses and apartments."

"Thank you for agreeing to do that with me," Jez said. "I feel so much better knowing I won't be making that decision alone."

"I'm proud of you for being so courageous to take this step."

Before she had begun exploring the design of his space, they'd sat at his kitchen table for almost an hour peeling back the layers of Jezmeen's life choices. And Charles mentioned staying in a hotel wasn't a wise choice financially long-term. He suggested renting something for a few months until she knew where her career was headed. And he threw out the idea of taking on a female roommate to help with the rent.

"You're willing to change," Charles said. "Not everyone is, and many people take weeks or months to feel ready."

"Well, the little issue of not having a toilet and a shower certainly spurred me on," Jezmeen said jokingly but knowing it was the truth.

Jezmeen jotted down the length and height of the walls before moving to measure the television. Charles leaned against the wall, continuing to watch her work.

"My wife never would've approved of this TV," Charles chuckled.

"Why not?"

"Too big. Too much of a focal point in a small room."

"Was she one to sit on the couch and watch TV with you?" Jez asked.

"She was more of a reader. I like the big screen for football games."

"If you two didn't watch TV together, what did you like to do?"

"She always worked odd hours, so we were pretty independent. But we went to church together." He smiled, thinking about Katherine. "We loved finding little dives to eat at, and whenever we could we'd take walks at the park."

"You must miss her companionship."

"It's been agonizingly lonely," he said honestly. "We loved taking vacations each year—usually finding a beach."

"When was your last vacation?"

"Does the last four months count?"

"You mean moving here and opening a business?"

"Yeah."

"What do you think?"

"Probably not," he sighed. "I guess it's been almost three years. We took a trip to the Gulf Shores a few months after her diagnosis. She was still well enough to get away, and we wanted to do that together. It was the last trip we took."

"Did you know it then?"

Jezmeen asked the question casually as she measured the fireplace.

"Your bartender's counseling degree is shining through," Charles teased.

"Sorry, you don't have to answer that."

"No, it's fine. Refreshing actually. And to be honest, no. We both had such optimism that she'd beat the cancer. She'd been responding well to treatment at that point, and lots of people were praying for her. It wasn't until the last two months that I began to recognize the Lord might take her from me," Charles said, his voice softening.

"I bet the last year and a half without her has been hard," Jez said, stopping her work and looking at him.

"The darkest time of my life," Charles said flatly.

Jez waited in silence for Charles to continue.

"But working through my grief with my own counselor helped immensely. And moving here has been…" Charles paused searching for the right word, "transformative."

"I imagine not having to look at all the places you had memories…starting over…is good."

Jez jotted down the mantle measurements and went to put the pencil behind her ear, but instead it clattered to the floor and rolled towards Charles. He reached to retrieve it as Jez bent down to do the same, and they bumped foreheads.

"Oww," Jez cried, her hand flying up to her forehead.

Charles rubbed the spot on his head where they collided.

"I'm so sorry," he grimaced. "Let me get you an ice pack."

"I'm fine," Jez said standing back up.

"At least sit down for a second," Charles urged.

Jezmeen moved to the couch and leaned her back against the cushion.

"Are *you* okay?" she asked.

"Yeah. I'm hard-headed," he teased and then sat down beside her.

They rested in silence for a moment.

"Must be nice to have your own place," she said wistfully.

"You and your fiancé had a house, didn't you?"

"Yeah, I decorated, but he owns it."

"How come you left him? Was he abusive?"

"Ethan, no!" she exclaimed. "You'd like him— he's a Christian."

"So, what happened?"

Jezmeen got quiet. A majority of what she'd shared with Charles highlighted her mom's flaws, not her own.

"He was ready for marriage, and I wasn't," Jez said, only revealing a portion of the truth.

"I imagine, knowing a little bit about your past relationships, that trusting men is very hard. And with all that you've been through, you may not even *feel* anything."

197

Jezmeen said nothing.

"Both of those things are very normal, after what you've gone through and been exposed to."

"I think my head's better," Jez said, not wanting to explore that topic any further. "How about we go over the timeline for the project before I go."

Charles knew he'd hit a wall, and he vowed to explore it further when she was ready again.

The Sunday School classroom was buzzing with after-class conversations. Izzy was chatting away with an older couple at the table in front of them. Ethan would've liked to bolt, but Izzy needed the connections. He tried to look busy, staring at his cell phone, as Ariana headed his way.

"Hey Ethan! How was your Thanksgiving?" she asked as she pulled up a chair next to him.

"Quiet. My mom came over. Izzy and I tackled our first turkey," he said.

Feelings of nervousness about talking to a woman—a beautiful woman—came over him.

"Wow. That's impressive. I went to my mom and dad's. Their landscaping still looks gorgeous, by the way."

"Glad to hear it."

"Can you believe it's December already," Ariana said, reaching her hands to her hair, and then back down with a strange look in her eyes.

"I'm half thankful that business has slowed down and half wishing it was spring already," Ethan replied.

"You run like a quarterback for a couple of seasons, don't you? It must be nice to have a winter break," Ariana replied.

"Yeah, but with everything burning down–"

"Can you start rebuilding, or is it too cold?"

"It's not necessarily the weather, although that doesn't help," Ethan said, not wanting to reveal that it was mostly financial.

There was a pause in the conversation, so Ethan took the opportunity to escape.

"Well, I better get Izzy some lunch. She's got homework to finish this afternoon."

"Right," Ariana replied, sounding disappointed. "Hey, before you go, I have a favor to ask you."

"Sure," Ethan said.

Her hands flew to the nape of her neck and then back down.

"I've got this company Christmas party in two weeks, and I'm like the only employee in my office that's single. I really don't want to go alone."

"You want to take Izzy?" Ethan teased, knowing she was asking him, but not wanting to respond.

She laughed. "I was thinking about someone a little older."

"Two weeks, huh? I think we're going to pick up my dad that weekend. He's been...out of town."

"Are you going to be gone on Saturday *and* Sunday? 'Cause the party's on Saturday, and we wouldn't have to stay long."

"I think–" Ethan began.

"Ethan," Izzy called from the table in front of them, "we're going to get dad on Sunday December 12th, right?"

"Yeah, I think so," Ethan mumbled.

"Okay, thanks, just wanted to let Doris and Howard know, so they can pray for us," Izzy replied, before turning back to their conversation.

"I think that I am free on Saturday," he replied with a sheepish smile, wishing Izzy hadn't blown his cover.

"Great," Ariana replied. "I guess I'll need your cell number, so I can text you more details."

Ethan shared his number, and she typed it into her phone.

"Well, if nothing else, I hear we'll have a fantastic dinner," she said.

"Sounds good," Ethan said, trying to sound more upbeat than he felt.

"Thank you," she said softly, touching his forearm. "Really."

Chapter Twenty

Jezmeen would have loved this type of party, Ethan thought, as he stood in line at the bar waiting to order two colas. The administrative staff at the medical complex where Ariana worked had rented out a banquet room at one of the nicest hotels in town. Most of the crowd sat at the circular tables which were decked out in cream linen and crystalware. A few others milled about, socializing, and while everyone was dressed to impress, Ariana, by far, was the most beautiful.

She always looked great on Sunday mornings, but she literally sparkled in her gold sequined dress with a V-cut neckline and rouching along the left side. Ethan didn't own a suit or a tuxedo, so he shelled out over a hundred dollars to rent one, all the while mentally grumbling about the hassle of the whole evening.

Even when Jezmeen hosted dinner parties at their home, Ethan didn't enjoy them. Now he was in a room full of strangers with a woman he barely knew. He hoped his lousy attitude wasn't emanating, but the ride to the Crowne Plaza had been stilted. Ariana bubbled over with excitement, but Ethan's anxieties caused him to clam up.

After doling out fifteen dollars for two drinks, Ethan's attitude didn't improve. Besides wondering how he'd make it through the night, he was also concerned about the drive to pick up his dad the next day. They had a three-hour drive to Wayne's rehabilitation center. He and Izzy would be starting out early, missing church.

They would have a private therapy session with Wayne and his counselor before driving back to Springfield. During their last phone conversation, Wayne revealed part of the relapse was caused by his fears of taking care of Izzy full-time. He'd never had to be fully in charge of her care, and he was concerned he couldn't do it well enough.

Ethan had agreed to let Izzy stay on with him as long as Wayne needed. With business slowing down, transporting her to and from school wasn't much of an issue. He'd even taken Izzy to see her grandma twice in the last month, but he figured Wayne could help with that once he got back.

Laughter erupted as Ethan sat down at the table. He handed Ariana her drink before taking a sip of his own.

"Kelly was just telling us a funny story. She didn't know B-e-a-u was actually pronounced Bo," Ariana explained with a giggle.

"Ariana, here, would never get a name wrong," Kelly replied from across the table. "She was actually the admin employee of the month for November."

"That's great," Ethan said.

"She always goes out of her way to give everyone excellent service," Kelly said.

Ariana's cheeks reddened at the attention and compliments. The conversation continued to swirl around him for the next fifteen minutes until the salads were delivered. The women at the table, all administrative employees, chatted about work, while the men tried to make small talk about football, their jobs, and the upcoming Christmas holiday. Ethan watched the dialogue ping-pong and began to get a headache from the noise mixed with the concentration required trying to keep up.

By the time the dinners were served, Ethan's temples were throbbing, so he excused himself to go to the restroom. As he ran his wrists in cold water, to see if cooling off would help, he said a short prayer.

God, I don't know why I'm here. I'm trying to be kind to Ariana, but I'm miserable and just want the night to be over. Please help me to have endurance for this thing. I don't want to ruin her evening.

When he stepped back into the hallway, he saw Ariana sitting on a padded bench in front of the bathrooms fiddling with a gold bangle on her wrist.

"You okay?" she asked.

"Yeah, why?"

"You seemed quiet in there."

"I've got a headache, and I'm not great at small talk."

She patted the space next to her on the bench.

"I've got some pain reliever in my purse." She retrieved a little white bottle and handed him a capsule.

"Thanks," he said, swallowing the pill without water.

"We don't have to stay long. After dinner, they do a couple of drawings for gift cards, and then we can go."

"I don't want to spoil your fun," Ethan said, noticing he was a good head and shoulders taller than the petite beauty sitting next to him.

Ariana laughed. "You think this is fun for me?"

"It isn't?" he asked, surprised.

"No! I hate these kinds of things. I'm just here because I feel obligated."

"So, if you weren't at a fancy party on a Saturday night, what would you be doing?" Ethan asked, relaxing for the first time.

"Wearing sweatpants. Watching a Christmas movie. Maybe trying out a new cookie recipe. I love to bake."

"That sounds like my kind of night."

"You like to bake, too?" Ariana teased.

Ethan laughed. "I like to eat cookies."

"Favorite kind?" Ariana asked.

"Well, I'll never pass up a classic chocolate chip, but I also really like this certain kind my grandma would make. They were called Divinity, I think, but they had chocolate chips in them."

"You mean the kind that's made with egg whites, and they look like little puffy white mountains?"

"I don't know what they're made with, but the description sounds right. All this talk about food makes me think we better get back in there," Ethan said, secretly thankful for the medicine and the promise to leave early.

Ethan started to stand up, but Ariana put a hand on his knee.

"Hey, before we go back in there with everyone, I also wanted to ask about your trip tomorrow. I know you said you were going to get your dad. Was he away on business?"

Ethan wasn't sure how much he wanted to share.

"I only ask because you've been pretty tight-lipped about the whole thing, and I want you to know that I care about what's going on in your life," she said.

She stared at him with brown eyes that were filled with compassion, and her hands were quiet for once.

"Thanks," he said sincerely. "My dad's been working on his health."

When he didn't say more, Ariana continued, "Well, I'll be praying for your travels, and if you ever want to talk, please know I'm here for you."

This wasn't the first time Ariana offered to listen. Maybe one day he'd actually take her up on the offer. He let her lead them back into the banquet room, and true to her word, Ariana whisked them away as soon as they officially learned neither had been chosen for any prizes.

Ariana and Ethan talked about Izzy the whole ride back to Ariana's apartment, and when he dropped her off, she thanked him again for accompanying her.

Before she shut the passenger door, she leaned back into the warm car and said, "Ethan Adams, you're one of the best men I know. Be safe tomorrow because I can't imagine this world without you." With that she headed into the apartment building, turning to wave goodbye at the entrance. Little snowflakes had begun to swirl, and the exterior lights gave Ariana a warm glow.

As Ethan drove away, he thought about Ariana's words. *One of the best men I know.* What had he done to deserve such praise? Ethan had never felt special, or good, or kind. Even after becoming a Christian, he still struggled with self-worth.

The birthmarks on his face had been removed, but the scars from his friendless childhood were still etched on his soul. Would he ever be able to receive and give love the way God intended?

Chapter Twenty-One

The chimes on the door sounded as Jezmeen stepped into *Style Street*. Gabrielle was ringing up a customer's purchase at the counter, so Jezmeen sauntered around the storefront while she waited. She spotted the blanket she'd used when she'd slept on the floor of the office.

Had she really gone from homeless to apartment renter in a matter of three weeks? Charles had spent a whole morning touring properties with her. He took notes on each place and asked about potential discounts or hidden fees. Hours later, he talked through the list, while they sat in her car. He helped her rule out the lowest cost option because it was in a shady part of town, and with a student discount, she was able to afford a studio apartment on the west-end, as long as she signed up for online classes.

She went back to Poplar Place by herself and reluctantly parted with over a thousand dollars, which was two months of rent. She could get back the security deposit when she moved out...if she kept the place in good condition.

By dinner, she was living on her own for the first time ever. Jezmeen felt neither nervous and scared nor liberated and free. She figured it was because she'd moved so many times, that the new change would take time to sink in.

After sleeping on the floor for one night, she purchased a box spring, mattress, and bedding set the next day from a consignment shop. Then she hit the thrift stores where she purchased some inexpensive dishes, a card table and chairs. She couldn't bring herself to spend anymore of her savings, so her furnishings were sparse. But they were all her own.

Back at *Style Street,* Jezmeen picked up a small wooden bird and flipped it over to see the price tag. It was $15.99 with a twenty-five percent-off sticker. Next to the hutch topped with birds, sat a black leather chair. She ran her hand over the back and spotted another discounted price. As her eyes scanned the store, she noticed everything was on sale, and she was surprised there wasn't more of a crowd.

"Thanks for coming in," Jezmeen heard Gabrielle say, and Jez headed towards the counter.

"Hey, Marie," Gabrielle said as she approached.

"How are things going? Did Monica hire anyone to replace me yet?" Jezmeen asked.

"Not that I know of. She didn't even ask me to put an ad in the paper."

"That's odd," Jezmeen said. "Who's finishing up the three new jobs I brought in?"

"Monica. But one client cancelled since you left, leaving her with just two projects right now," Gabrielle replied. "It's a good thing you came on a weekday. She's been here every weekend since you…left."

"Got canned," Jezmeen winked.

"Like the five before you," Gabrielle sighed. "To be honest, you brought in the most new business by far. I was shocked when I heard you'd been fired."

209

"Me too."

"I think she was just threatened by you," Gabrielle said. "She doesn't like anyone to upstage her, and you're a good decorator."

"Wow," Jezmeen said, taking in the compliment. "Thanks."

"You here to get your paycheck?" Gabrielle asked.

"Yeah."

Gabrielle pushed a button on the register, opened the drawer, pulled out the money tray, retrieved a white envelope, and handed it to Jez.

"Did you get a new job?"

Jezmeen didn't know if she should admit the Turners hired her. Monica could make trouble if she found out.

"I decided to try working for myself in the field," she admitted honestly. "I'm thinking of taking some online courses to get my certification."

"Good for you," Gabrielle said, then greeted a couple who came in the door.

"I'm surprised you aren't busier with the sale going on," Jez said watching the couple check out a coffee table.

"Business has been slow," Gabrielle said, emphasizing the last word. "Usually before Christmas we're swamped. "

"That's too bad," Jez replied. "Wonder why?"

"I think Monica's been pulling back on the advertising budget."

"Sorry. I bet the hours drag."

"They sure can."

"Excuse me, Miss," the woman who had entered called from a dining set. "Could you help me?"

"Well, I'll let you get back to it. Thanks for everything," Jez said, not knowing what else to say, and with her final paycheck from *Style Street* in hand, she exited out the door for what she thought would be the last time.

Ethan rang the doorbell at the Rogers' farmhouse. Claire Rogers, his cute, red-headed neighbor and office manager, was leaving for China in a few weeks with her fiancé. Claire had met her fiancé Tyler when she went to teach English as a second language in Tianjin the year before. When her dad had a stroke, she came back to Springfield and resumed her position as Ethan's employee. With Christmas approaching and Claire's imminent departure, Ethan wanted to share some gifts.

"Hey Ethan," Claire said, answering the door.

He held up a red gift bag covered with a white snowflake pattern and a smaller one with polar bears dancing with candy canes.

"I brought you and your parents a little something," Ethan said.

"That was so thoughtful," she said with a smile. "You want to come in? My parents went to do some errands, but I'll tell them you stopped by. Do you want a cup of coffee?" she asked.

"No thanks," he replied, following her into the kitchen.

"Is Tianjin as cold as Springfield in the winter?" Ethan asked, shivering from his short walk over from his house.

"Well, it's in the northern part of China, so it's pretty cold. At least I've been told. I was only there in the summer. And the weather was lovely then."

"How's your dad doing?" Ethan asked, knowing he had intense speech therapy after the stroke.

"Great," Claire replied. "Every so often he'll forget how to pronounce a word, but overall, you'd never know."

Ethan sat down at a counter stool, and Claire stood across from him at the kitchen island.

"And you?" Ethan asked with concern. "How's your health?"

Earlier in the summer, he'd found out that she'd managed Type 1 diabetes since she was a young girl.

"Stress can make my numbers go crazy, so with Tyler coming and us heading to China, it's been a little unstable, but that's to be expected. Anything new with the fire investigation?" she asked.

"Nothing since the last time we talked."

"So, it was just some natural cause, and we may never know how it started?"

"That's it in a nutshell."

Ethan took off his gloves and put them in his coat pockets.

"Do you want me to take your jacket?" Claire asked, aware of his movement.

"Nah. I won't stay long. I just wanted to bring you and your parents a Christmas gift since I can't go to their party this year."

"Are you hosting something yourself?"

"Kind of. I'm having my dad and mom over. And Izzy, of course."

"So she's still with you?"

Ethan nodded in affirmation.

"Why don't you open your gifts," Ethan said pointing to the snowflake package.

"Okay."

She pulled out the tufts of red tissue paper and set them on the counter.

213

"A couples devotional," she exclaimed cradling a hardcover book. "Thank you."

"You're welcome. There were a bunch of them at the Christian bookstore, so you can always exchange it, if there's something else you'd like."

"No, this looks great," she said, flipping through the pages.

"There's more," Ethan said.

She reached in and lifted out a plaque.

"Adams Landscaping employee of the year," she laughed.

"You've always been the encouraging one at work," Ethan said, remembering how she used to write employees notes when she received feedback from the customers about their good work.

"This is special," she replied.

"I know there weren't many employees to compete with," he chuckled, "but seriously, you've been an amazing assistant, and I'm going to miss you so much."

"Thanks, Ethan. I've been praying for your business." She put the plaque and devotion back into the bag. "At least you've got the debris all cleared," she said.

"Maybe someday I'll be able to rebuild. For right now, I'm trying to see how God's working in the wilderness."

Claire gave him a quizzical glance.

Ethan laughed. "Our pastor gave a sermon on the Israelites in the wilderness last Sunday. He talked about how to live in the land of 'in-between.' When we're not where we want to be, how we can trust God's still leading."

"Sounds like a good message," Claire replied.

"It was. Especially since I feel like every place I turn; things aren't working out how I thought they would."

"Are you referring to Jezmeen leaving? 'Cause if so, I think that's for the best."

Ethan instantly recalled how sick Claire looked when Jezmeen had accidentally messed up her insulin dosing back in August.

"I can imagine you don't think that highly of her."

"True, but I also think you need someone who's living life with an upward call, like you."

"It's not just the break-up with Jez though. It's my dream of growing plants going up in smoke— literally. And taking care of Izzy. And worrying about my dad."

"How many more days till he's back?" Claire asked. Ethan had shared with her that he had taken him to southern Illinois for rehab.

"Izzy and I picked him up yesterday," he replied.

"How'd that go?" Claire asked before taking a drink of her water.

"I learned a lot. We had this therapy session before he left, and I had no idea that one of the signs that he was slipping was that he'd taken up smoking cigarettes again. So, I know to watch for that now."

Ethan played with the saltshaker on the counter.

"He was really moody a lot before he relapsed. I guess he was struggling with worry over taking on Izzy full-time, and he was really stressed about doing things right with me. I was shocked he was so burdened by our relationship. I feel bad–"

"He doesn't regret having you in his life?" Claire asked with concern.

"No. It's just that he feels so much guilt about not being there for me, and the more pressure he was putting on himself to be perfect, the more he felt like he couldn't uphold his image."

"Poor guy."

"I know, right? So, the counselor said it's helpful for me to be encouraging with my dad, that he's enough the way he is."

"Is that okay with you?"

"Sure. It's just that nothing right now is how I would've dreamed it to be. Supporting my dad. Taking care of my sister. Breaking up with my fiancé. Living in the country without all my plants."

Claire moved to the open bar stool next to Ethan and sat down. Sunlight from the winter morning streamed in the three large windows by the kitchen table, and Ethan felt a pang of sadness at the thought of Claire leaving. She'd become a true friend.

"So, what'd your pastor say?" Claire asked, swiveling her stool to face Ethan.

"Huh?"

"About living in the land of in-between?"

"Oh, right. Just that if God led His children with a cloud by day and a pillar of fire by night, one step at a time, He'll do the same for us—for me. I don't have to know the end, just walk in the now."

"Not easy," she smiled.

"You been there before?" Ethan asked.

"Lots of times. Even now. Tyler and I are finishing off the school year in Tianjin, then coming home this summer, but after that we don't know what we'll do. Live in Springfield by my parents? Go to Iowa by his? Return to Tianjin? If so, for how long?"

Claire flattened a piece of red tissue paper beneath her fingers as she continued.

"But in the meantime, we're praying, and we're walking forward. And you know what, Ethan? You learn the most in the wilderness. When you get to the Promised Land, you'll be strong and lean and healthy because of all that walking."

"I'm going to miss you, Claire," Ethan said, his voice breaking. "I'm a better person for knowing you."

She patted his hand, resting on the counter, twice. "It's not like I'm going to be gone forever.

217

There's already a wedding invitation with your name on it."

"Literally?" Ethan asked.

Claire laughed. "No, not yet, but there will be."

Chapter Twenty-Two

Charles poured himself a second cup of coffee and topped off Jezmeen's mug at the same time. He had yet to admit that their weekly sessions were therapy, but Jezmeen knew exactly what they were. Now on their fifth one, Jezmeen felt...different.

With Charles' support she enrolled in Ashworth College's online interior design certification program. If she worked diligently, she could complete the program in only four months.

Balancing classes and working for the Turners would be Jezmeen's new normal. She'd met with the Turners, setting a timeline, budget, and signing a contract for the job. She'd begin decorating the first week of January. So, for the time being she was living off her savings, which made her feel uncomfortable, but Charles constantly reminded her God was in control.

She had yet to decide if she'd actually charge Charles for the work she was doing. They hadn't discussed payment, and they'd purchased everything for his space during one shopping spree together, never exchanging any money for the job. But the way he listened, validated, and offered sound advice was compensation beyond what she was offering him.

Charles returned the coffee pot to its base on the kitchen counter. "Well, I'm glad to hear living alone is going just fine. Not that I doubted you'd have any trouble."

"With Christmas coming up in a few days, do you have any plans?" he asked.

The sky was pearl gray out of the alcove window, and Jez watched a squirrel scurry up the large tree trunk in the middle of the backyard.

"Not really. It's a family holiday, and well, you know, I don't have any family here."

"How about friends?"

"I know this sounds pathetic, but not really," she said, making light of it by laughing.

"Why do you think it's hard for you to make friends?"

"Girls never seemed to like me. And guys, well, I tend to run out on them, or they run out on me. So, it's not like anyone is staying in touch."

"Do you get lonely?"

She shrugged. How could she explain to Charles that she felt the same way her whole life. Empty. Dull. Sad. Until the last few weeks. The last few weeks she felt hopeful. Like life was entering her dry bones. Even her headaches and stomach aches began disappearing.

"When you were growing up, how did you celebrate Christmas?" Charles asked.

"Every year was different," Jez replied, cradling the mug in her hands.

"Did you have a favorite?"

Jezmeen pursed her lips to one side and thought.

"I guess the year I got a Barbie Dream Mansion. My mom was dating some guy who had money. Of course, when she broke up with him, there wasn't enough room in her two-door car for that toy. She'd packed up our lives when I was at school. So, I never saw the thing again."

"Do you think that's why all you've traveled with, since you've been an adult, is your suitcases of clothes?"

"Never thought about it."

Charles rested his hands on the table.

"Have you ever forgiven your mom for all the hurtful things she did to you?"

"You mean let her off the hook for all the toys I had to abandon?" she said trying to sound funny even though she felt sad.

"Sure, but even deeper, forgive her for the example she set that shaped you."

"I'm really different from my mom, Charles," Jez said, her voice garnering an edge.

"You've told me that she let men use her so she could get something in return, right?"

"Yeah, why?"

"Have you done the same?"

"I guess you could see it like that," Jez said, twirling a curly brown stand of hair around the end of her fingers, "but I've been saving my money. I've been in control. It's been like a career."

Jezmeen didn't like being accused of being like her mom. Sherry had been called a whore, slut, prostitute. Jezmeen was smarter than her mom. She was... As Jezmeen tried to build herself up mentally, Nick's words flashed through her mind, "*You're a piece of trash.*"

"Did you ever give your body away when you didn't want to?"

"Depends on what you mean," Jez said flatly. "Can we talk about something else?" she asked, desperate to change the subject. She adored Charles and didn't want to talk about the dark side of her life.

"Sure, but can I ask one more question?"

"I guess."

"Did anyone ever just take intimacy from you when you didn't offer it?"

Jezmeen shifted in her chair. Did he mean in the middle of the night when she was thirteen, or from one of the losers after a bartending shift, or...she didn't want to remember anymore.

"Men like to take, Charles. And I like to give," she said with a light-hearted lilt.

"Do you think *all* men like to take?"

"Absolutely," she replied promptly. "Given the right circumstances."

"I'm sorry," he said softly.

"For what?"

"For the ones that took from you what they had no right to take."

"It's okay. I can compartmentalize. It's not like it means anything to me."

"Do you think it should?"

Jezmeen shrugged again. She didn't think she'd ever have the capacity to trust a man fully.

"You've been brave and strong to make so many changes, Marie. And I believe you can learn to trust. But it's going to require a lot of forgiveness. There's freedom in letting people off the hook, even when they don't deserve it. I think that you start with your mom, and then go to every man who's mistreated you. That will be a big undertaking. You can write to them and hold onto the notes, or journal, or pray. However you do it, I think you'll be amazed at what happens in you."

Jezmeen crossed her arms. She'd love to believe Charles, but it didn't seem so simple. She hadn't trusted anyone since her first boyfriend Steven, except maybe Izzy. She missed Izzy so much.

"The last person I trusted was a thirteen-year-old girl. What's that say about me?" Jez said, trying to laugh.

"That there's hope," Charles replied.

"So if I do all that forgiveness stuff, then I'll just start trusting people?"

"Not necessarily. But you'll be able to give people a fresh chance, without looking at everyone through the lens from your past."

"Charles, when I was in fifth-grade my mom dyed my hair blonde. I didn't want it to be blonde, but she thought it would look cute. It looked good for a while, but my roots grew back chocolate brown," she said.

"What are you trying to say?"

"No matter what I do, I'm still going to have the same roots."

"That's a good analogy. And you're right. Your past will always be a part of you, but you don't have to let it define your future."

Jezmeen watched a squirrel jump from one wobbly branch to another.

"Marie, there was a woman in the Bible named Rahab. She was a prostitute. But she had an encounter with some of God's followers and she chose to side with God—even putting her life and her family in danger to do so. And God made Rahab a part of the holy lineage of Jesus. God's own son, Jesus, came from a line with a prostitute in it. Doesn't that show that God can forgive anyone? Use anyone?"

The squirrel landed upside down unto the new branch and held on for dear life. Jezmeen wondered if that's what she looked like maneuvering through life. She'd gotten her own place. Signed up for college classes. Taken on a new job. Was that the extent of the changes for her, or could she really have victory over everything that defined her?

224

Charles waved to Jezmeen and pointed to the open seat next to him. Thankfully he'd reserved her a space at the end of the row, so she wouldn't have to shuffle past so many people.

"I'm glad you came," he said as she sat down beside him.

A woman with a tiny button nose, dark glasses, and jet black, thinning permed hair leaned across Charles' body.

"Marie," she said, "so nice to finally meet you."

"Likewise," Jez greeted Charles' sister, Nancy.

"This is my husband, Dwayne," Nancy said.

A portly man with a graying beard reached over Nancy and held out his hand. Jezmeen shook it.

"Merry Christmas," Dwayne bellowed to be heard over the din of the crowd in the sanctuary.

"Can you say that already?" Charles asked.

"Sure. We're only hours away," Jezmeen grinned at Dwayne. "Merry Christmas," she replied in return.

Nancy and Dwayne leaned back against the cushioned pew, and Jezmeen began to take off her cream winter jacket. As Charles saw her wiggling her arm out, he reached over and helped her.

"Thank you," she said.

A small orchestra on the platform began playing a Christmas hymn. Jezmeen recognized the tune. Not because she'd grown up listening to Christmas music, but because she listened to the Christian radio station all month, and they'd been playing holiday songs.

"Are you doing okay?" Charles whispered.

He smoothed down the back of her coat against her chair as he glanced at her.

"Sure," she lied. She'd been nervous all day, thinking about backing out since she left her "session" with Charles where he had invited her to go to his Christmas Eve church service.

She'd never been to church before, and she wasn't sure she wanted to break her perfect record. But being alone in her tiny, sparse apartment seemed unbearably lonely, and something inside her was relentlessly whispering that she needed to go. She purposely left her apartment as late as she could, while still making it there on time. And when she got out of her car to go in, she turned around twice, before deciding to follow through.

The congregation stood up to join in singing, and Jezmeen followed suit. After four verses of "Joy to the World," the music came to a close and everyone sat down. The lights on the platform dimmed and a young woman dressed in cream cotton robes and a headpiece slowly walked to center stage. Jezmeen doubted she was really pregnant, but rather she was depicting the Biblical Mary.

A low hum from the string section stirred to life in a quiet introduction before the piano layered over their melody. Then the young woman began to sing a ballad Jezmeen had never heard before.

226

Alive in me. The lyrics repeated many times throughout the song. The woman's beautiful voice haunted Jezmeen, but the words `I *surrender. Mighty King. Alive in me,"* resonated after the talented singer walked off the stage.

With quiet reverence, matching the mood in the sanctuary, the pastor made his way to the podium and spent the next twenty-five minutes speaking directly to Jezmeen. At least that's how it felt to her. It was as if the other five hundred or so people in the room weren't present. Everything he said seemed offered just for her benefit.

The pastor asked all the questions she was struggling with, as if he knew she would be here tonight. Was her past one that made her feel like God could never truly accept her? Had she held God at arm's length because of her sin? Could she sense there was more to life, but she was afraid to surrender?

The pastor tied the song into his sermon, asking the congregation to open their hearts to the Holy Spirit. Like Mary—be open and available. He closed in prayer, petitioning listeners to accept Jesus as their Savior.

And with an 'amen,' the hush in the room was lifted, and the orchestra burst into a lively tune. Announcements were made, a final hymn was sung, and the service came to an end. Jezmeen went through the motions of putting on her coat and making small talk with Nancy and Dwayne as they shuffled out of their seats, but her mind wanted to take her body to a quiet place to retreat and think. She needed to process all she'd heard and experienced.

As they made their way slowly down the crowded aisle, Nancy invited Jezmeen over for hot chocolate and cookies, but she politely declined. The wrestling inside her soul was too heavy for light-hearted socialization.

When they got to the church lobby, Charles offered to walk her to her car. Again she tried to withdraw alone, but Charles wouldn't hear of it. The December night was still, cool and crisp, and the smell of burning firewood wafted in the air. With a nearly full moon shining above, all Jezmeen's senses quickened.

"Did you enjoy the service?" Charles asked as they walked onto the blacktop.

"Very much," she replied.

"You're lost in thought," Charles said.

"How can you tell?"

"A by-product of studying people for a living," he smiled.

Jezmeen noted that his slender frame was made fuller by the thick brown coat he wore, a decade behind the trending style.

"Do you want to share?" he probed.

Did she? It seemed as if she was meant to take up a seat in the sanctuary. Meant to hear those words. Meant for her soul to stir. But if she "crossed the line," she'd plunge into Christendom. And for her that meant a whole new lifestyle.

She didn't really want to go back to living with men. Using them. Being used. But what if the interior decorating thing didn't work out? If she couldn't pay her bills, what would she do?

The pastor said Jesus was perfect. Pure. Holy. Unlike her. Yet he still loved her despite her imperfections. He lacked for nothing and still He wanted her...the way she was. She didn't have to go home and get cleaned up first. He did the cleansing.

Jezmeen hadn't spent much time contemplating the meaning of life. What would happen when she died, or who created the world. Her adopted son went to church, and she had spent every Sunday watching him walk into a building, but she'd thought little about God until Ethan became a Christian. And now the lyrics, *"Alive in me,"* were stuck in her head.

Charles and Jezmeen arrived at her car.

"Given your silence, I guess not," Charles chuckled.

"Oh sorry," Jez replied, unaware they'd walked so far without saying a word.

"It's okay. Thanks again for joining me tonight. I'm glad you got to meet my sister and her husband. They've been hearing a lot about you."

Jezmeen raised an eyebrow.

"Uh oh. Have you been telling them all about your 'messed up' friend?"

"No," he said, taken aback. "They saw my office, and I showed them the new family room furniture."

"Oh," she said, relieved. "All I have left to do is hang the artwork, and your space will be finished."

"Are you busy on Saturday afternoon? I don't have any clients then."

"No. That should be fine."

Jezmeen opened her car door and slid into the driver's seat.

"Merry Christmas," Charles said lingering by her car door longer than he should.

"Merry Christmas," she replied.

Jezmeen began to cry as soon as she pulled out of the church lot. She didn't know why, but she couldn't stop the tears. It was as if a dam broke, and the current was untamable. She kept driving, and she was thankful traffic was moving slowly out of the crowded lot.

When she halted at the four-way stop, she pulled a napkin out of her glove compartment and blew her nose, but the tears continued. She swiped another napkin across her eyes, smearing her mascara and eyeshadow, but she didn't care. There was no one waiting for her at home.

Ten minutes later she arrived at her apartment complex, and she pulled into an open spot right in front of her building. With an emotional sigh, she turned off her car and sat in silence. She couldn't go any further without addressing the One who had her restless and riveted.

God? You've got my attention.

She waited for what felt like an hour, but only minutes passed, and yet no audible—or inaudible—voice was heard.

Do you really love me? She whispered into the air.

Again, no words were uttered in response, but instead a warmth filled her like the sun. Her whole body was bathed in unspeakable peace, and she felt as if she radiated light.

Oh God. You're real. You're here.

And as she realized a Holy One was in her presence, she shut her eyes.

Forgive me. Forgive me.

The glow within continued, not hotter or cooler, just continuous. Jezmeen felt so safe in that moment, she never wanted it to end.

Alive in me.

Chapter Twenty-Three

Ethan knelt by the hearth of the fireplace and added a small gift to Izzy's pile. Earlier in the day he'd found the lipgloss she asked for, and he'd finished wrapping it. Stretching out his legs as he stood up, he looked at the poppy picture on the wall and thought of Jezmeen.

She'd crossed his mind so many times over the past two months, and yet no word from her came. After a few weeks passed without her, he called *Style Street*—to make sure she was okay. But the receptionist said she no longer worked there. He was shocked. Did she move or just get a new job? He thought she loved *Style Street*. He'd driven through the Finnegan's Taphouse parking lot multiple times looking for her car, just in case she'd returned to her old job, but it was never there. And he called her cellphone many times, but she never answered.

Maybe if they'd parted on more amicable terms, he wouldn't feel so troubled. Was she still in Springfield? Did she have a place to stay? He prayed for her daily—that she would come to know the Savior who changed his life. Ethan still remembered how God showed him a primrose plant blooming within the weeds, and he knew Jezmeen was that rose.

Temporarily overcome with emotion for the woman, he uttered a prayer. *Father, wherever Jezmeen is tonight, show her how much you love her. Help her to know you've never given up on her, and that You are from everlasting to everlasting.*

Moving to the kitchen to get a glass of water before bed, Ethan's gaze fell upon the tin of cookies from Ariana. She'd sung a beautiful solo at the Christmas Eve service hours earlier. Wayne, Izzy, and even his mom, Suzanne, had attended. After service, they chatted in the lobby. Wayne and Suzanne, his biological parents, had only reunited months earlier, and rarely talked unless Ethan brought them together.

Izzy didn't mind being the center of attention, so they conversed about her grades and acting aspirations. While they visited, Ariana approached. Her two-inch heels brought her chest-height with Ethan.

He introduced her to Wayne and Suzanne, while Izzy gushed over Ariana's red dress and her powerful voice. Ariana told them she'd be celebrating Christmas with her parents and sister's family, and before they parted, she handed him the tin, which was filled with chocolate chip cookies and divinity.

She'd taped a card to the top but told him not to open it until Christmas day. However, as he went for his third helping of divinity of the evening, he couldn't resist opening her letter. Tomorrow, he was hosting Wayne, Izzy and Suzanne for lunch. He didn't want to forget, he reasoned.

Sliding his finger under the sealed portion, Ethan pulled out a card with angels trumpeting on the front.

Merry Christmas, Ethan.

I hope you enjoy the cookies. The divinity were surprisingly easy to make, so I'm happy to refill the container whenever you'd like me to. I also wanted to thank you again for accompanying me to my work party. It meant so much to me, but that's just the kind of person you are. You are kind and giving. You are a caretaker, and you help others. Since the first day I met you, I've wanted to get to know you more, and I hope in the new year we can do just that.

Much love,

Ariana

Letting the delicate white cookie melt in his mouth, Ethan thought about Ariana's advances. He was flattered that this attractive woman, who could bake and sing, liked him. But even more important, they had the same faith foundation. When she talked in Sunday School class, he could tell she knew the Bible well. Certainly better than he did. Was he ready to take their friendship to another level?

He'd learned from dating Jezmeen that a relationship had to be based on something greater than exterior appearances, and he definitely would have boundaries this time around. Ethan grabbed one more cookie before shutting the tin. Whatever was ahead, he determined he wanted God to lead.

"A little higher," Jezmeen said from the entry between the kitchen and family room. "Okay, good. Just hold it there."

Jezmeen rushed forward with a pencil and marked the corners where the picture was resting against the wall. Then she told Charles he could lower the frame. Jez grabbed a nail from her pocket and began hammering. When the canvas, featuring a sunset over the mountain range, was securely in place, Jezmeen sat down on the couch to see how it looked.

"What do you think?" she asked Charles.

"Perfect," he said, stepping back from the wall.

"Come see it from here," Jez said.

He sat down beside her.

"Still looks good," he chuckled.

"I can't believe we're done. Are you happy with the room?"

"I love it. It's a perfect balance of sophisticated and classy, but comfortable and welcoming."

"And the little clock that your parents got you for Christmas looks great on the mantle," Jez commented, eyeing the fireplace.

"Oh, that reminds me...wait here," Charles said.

Charles hopped off the couch, hustled to the kitchen and returned with a gift bag in hand.

"What's this for?" Jez asked as he handed her the bag and sat back down.

"It's a Christmas and 'thank-you for all your work' gift."

She opened a small cardboard box and withdrew the silver cuff bracelet, holding it up to read the words.

"Through deep waters I am with you. Isaiah 43:2."

Jezmeen put it on and rotated her wrist from side to side, admiring the new piece of jewelry.

"Beautiful. Thank you," she said, looking into his eyes.

Charles gazed at Jezmeen warmly.

"Marie, I'm so proud of all the changes you've made in a short period of time. You're truly inspirational, and I'm rooting for you."

"Thanks," she said breathlessly, taking in his praise. "I have something for you, too. Hold on."

She retrieved her oversized purse from the kitchen table and returned to Charles carrying two wrapped gifts. She handed him the larger gift first and then sat down.

"Hazelnut Coffee!" Charles exclaimed after tearing open the paper.

"It's a refill. For the amount of times you've shared, I figured I owed you."

"Well, thank you."

"And here's gift number two."

She passed him a rectangular package.

"A Bible," he mused, setting the wrapping paper on the couch cushion between them after he'd opened it.

"You see that stack of books on the top shelf over there?" Jezmeen asked, pointing to a few angled books resting on the bookshelf.

"Yeah."

"I purchased the Bible a few weeks ago because it was the right color and size to fit on the top of the stack."

"Again, thank you."

He flipped through the pages.

"Oh, you personalized it," he said, noticing her handwriting on the inside of the front cover.

"You don't have to read that now," Jezmeen said, seeming embarrassed.

"For new direction in so many areas, thank you. Alive in me. December 24, 2014. J.M.W." Charles read aloud. "What?" he asked with wide eyes, looking up for the inscription.

"Thank you for the invitation to church," she said, busying herself with folding the used wrapping paper into smaller squares.

"You've given your life…" Charles paused searching for words. "You're a believer?"

Jezmeen nodded her head in affirmation before stuffing the paper into her purse.

"This happened when we were at church on Christmas Eve?"

"No. Afterwards," Jez replied with a short answer, uncomfortable talking about her new faith.

Charles leaned towards her then stopped. "Can I hug you?" he asked.

"Sure," she replied, drawing out the word, unsure why he would need to ask.

He drew her into his arms, and she smelled a light scent of cologne on his neck. She felt comfortable. Safe.

"I wanted you to have an everyday reminder that you were a part of that," Jez said when she pulled away.

She picked up the Bible and walked it to the stack, setting it atop the other two books.

"Why J.M.W." he asked.

"What?"

"The initials inside the Bible?"

Jezmeen was ready to be truthful.

"I should have told you this months ago, but my name isn't really Marie," Jez said softly. She was tired of him calling her by her middle name.

"Remember Monica? She wanted me to go by my middle name, Marie. Said Jezmeen didn't roll off the tongue."

"Your first name is Jezmeen?"

"Unique, huh?"

"So, all this time I've been calling you Marie, and you're really Jezmeen," Charles said, still in shock from both announcements. "How'd your mom come up with it?" he asked.

"She wanted something flashier than Jasmine. Something people would remember."

Jezmeen returned to the couch and began to clean up the tissue paper.

"Well, you certainly are one to remember," he said, smiling at her while she worked. "Speaking of remembering, did Ethan call you on Christmas?"

They'd talked about Ethan in her past sessions, and Charles knew she'd been avoiding his calls.

"No, I think he's gotten the point and given up."

She headed into his kitchen and opened the cabinet under the kitchen sink to throw away the paper. Having spent so much time at his home, she knew her way around.

"Have you found yourself missing him?" he asked when she returned.

"I don't know?" she shrugged.

Jezmeen felt so guilty about the way she parted with Ethan that she tried not to think about him because it brought up so much shame.

"Do you miss Katherine?" she asked.

She picked up the box for the bracelet she was wearing and put it in her purse before sitting down next to Charles on the couch.

"All the time."

"Do you ever think about getting remarried?" she asked. Jezmeen leaned her head against the back of the sofa and stared at the newly hung picture.

"Why do you ask?" Charles replied with curiosity in his voice.

"Well, you're young—"

"How old do you think I am?" he asked with a playful glint in his eye.

The bartending Jezmeen would have been flattering, this Jezmeen chose to be honest.

"I'd say mid-fifties."

"Fifty-four," he replied.

"See? Young. Did you and Katherine talk about the possibility of you remarrying?" Jezmeen asked, knowing Charles liked it when she showed interest in him.

"Yes, and she encouraged me that if I found the right person not to hesitate."

"And what would that look like for you?"

Jezmeen wondered if she crossed a line. They'd never talked about his love life.

"Well, she'd be kind. Loving. Compassionate. A good listener. A Christian...a lot like you." He threw in that last line casually, and Jezmeen wondered what to make of it. She didn't want to explore that topic anymore with him. Charles was her most trusted friend and companion. She didn't want to lose him for anything, and she'd never had a relationship last.

Chapter Twenty-Four

March 2014

The first day of spring was like a moody cat. It started out spitting sleet in the early morning hours. But by noon the sun was out, and the temperature rose steadily until it reached forty-eight degrees, warming up like a feline to company. Jezmeen had dressed in layers, and by mid-morning she'd shed her light blue sweater as she worked in the Turner's walk-out basement.

She'd spent the winter months happily decorating the first floor, and now she was transforming the lower level. All morning she'd been wallpapering the risers—the vertical portion between each stair to the basement. Weeks earlier, Jez had come across pictures of cool-toned, wood-like wallpaper that gave stairs the look of reclaimed materials.

After showing the images to the Turners, they jumped at the idea because it was budget friendly and captured the feel of lake living. Although Jezmeen had never wallpapered stairs before, the paper was easy to work with, and by lunchtime she was three-fourths done with the project.

So far, the remodel had gone according to schedule, but the Turners purposely waited to do their kitchen last. They wanted to be able to grill outside while their kitchen was ripped up, so they didn't always have to eat at restaurants. Soon Jez would be overseeing the kitchen remodel and redoing the lower level at the same time. That pleased the Turners.

Having someone in the home while subcontractors were coming in and out saved them from running back and forth from their own jobs.

While January and February had been brutally cold and endlessly gray, Jezmeen had never enjoyed a job so thoroughly. Even when she was physically spent from a long day moving furniture around or running endless errands, she couldn't wait to wake up and do it all again.

And even though her body was tired from bending over all morning, she wanted to get back at it as soon as she was done eating her packed lunch. With the weather warming up, Jez decided to eat outdoors. The Turners had an old set of black wrought-iron furniture on their brick patio. After Jez threw on her sweater again, she pulled open the glass door, wiped a chilly seat with her napkin, and sat down. She just finished praying when she heard the sound of two men talking to each other nearby.

Not frightened in the broad daylight, Jez mentally calculated who it could be. The demolition of the kitchen didn't start until tomorrow, and she didn't expect any other work crews today.

"Hello," she called from the low-lying patio, as the men rounded the corner of the house.

They waved and headed towards her. Within seconds, her heart began to race. Ethan. VJ. Why were they at the Turners? As soon as Ethan recognized her, he stopped in his tracks. However, VJ, Ethan's longtime co-worker, raced forward to return the greeting.

"Jez," he said, stepping onto the patio. "Long time no see."

"How've you been?" Jez asked, trying to appear more composed than she felt.

"Good. Good. Glad to get back to work. I picked up some side jobs doing remodeling in the winter, but I was ready to be outside again."

"I'm glad you and Ethan are back at it. Where's Mark?" Jez asked, knowing that Ethan's other assistant often ran with the pair.

"Honeymoon," VJ answered. "He got married a week ago."

"That's great," Jez murmured, noticing that Ethan had gotten closer but still wasn't standing on the patio.

"Hey, VJ," Ethan said, making VJ turn to look for his boss. "Why don't you go ahead to lunch. I think I can get these measurements all by myself."

"You sure?" VJ questioned. "This is a big job."

"Yeah. I'll be fine."

"Okay," VJ said. He seemed to understand that Ethan wanted him to leave. "Good to see you, Jez."

Jezmeen watched him go, and then took in the sight of Ethan. He wore a long-sleeve brown work shirt and his signature fedora, the one that shielded his sensitive skin from getting too much sun. He was so unchanged, and yet she felt nervous in his presence.

"How've you been?" she asked, standing up next to the wrought-iron table.

"Fine. You?" Ethan replied from six feet away.

"Same," she answered. "I was just about to have lunch. You want to sit down?"

"Nah."

Jezmeen wondered why he was afraid to get close, but she returned to her seat anyhow.

"Is this your new boyfriend's house?" Ethan asked with a little bite. "Sorry, I shouldn't have asked that," Ethan quickly added.

"It's okay," Jez replied. "I'm guessing Tom Turner must have hired you, and that you've never spoken with Denise...his wife."

"Oh, sorry," Ethan said with embarrassment.

"I'm their interior decorator," Jez said.

"Really?" Ethan asked, cocking an eyebrow. "I called *Style Street*, but they said you were no longer there."

"I work for myself now."

Jez could see anger and anxiety etched in Ethan's eyes.

"You don't trust me, do you?" she asked.

"You wouldn't answer your phone when I called, and I wanted to make sure you were okay," Ethan replied, fielding the question without answering hers.

"I thought it would be best if we had a clean break."

A light breeze blew some brown leaves around the patio, and Jezmeen pulled her sweater against her arms. Even though the sun was out, the wind made it chilly, and sitting on the wrought-iron chair didn't offer any warmth.

"Did you find a place to stay?" Ethan asked, noticing that she seemed cold, but not doing anything chivalrous.

"Eventually. I'm actually living on my own now."

"Gotcha," he said sarcastically.

"You don't believe me, do you?" Jez said softly, noting his tone.

"Living alone certainly wasn't your pattern in the past," Ethan shrugged and picked up a small, brown stick at his feet.

"People can change."

When Ethan didn't reply, Jez asked a question of her own.

"How's Izzy?"

"Fine."

"Has she done any more acting?"

Ethan chipped at the stick's loose bark with his fingernail.

"She got a part in the school's spring musical. I guess it's not a big role, but she said it was fair since she claims she's not a strong singer."

"Tell her congratulations."

"I will."

There was a lull in the conversation.

"I guess you're doing landscaping for the Turners?" Jezmeen said, putting it all together.

"Yeah. They want this old brick patio torn out and a stamped concrete patio put in. A gazebo by the water, new landscaping front and back, and new steps to the boat slip."

"Sounds like a big job."

"Big enough that I had to hire another crew member."

"I'm happy business is going so well."

When another cool breeze swept Jezmeen's hair across her cheek, she shivered.

"It's a lot colder out here than I thought it would be. Do you want to join me inside?" she asked.

"No thanks. I better get going on the measurements."

"Good to see you," she said, picking up her lunch bag.

As she pulled at the heavy glass door, Ethan called to her.

"What you did to me was wrong, you know?" he said from his standing position at the edge of the patio.

She turned around.

"You're right," she said softly.

"Faking a pregnancy. Making me think I was going to be a dad. Do you know how hard that hit me, finding out you lied?"

For the first time since their greeting Ethan made eye contact.

"Using me for my money. Stealing from me last year. You hurt me, Jez." He sucked in his breath. "A lot of disappointing things happened this fall, but you walking out was the worst."

"I know these are just words, but I really am sorry," Jez replied. "Maybe one day you'll be able to forgive me."

"That's the thing, Jez. I've been praying about this moment for months. And I thought I had forgiven you—really I did. But you standing here before me—looking as beautiful as the first day I met you—everything I'd rehearsed has left me."

"What can I say that would make you understand that I know I was wrong?"

He shrugged.

Jezmeen started towards Ethan, but as she approached, he moved away.

"You can't even be near me?" Jezmeen questioned.

Ethan didn't respond.

"If I could rewind everything-" Jez started.

"Look, I've got a lot of measuring to do," Ethan replied curtly.

"Do you want help?" Jez asked, knowing he sent VJ away.

"Nope. It seems I do best alone."

For the first ten minutes of the drive to his house, Izzy waxed and waned about whether she liked Cody or Dylan better, even though she swore neither of them liked her. Since he was still helping his dad with Izzy, Ethan had picked her up from school.

"If Jezmeen was here, she'd help me know. She had that radar, you know."

"I saw her today," Ethan said casually.

"I can't believe you let me ramble on and on about Dylan and Cody instead of telling me about Jezmeen! Where did you see her? How's she doing? Did you ask her over?" Izzy peppered.

"On a job. Fine. No," Ethan replied curtly.

"Ethan, this is the biggest news of the day. I need deets."

"Deets?"

"Details."

Ethan chuckled. "There's not much to tell."

He glanced in the rearview mirror to see a truck quickly approaching his bumper and he sped up a little.

"Why was she at your job site?" Izzy asked.

"She works there, too."

"You mean she's a landscaper now?"

"No," Ethan laughed. "She was hired by the same people to decorate their home."

"That's awesome. But I thought she wasn't working at *Style Street* anymore."

"She's not. She got hired on her own."

"That's so great. So, you'll be landscaping outside, and she'll be working inside. You two have got to get back together. See what a good team you make?"

Ethan gave Izzy a quizzical look.

"Your business could do so much better if you offered interior *and* exterior services."

"Creative idea, Iz, but there was no talk of reuniting."

"Why? Is it because you're seeing Ariana?"

"Seeing Ariana? Izzy you are full of it today."

She's been over to the house like every week all winter. And I've seen you holding hands," she accused.

"We're just friends."

"There's this girl in my gym class, Emily. She really likes this boy, Adam. Every time we're on teams, she's always gravitating to him. Touching his arm. Flirting with him. Ariana's the same way with you."

"Can't a guy and a girl just be friends?"

"Maybe in first grade," Izzy retorted, and Ethan laughed.

"Even then, it's iffy," Izzy continued.

"So, what should I do, because everyone should look to their thirteen-year-old sisters for relationship advice," Ethan teased.

"You need to be honest with Ariana. You don't have intentions of getting more serious with her, do you?"

"Well, now that you mention it, maybe I do." Ethan replied jokingly.

"What?" Izzy burst out.

"I thought you liked Ariana," Ethan said.

"I do, but you need to end up with Jezmeen."

"Why?"

"Because you two fit."

"How so?"

"She's a talker, and you're quiet. She's been hurt a lot, and so were you. You're both sensitive. And of course, I already told you that you'd make a great match with your careers."

"But she's not a Christian, Izzy. And she's done some pretty dumb stuff."

"Hurt people hurt people," Izzy replied.

"What?"

Ethan looked at his little sister again.

"Hurt people hurt people. I learned that in my peer leadership class. Jezmeen's been hurt a lot, but she's got kindness in her. I know it."

"You're something else, Izzy," Ethan replied, turning to smile at her.

"So, when are you going to see Jezmeen again?"

"I don't know."

"What do you mean you don't know? When are you working at that job site again?"

"Tomorrow."

"Then you're seeing her tomorrow."

"She'll be inside, and I'll be outside."

"So, make up a reason to go inside—use the bathroom or something."

"I don't think so, Iz."

Ethan put on his turn signal and began to brake as Farmingdale Road came into view.

"Why not?"

"The sun will shine where it will. It needs no help from me."

"Huh?"

"Just trying to be deep like you, sis."

"Only your comment made no sense."

"What do you mean? I thought it made perfect sense. If it's meant to be, it will happen—that kind of thing."

"The sun shines every day on everyone, Ethan, even when it's cloudy."

"You're ruining my moment."

"That's what little sisters are good for," Izzy teased as Ethan pulled into the long driveway leading home.

Chapter Twenty-Five

Can I come over? Jezmeen texted Charles. She knew he didn't see clients on Monday evenings, and she needed to talk. After Ethan walked away, Jezmeen replayed their conversation while she finished wallpapering the stair risers. But her heart kept racing, and she couldn't get it quiet. Charles would know what to do.

Having a friend who was a counselor was the biggest blessing God had given her, besides salvation. Throughout the winter months, she found herself faithfully attending weekly therapy sessions at his house, and she sat by him at church on Sunday mornings. He kindly switched service times, just so she could continue to see Ace walk into *his* church first.

Even though Charles tried to help her loosen up about seeing Ace each week, he didn't say she was crazy for wanting that connection. When Ethan found out about Ace, he hadn't asked her to give it up either. Looking back, Ethan was surprisingly patient with her.

He'd gone along with her selfish idea to build a huge home, when he'd originally wanted something small and affordable. Then when she'd asked for money to decorate it, he'd opened a savings account, and she'd spent every penny of his thirty-thousand. Once they moved in, she threw dinner parties for "important" people she'd met as a bartender, even though Ethan disliked socializing…especially with strangers.

As if that wasn't enough, she'd grown jealous of his assistant, Claire's, relationship with Ethan, so she messed with her insulin pump, but he forgave her. And then there was the fake pregnancy. She had hoped he'd let her stay at his house after that, but she had no idea he'd propose...or fall so in love with the thought of being a dad.

The only thing she'd done well was adore his sister, Izzy. Why had Ethan been so kind to her, when the majority of her choices harmed him? At first, he really liked her. She could tell he was taken with her from the moment they met. But the shine wore off, like it always did, and then he tolerated her.

But after he became a Christian, he was kind. Loving. Gentle. Patient. Good. Seeing Ethan was like drawing back a blanket on a sleeping child. She was jarred into the reality that she'd wounded him and walked away.

Charles had given her an assignment many months back to forgive people who wounded her. She had a folder full of notes, after writing out her thoughts to Sherry, Steven, and others, but she had yet to write to Ethan. Every time she started, she didn't know what to say. It wasn't as if he was perfect, but she'd been the one to coerce him into...everything. Was she really just a wicked person? Charles would get to the bottom of it.

As she drove to Charles' house, traffic was heavy because of the five o'clock hour. While she waited at a light, her thoughts drifted to Charles. A few weeks ago, on a gray, sleeting morning they'd eaten brunch at his parents' assisted living home. He'd invited her, and she didn't know what to make of it.

As usual, Charles was caring and attentive, not only to her, but also to his parents—making sure their drinks were full, everyone had the desserts they wanted, and that the conversation flowed easily.

They'd driven together, leaving from the church parking lot. So when he dropped her off and it was still drizzling, Jezmeen sat in his car for a minute before making a run to her vehicle. In a rare change of events, Charles talked about himself, telling a story about how he ended up playing the French Horn in grade school because he thought it was really a fancy trumpet.

As she attentively looked on, he explained that his parents made him stick with it until the end of junior high. Charles said his parents still had the French Horn, hoping he'd take it up again one day. When he finished, he smiled at her. And in the turn of his lips, the crinkle of his eyes, the unspoken emotion filling the small space, she knew that he loved her.

And she didn't like it. She'd known for a long time that Charles felt *something* for her. But he never said anything, and she didn't want to ask. Anything romantic would ruin the good thing she had with him. Plus, he was fifty-four and she was thirty. He was old enough to be her father.

Pulling into his driveway, she grabbed her purse, locked her car, and headed to the front door. She knocked twice before he answered. She found him still dressed in work clothes—khaki pants, a blue and white plaid shirt, his thinning hair combed to one side.

"Did they hate it?" he asked as she entered.

"What?"

Jezmeen walked with ease into his kitchen and sat down at the table in her "usual" seat across from the bay window looking out into the backyard.

"The wallpaper on the stairs."

Jezmeen laughed, remembering that she'd told Charles about the wallpapering project.

"I left before they got home. Which reminds me, I have to keep my phone close by in case they call with feedback."

Jezmeen noticed the glass of water sitting on a coaster at her place.

"Thanks," she said while taking a drink.

"I knew you wouldn't want coffee this time of day. So, if it wasn't the wallpaper, is it my sister?" he asked, sitting down in his standard spot, caddy-corner to her.

After she'd finished his family room, he recommended her to his sister, who hired Jez to do hers. Between working for the Turners, Nancy, and taking online classes, she was busy.

"No, your sister is great. It's not work. It's my ex."

"Ethan?"

"Yeah. You'll never believe this—I barely do—but he was hired by the Turners to landscape their backyard."

"Wow. That's an amazing coincidence," Charles said, a cloud of concern crossing his face. "How'd you find out?"

"I'd just taken my lunch to the patio when I heard somebody coming around…and it was Ethan and his co-worker, VJ ."

Jezmeen grabbed an unused coaster that was resting in a stack in the middle of the table and began running her fingers over the grooves. As usual, Charles didn't interrupt, and she continued ahead.

"Somehow Ethan got VJ to leave pretty quickly, and then it was just him and me standing on the patio. Well, he never really got that close. It was like I had the plague."

"And how did the reunion go?"

"I don't know. At first it was awkward. You know, seeing someone you didn't expect to see. You don't really know what to say."

"So why are you troubled?"

"I guess because he was so upset. I've broken up with lots of guys before, but I think I feel worse about this one."

"How come?"

"Ethan is…Ethan."

"Can you explain that a little more?"

"When we first met, I was bartending at Finnegan's, and he came in one night carrying his silly fedora. This tan hat, that makes him look like Indiana

Jones, he wears to keep his face from getting back his birthmarks. Port wine stains, I think he called them. He used to have these purple marks on half of his face. He showed me pictures, when we were first dating."

She tapped the coaster again, realizing she'd gotten sidetracked.

"Anyhow, Ethan is…was…pretty nerdy. Shy. Quiet. Insecure. Before we met, he barely went out. He was really a recluse."

"Has he changed?"

"Actually, he has," Jez said, realizing the truth. "I kept doing these dinner parties last summer. He hated them. But I don't think it was that. I think it was meeting his dad and sister that changed him. He loves being with them."

"So, you feel bad because he's different now?" Charles asked, trying to understand.

"No. It's not that. I'm happy he's more confident. He's still quiet, but less insecure. I think I feel so guilty because I was really horrible to him."

Jezmeen had never really shared all the horrible things she did to Ethan, but she needed to get the weight off her back. So, she poured it all out. Every detail, even though each word incriminated her. When she finished, she felt dreadfully shameful and lighter at the same time.

"No wonder you had so many headaches and stomachaches when I first met you," Charles said, his eyes lighting with realization. "Guilt is one of the hardest things to carry. It physically affects the body after so long."

"I'm such a horrible person," Jez said, biting the inside of her cheek until it started to bleed.

"You're not a horrible person. You made some poor choices, but that doesn't make you bad. You know we've talked about how you valued having a place to live so highly that you would do whatever it took to make it happen. You've recognized your wrongdoing, and that is a sign that you have a moral compass."

Jezmeen took a drink of water to wash down the blood in her mouth.

"Sometimes when I lie in bed and I can't sleep, I hear this guy, Nick's, words over and over, *'You're just a piece of trash.'*"

Jez didn't want to make eye contact with Charles, so she stared out at the dusky sky. The daylight was lengthening again.

"I think it's time to start combatting that lie with truth," Charles said, keeping his gaze upon her. "You are a woman of high value. Jesus has forgiven *all* your sins. Past. Present. And future. All that you've done...and ever will do...is as far as the east is from the west. Do you grasp that?"

A tear slid down the side of Jezmeen's nose.

"The east and west never meet...these burdens. Mistakes. They're completely removed. God's mercy is upon you. That is freeing grace."

More tears fell.

"You never got to know your biological father, and most of the men that played that role were ones I should've been seeing in my office because of their own brokenness. You're learning to live differently now…getting to know your Good Father."

He stopped talking and paused, thinking.

"Do you sense God loves you?"

Jezmeen grabbed a napkin out of the holder in the center of the table and dabbed her eyes and nose.

"Yes," she said weakly. "From the moment I surrendered to Him, I have felt His presence. I'd always thought he'd reject me because of how I've lived, but it's like he's been nursing me back to health, not pushing me away."

"I'm glad to hear that."

"I just wish I never would've gotten involved with Ethan. I used him so much, and he was so naïve."

"But don't you see how God was directing you even then? He used Ethan to introduce you to Christian music and radio. He was breathing new life into Ethan, and you saw that. There was cultivation of the fertile soil of your heart happening. And the experience decorating his house showed you how much you enjoyed it and what a talent you have. Even his encouragement to work at *Style Street* shaped your life. God used Ethan greatly."

She started to tear up again.

"Maybe that's why I feel so awful."

"Have you stopped to recognize how God might have been using you in Ethan's life, too?"

She laughed cynically.

"You mean to ruin it?"

"You told me you introduced Ethan to his dad. You made that connection for him and see how he's gained a sister as well because of you. If you hadn't met Ethan that might never have happened. And you told me you built a relationship with Izzy. Maybe you showed him how to do the same."

Jezmeen warmed at these thoughts.

"Did you ever truly love Ethan? You said 'yes' to his proposal, but did you intend to marry him?" Charles asked with great seriousness.

"No," Jezmeen sighed. "I don't *ever* want to get married."

"How come?"

"Men are users," Jez said, and then her hand flew to her mouth. "Besides you, of course."

"Was Ethan one of those 'users?'"

"At the beginning, he was just like all the others. And then he changed."

"If someone came along who loved *you*, and not your body or what you could…provide…could you open yourself for that gift?"

Jezmeen laughed cynically. "It's hard to believe love could be a gift."

"Having lived it, I know that it can," Charles said softly.

"I don't know."

"That's a fair answer. Just be aware that the right relationship can be a blessing from God."

Jezmeen nodded her head affirmatively.

"Now back to Ethan," Charles continued. "You may run into him a few more times, since you'll be working at the same place. It may help to write him a note, telling him your regrets. Ask for his forgiveness. Sometimes the written word is as powerful as the spoken word."

"I can do that," Jez said, and then they both startled as her cell phone rang. "I better take this. It's probably the Turners."

Swiping her finger across the screen, she opened the call.

"Oh hey, Gabrielle," she said aloud. She bit her lip as she listened to her former colleague from *Style Street*. "You can't be serious," she gasped.

Chapter Twenty-Six

For the first time since he opened his landscaping business, Ethan didn't look forward to going to work. All that would stand between him and Jezmeen was a sliding glass door, which was why his stomach was in knots. His team was tearing out the old brick patio, and he estimated that would take most of the morning. Then they'd level the ground and start making the form for the new patio in the afternoon.

He hoped if Jezmeen made an appearance, VJ or his new assistant, Karl, would be around as a buffer. When he pulled up to the Turners at a quarter to eight, Jezmeen's car was nowhere in sight. Could it be that Jezmeen wasn't working at the Turners today? Perhaps she had other clients, too. He sincerely hoped so.

The other day, he didn't even think to look for her vehicle. Now he knew better. Even though Ethan prayed constantly since their reunion a few days earlier, he felt ashamed that he hadn't been kinder to her. He wanted to reflect Christ's love, and he'd failed. All he'd been was angry.

Before his dad went into rehab, this would have been something he would've brought up with him. But since Wayne had been back, Ethan hadn't talked about anything of depth. Ethan was too concerned he'd say something that would trigger Wayne into drinking again.

Plus, it felt like he was always carrying around an unopened envelope when he was with Wayne. They'd resumed their Sunday lunches, but neither spoke of the cause of the fire. However, Wayne talked passionately about helping Ethan rebuild the greenhouses and the storefront, but Ethan didn't have the funds.

His home mortgage was weighing him down like a weight of bricks. Winter meant a complete standstill of income, and even the royalties from the pergola sales were down. If he had insurance, he would have claimed a $30,000 loss of product and structures. Now, all he had to show for three years of owning twenty-three acres in the country was a huge house that sapped all his funds, a long driveway, and a pile of ash.

Throwing open his truck door, he grabbed his level off the passenger seat. After rolling a wheelbarrow down the ramp off his trunk, he headed to the back to begin ripping out brick.

Using his favorite razor-back shovel, he got right to work pulling up the old, chipping bricks. Thankfully they were just embedded in sand, which made the job relatively easy. And by the time VJ and Karl arrived a little after eight, he'd already loaded the wheelbarrow once and hauled them into his truck bed.

The March morning was beautiful. Sunny. Not too hot. Not too cool. But he was stuck in his head. When VJ asked him twice if everything was alright, he knew he must be worse than he realized, even though he hadn't caught sight of Jezmeen beyond the glass.

Stopping midmorning to take off his sweatshirt, he also shed some of his worry. It had been hours, and Jez hadn't appeared. But as soon as he picked the shovel up again, he overheard Karl speaking to VJ in a whisper.

"Hey, VJ, look at that babe."

In a normal speaking voice VJ retorted, "You better watch what you say. That's Ethan's ex." And then VJ waved to Jezmeen.

Jezmeen slid open the glass door but didn't step outside. The ground was too torn up to be inviting.

"Well, if it isn't the hardest working landscaping crew in town," she said from the door. "Who's the new recruit?" she asked, throwing her eyes as Karl.

"Karl. Jezmeen. Jezmeen. Karl," Ethan interjected, introducing the two from afar.

"You want to come out and help us?" VJ asked playfully.

"Thanks for the offer, but I think I'll stick with the inside and leave the outside to you guys."

"If you change your mind, I'm sure I can find you a shovel," VJ teased.

Jez laughed. "And if you want to come inside, I'll hand you a paint brush."

"Oh yeah?" VJ retorted. "Painting some walls?"

"Nope. Some built-in bookshelves. Going from oak to white."

"What'd ya say, boss," V.J said, turning to Ethan. "Should I help the lady?"

"I think we should all stick with what we were hired to do," Ethan responded.

"Have fun," Jez said, slowly sliding the door shut.

The rest of the day went by without any appearances from Jezmeen. He went to lunch with Karl and VJ, even though he rarely ate out. All to avoid any run-ins with Jezmeen.

Ethan trusted he'd be less nervous when there was more distance between them. And by the close of the day, he was exhausted physically and mentally. He rolled the wheelbarrow into the truck bed and then realized he'd forgotten his level in the backyard.

He found the level in the grass beside the frame they'd built to hold the concrete, which they would pour in the morning. Ethan bent down to pick it up and caught a glimpse of Jezmeen trying to push a couch inside using the weight of her slender body. Acting as if he was checking one of the boards he already laid, he continued to watch Jez struggle against the heavy piece of furniture, and he sighed.

Carefully treading between the slats of rebar along the ground, he reached the glass door and rapped on it a few times. Jezmeen straightened and headed to the door.

"Need help?" Ethan asked when she slid it open.

"Oh man. You saw that?" she groaned.

Ethan laughed, and the sound softened the tension.

"I've been waiting all afternoon to move the couch and loveseat. I didn't want you guys to see me."

"Forgot my level," Ethan said, holding up the tool. "If I take off my boots, I won't track in much."

"Okay," Jez said, moving aside as Ethan stepped in and took off his boots near the door.

"Where do you want the couch to go?" he asked, taking charge, as Jezmeen watched him quietly.

"It needs to face the sliding door."

"I thought these little furniture sliders would do the trick," Jez said, repositioning one that fell out from under a claw.

"They'll be helpful, but I think this is a two-person job. I'll push. You pull."

Ethan's muscles contracted as he used his upper body to direct the sofa.

"That's good," Jez said.

She stepped back and observed the placement.

"Perfect," she said.

"Now the loveseat?" Ethan asked.

"If you have time…and don't mind."

"Happy to help," he replied.

"Ever thought about hiring someone?" Ethan asked as they pushed the next piece into place.

"Can't afford it. Plus, I've found there are relatively few things I can't do by myself," she replied with a hint of pride.

"How come you don't want them facing the fireplace?" Ethan asked, noting they were moving them away from their original positions.

"With this view?" she asked incredulously.

"Good point."

She stepped back again.

"I think the loveseat needs to go to the left a half inch and then back a little."

He followed her directions and paused in anticipation for feedback.

"Now just a tad to the right...Excellent."

Ethan stood up and waited again, watching her brow furrow as she analyzed the room. Surprisingly, he didn't feel angry or anxious at being alone with her for the moment, and he offered a silent prayer of thanks for his renewed attitude. Besides observing her wait on customers at Finnegan's Taphouse, he'd never seen her in action on a decorating job. Not even when she did his home. And her focus made her exceedingly attractive.

He shook his head as if to release the thought.

"If that's all, I better be going."

"One more favor?" she asked. "Can you sit down and tell me if you can see the lake?"

"I'm not sure if I should," he said, eyeing the dirt on the knees of his jeans and the white couch in front of him.

"Good point," she chuckled.

"Could you wait until I try it out? I may need to move both pieces back."

Jez picked the middle cushion and slid back.

"Ahhh," she sighed. "This is what half a mill gets you."

"You like it better than the view of a rolling cornfield?" Ethan asked from his position next to the arm of the sofa.

"The country was beautiful, too," she reasoned. "How is everything down on Farmingdale Road?"

"Changed."

"Claire left for Tianjin?" Jez asked, knowing his assistant was going to China after Christmas.

"Yes, but that's not the biggest difference."

"Did you add a few more hoop houses?"

"Subtract is more like it."

"What do you mean?" she asked, turning her body to face him.

"There was a fire on the property."

Jezmeen gasped. "Oh my…"

"The business…The storefront and greenhouses…everything burned down."

"The house too?"

"No. Thankfully the firefighters got it out before it spread to the Rogers farmhouse or our—my—place."

Ethan felt embarrassed by the slip of his tongue, so he stared out at the lake.

"Oh, Ethan, I'm so sorry," Jez replied with genuine sorrow in her voice. "How did it happen? I mean what started the fire?"

"Not sure," Ethan replied.

"Wow," Jez said, and sat silently for a second taking in the news. "When are you going to rebuild?" she asked, her striking hazel eyes upon him, causing his discomfort to grow.

"Don't have the funds," he said, noticing a piece of grass on the carpet, stooping to pick it up.

"But I thought—"

"That I was super rich," Ethan replied, trying hard not to let his tone sound biting.

"Well, I…" Jezmeen fumbled to find the right words, so Ethan saved her.

"Just remember where we lived before the house was built."

Ethan had sold the trailer the same week they moved into the two-story.

Stillness filled the room.

"I'll let you get back to work," Ethan said, moving towards his boots.

Jezmeen got up from the couch.

"Thanks for your help. I'm actually glad that you saw me. I don't think I could have done it without you," she said softly.

"I don't know about that," Ethan smiled as he tugged the heel of his boot into place. "Like you said, there's not much you can't do alone."

The long driveway to Ethan's home made it easy to see if he had company, and even from the mailbox he knew Ariana had stopped by for a visit. She'd only done that once before, bearing cookies. So, when she stepped out of her vehicle holding a container, Ethan wasn't surprised.

He'd spent the twenty-minute drive home thinking about Jezmeen. Part of him wanted to draw her into his arms and hold her until they both would hurt no more. The other part wanted to run far away from whatever direction she was headed. And even though Ariana was waving to him, Ethan was still stuck in his head as he put the truck in park in the circular driveway. She approached his side, and he rolled down his window.

272

"It was a food day at work, and I made an extra two dozen cookies for you," Ariana bubbled.

Ethan took the Tupperware container from her outstretched hands through the window.

"Do you want to get in?" he asked, noticing she looked cold dressed in a sheer mint-colored top and navy pants.

"Sure."

Ethan didn't want to invite her inside his house because she would often overstay her welcome, and he didn't know how to ask her to leave.

"How'd you survive in a t-shirt all day?" Ariana asked as she slid into the passenger seat.

Ethan pointed to the floor by her feet.

"Oops. I hope I'm not stepping on it," she said, pulling her heels away from his sweatshirt.

"It's fine. It's dirty already."

"Thanks for the cookies," he said, taking off the top. "Mind if I have one?"

"Not at all."

"You want one?" he asked, reaching the container towards her.

Ariana fiddled with a gold bracelet around her wrist.

"No thanks. I think I ate a few too many desserts today as it is."

"Why was there a food day?" Ethan asked.

"It's a co-worker's birthday."

They sat in silence for a moment before Ariana moved the conversation forward.

"Did you have a good day?" she asked.

"It was okay," he replied flatly.

"Something bad happen?"

"Well," Ethan paused. He didn't know what to tell Ariana. "I saw my ex today."

"Really? Where?"

Ariana's hand flew to the nap of her neck, and she set it back down into her lap.

"We both got hired by the same people. She's doing the interior decorating, and I'm doing the landscaping."

"Wow. What a coincidence," Ariana replied with a hint of frustration. "Did you talk to her?"

"A little."

"I know the first time I ran into my ex after the divorce, I was pretty shaken up. It was hard to see him again."

When Ethan didn't say anything, Ariana continued.

"We've never really talked about…what's her name?"

"Jezmeen."

"Yeah, Jezmeen."

"True."

"Do you miss her?" Ariana said, treading lightly into deep water.

"To be honest, I wanted to be rid of her so many times before we broke up, but then once we did, all I could do was think about her."

"Why?"

"I don't know. I guess I was worried about her."

"But she's doing okay?"

"Yeah. She seems to be…"

Ariana pulled at the tiny hairs on her arm.

"Where's that leave us?" Ariana asked, looking straight out the windshield.

Us, Ethan thought. He didn't even know there was an "us" with Ariana. They were friends, but that was all, at least according to him. How would he proceed? This was uncharted territory for him.

"What do you mean?" Ethan asked.

"I thought we were heading somewhere. I mean, we've been seeing each other for three months. But if you still like Jezmeen I need to know."

Ethan realized Izzy had been right. He thought hanging out and watching movies with Ariana a few times a month equated to an innocent friendship. She obviously thought it was something more. He wished his thirteen-year-old sister was here now to walk him through this conversation. Knowing he needed help, he offered up a silent prayer to God.

"Ariana, you're practically perfect. Beautiful on the outside...and the inside. A woman who's smart and can sing, and cook, and knows the Bible..."

"But?" Ariana interjected.

"But that's just it. You're too perfect for me. I'm still a mess on legs," Ethan chuckled, trying to lighten the mood in the cabin.

Ariana laughed cynically. "You think I'm perfect?"

She tugged at the hair on her forehead and began to pull it back. Ethan stared aghast as she continued to gently remove what Ethan now realized was a wig. A large bald patch in the middle of Ariana's scalp made him wonder what was wrong with her. Did she have cancer? *"Please God, help it not be cancer,"* Ethan prayed.

"Are you okay?" he asked.

"Depends on what you mean by 'okay.' I have trichotillomania. It's a hair-pulling disorder. I had it under control for a long time, but after the divorce it got really bad. So now I wear a wig."

Ariana quickly pulled the wig back into place.

"So, if you've ever wondered why I fidget so much with my hands, jewelry, skin, now you know. I have a hard time keeping my fingers quiet."

276

"I had no idea."

"I don't tell many people. It's so embarrassing. But at least you have proof that I'm far from perfect."

"Ariana…" Ethan began.

"Don't say anything else," Ariana interrupted. "I can tell Jezmeen holds what I want. I've had to do a lot of chasing with you, and I'd rather be the one being chased."

She grabbed the door handle and began to open it. After hopping out, she stopped and looked back at Ethan.

"I hope she realizes what a good thing she's getting."

Chapter Twenty-Seven

Charles and Jezmeen scored a table by a window at Papo's Café after church. They'd already discussed the sermon and Charles' Saturday visit with his parents while waiting for their food to arrive. And once the pecan apple salad and turkey wrap were delivered, Charles prayed.

"Thanks for doing lunch today," Jez said.

She speared a candied pecan and coupled it with the green leafy lettuce mix.

"I've been patiently waiting all week to hear what you decided about *Style Street.* I still can't believe Monica offered to sell you the Springfield franchise."

"I know. She obviously thought I was much wealthier than I really am. But the first thing she said when I talked with her over the phone was that my fiancé would probably want in on this deal because it was so hot."

"Did she know Ethan has his own business?"

"Yeah, I told her in my interview that he ran a landscaping company."

"So, she thought you two were still together?"

"I never told her otherwise."

"Did she ever say why she was selling?"

Charles opened a bag of kettle-baked potato chips and popped a few into his mouth.

"Only that her business in Schaumburg was 'booming,' and it needed her full attention. But after I talked with her, I called Gabrielle, and she seemed to think it was because the Springfield location is failing and supposedly has been for months."

"Did you entertain the idea, or was the price completely out of your league?"

"It would take my whole nest egg, but it's doable."

"And you prayed about it?"

"Of course."

"And…"

Jezmeen sipped her water, leaving burgundy lipstick stains on the straw.

"For a while all I could hear were my own doubts. Imagine me, a girl without a degree, less than a year of experience, no real credentials, owning an interior decorating business."

"But you'll have your certification in just a few months, and you're a natural. You won over the Turners, and you were competing against two other companies."

"You're so encouraging," Jezmeen said with a smile.

"So, don't leave me hanging any longer, what did you decide?" Charles asked fervently.

"I didn't know what to do…until Thursday."

"What happened Thursday?"

"I spoke with Ethan again."

Charles sounded surprised. "Oh, really. Did he give you advice?"

"No. I didn't even mention *Style Street*."

"So how did that help?

"Did you know his business burned down?"

"No!"

"He lost everything. All the greenhouses he built by hand. His brand-new storefront. Gone. And he doesn't even know what caused it."

"That's devastating."

"And that's when I heard, '*make it right*.'"

"What do you take that to mean?"

"You know how badly I manipulated Ethan. How I got him to build a bigger house and spent a ton of his money furnishing it. Making it right means to help him now."

Charles had stopped eating and was listening intently.

"But he probably had insurance."

"Actually, he told me he didn't."

"Do you think he'll really take your money?"

"That's the amazing thing. I still have the routing number for the bank account he opened for me to use for house purchases. I'll just deposit the money into it, and he won't even know where it came from."

Charles paused in thought.

"I'm guessing if you give him a chunk of your nest egg you won't have the finances to purchase *Style Street?*"

Jez pursed her lips and nodded affirmatively.

"And this is the direction you think God is leading you?"

"Does it sound crazy?"

"You'll be giving up your dream to make his happen."

"Not really. I can keep doing what I'm doing. I'll just have to grind harder to make myself visible. Which is probably better. Acquiring a business is risky, and I don't think I would've been comfortable doing the deal anyways. You know how much I value my savings and how hard I worked to build it up."

"That's why I'm shocked you're willing to part with a substantial amount of it for Ethan. He's using the furniture you bought him, and he could sell the house if he didn't want to live there anymore. It's not like you really owe him."

Jezmeen was surprised. This was the first time his neutrality seemed to waiver in his counsel.

"Do you think I'm making the wrong decision?" she asked, genuinely wanting to know.

"Before Ethan became a Christian, he was good to you, right?

"What do you mean?"

"Never hit you. Took advantage of you. Treated you with kindness?"

"Yeah, why. What's that have to do with making it right?"

"Just wondering. That's all," Charles said, the clouded look in his eyes clearing. "I think it's very mature of you to recognize how your influence on Ethan affected his choices. And if God is leading you to *'clear the board'* with him, I won't lead you in a different direction."

Jezmeen breathed a sigh of relief. "Well, that's good to know. I was worried you were about to tell me something else."

With the money deposited in Ethan's account, Jezmeen felt free, clean, so when she saw Ethan eating lunch on the lawn alone, gazing at the lake days later, she was drawn to him.

It was finally warm enough to be outside without a coat or sweater, and Jezmeen relished the feel of the sun on her arms as she carried her thermal tote down the sloping backyard. Not wanting to startle him, she called his name once she was in earshot. Jezmeen never noticed his light tan fedora had a brown band around it, matching his shirt well.

When he turned, Jez asked, "Care if I join you?"

"No."

"No, you don't want me to, or no it's okay?" Jez asked, concerned.

"It's fine," he replied.

"Where are your two side-kicks?"

"I think they went to Subway."

"What are you eating?" Jez asked, leaning over to look at what he was holding.

"An Izzy special. Turkey. Cheese. Banana peppers. Mayo."

"Izzy made you lunch?"

"Yep. It was my night to have her."

Jezmeen looked at Ethan quizzically.

"My dad kind of took a turn for the worst after the fire. Did a stint at rehab. He's back but still working on stability. I'm just helping with Izzy to take some of the load off him since her grandma couldn't do it anymore."

"That's really kind of you, Ethan. How is Izzy? You can't imagine how much I've missed her."

"She's good, and she's missed you, too. Izzy made me promise to ask you to come over for a Sunday lunch sometime."

"You told her we reconnected?"

Ethan shrugged. "Seemed like something she'd wanto know."

Jezmeen gazed at the deep blue-green water of the placid lake, bouncing back the brilliant spring sun.

"It may not be like a tropical beach, but it sure is peaceful out here," Jez commented as she took a container of yogurt out of her lunch bag. She peeled back the foil top and licked it. "Did you know I always wanted to live on the oceanfront?"

"I've never been to the ocean," Ethan said.

"Me neither."

"And you want to live there someday?" he chuckled.

"I used to."

"Not anymore?"

"I don't know. Just taking things one day at a time. How about you? Did you always want to have cornfields next door?"

"I don't know if I dreamed of cornfields, but I wanted to live in the country for most of my adult life. It took me ten years to save for the land."

"How's the gazebo going?" Jez asked, nodding to the freshly leveled ground to Ethan's left.

"VJ's pretty sad that he can't use the backhoe anymore."

Jezmeen laughed.

"I'm glad I don't have to hear the annoying beep every time the thing backed up."

"Yeah, me too," Ethan smiled.

Ethan's guard seemed to be coming down, and Jezmeen was thankful. Making things right was more than just depositing money into an account.

"How are things going with the decorating?" he asked.

"To be honest, I have no idea what I'm doing."

"What do you mean? You're great at this stuff."

"It's not that. It's the kitchen remodel. I'm not doing the work, but when something comes up... like the fridge we picked is not going to fit in the space, or the venting for the range needs to be moved over, I don't know what to do. I can't wait until May."

"Why?"

"That's when we're learning about kitchen designs in school."

"You signed up for classes online?"

Jezmeen swirled her spoon around the yogurt container and nodded affirmatively.

"That's great," he said, his voice laced with shock and pride.

Behind them, laughter erupted, and they instinctively turned to see VJ and Karl walking their way.

"I'll get out of your way," Jez said, quickly getting up and brushing off the back of her blue jeans.

Ethan didn't stop her.

"Oh," she said looking at the zippered pocket of the thermal tote. "I have something for you."

She reached into the compartment and pulled out an envelope.

"Read it later," she said. "And thanks."

"For what?"

"Sharing ground."

The envelope in Ethan's pocket burned against his thigh, and the angst he felt over spending time with Jezmeen caused Ethan to pound the floor joists with enthusiastic vigor. Thankfully VJ and Karl were staining boards on the driveway, so they didn't ask questions.

When three o'clock rolled around, Ethan left VJ
and Karl to finish up for the day while he drove to do
his first of three estimates for potential clients. And
when he stopped to fill up his truck for gas, he pulled
over into a parking spot after he paid the attendant.
That's when he took out the letter. It was crinkled and
warm.

Dear Ethan,

*When I was a freshman in high school, I went to
the state fair and rode the Orbiter. Did you ever ride
that one? If you did, you wouldn't forget it. These
pods twirl you upside down and all over. I screamed
the whole time. But I should have just sat there calmly
because the Orbiter was exactly like my life. So, you'd
think I'd be used to the motion.*

*Did you know that I went to three different
schools in first grade? And by the time I got into junior
high, I stopped counting how many different places my
mom and I stayed. The first time she got married I had
high hopes. Finally, some stability. But she was
divorced within a year.*

*I never wanted to be like my mom, and until
recently I didn't even realize how similar we were. For
a long time, I blamed Steven, my first boyfriend…the
one that left me pregnant with Ace. After him, I
bounced around from relationship to relationship,
telling myself there were no good ones. All men
weren't to be trusted.*

*But my lack of trust came from a place even
farther back than Steven. When my mom's boyfriend
crept into my bedroom and did the unthinkable,
muffling my shouts, I was only thirteen. That's when I
really broke. I met Steven a few months later, and he
was my ticket out.*

287

It would be convenient to say all my choices after that stemmed from this abuse. But to be honest, I made a fair amount of poor decisions all on my own. I pushed myself into your life when I realized I was in a dead-end relationship with the guy you met, Nick. I was good at jumping in and out of homes. But I never wanted to stay so badly until I got to yours.

Before I sat down to write this letter, I would have told you that my urge to stay was because I'd decorated the place. It was perfect and cozy and beautiful. But it wasn't that, because I've used that "magic wand" on my apartment, and it's not the same.

So, then I thought it was because I loved Izzy, and when she was there everything felt joyful. But Izzy came and went. She wasn't always there. So did Chewy.

Ethan smiled at Jezmeen's hand-drawn paw print next to Chewy's name.

Why did I kick and claw and fight and lie to stay when I've never had any trouble leaving anywhere else?

The only thing left was you.

If I could turn back time and redo all my past mistakes, I would in a heartbeat. But since life can't be put in reverse, all I can do is apologize again for the hurt, pain, manipulation. All of it.

Given my history, I wouldn't blame you if you didn't believe any of this. But I'm praying you will sense the truth, know I've changed, and truly forgive me. James 5:16

Jez

Chapter Twenty-Eight

The area rug Jezmeen had been waiting on for Charles' sister finally arrived. It was the last element needed for her living room make-over, and Jez stopped by after working at the Turners to see how it looked. Nancy was thrilled with the whole room and said she'd happily give Jezmeen a good review on her website, once she got one up and running. She and Nancy talked for a few minutes about their mutual interest, Charles, and then she said goodbye.

As she headed down the driveway, she saw Charles pull up along the side of the road in front of Nancy's house.

"Coming to check out the rug, too?" Jezmeen teased. She wondered if he even knew she'd be at Nancy's.

"No. I was coming to talk with my sister, but I'm glad to see you, too."

"Everything okay?" Jez asked, noticing Charles seemed distant and almost sad.

"I think it will be. Do you have a minute?"

"Sure," Jez replied, beginning to feel worried.

Charles sat down in one of the two wicker chairs on the covered front porch. Jezmeen sank onto a cushioned chair next to Charles.

"Should we call your sister outside?" Jez asked.

"I'll chat with her next," Charles replied without a smile.

Jezmeen felt her heart palpitate. Charles was never this serious.

"I'll start with the good news. Remember the spare office you helped decorate?"

"Of course."

"Well, I now have a partner for the practice."

"That's great. Tell me more…"

"Her name's Donna White. She lost her husband when she was in her twenties, and she became a counselor specializing in trauma and grief. She has two daughters in their twenties, and I think she'll be a great fit."

"I didn't know you were already looking."

"I wasn't," Charles replied, staring down at his brown dress shoes and scrubbing a spot with his thumb.

"So, she just appeared?"

"Not exactly. I'm needed back in St. Louis," Charles said, continuing to scrape at the scuff on his shoe without making eye contact.

"What do you mean?"

"My old clients need me."

"So, you're going to be in St. Louis a day a week or something?"

291

"It's a little more extensive than that. I'm moving back," he said, straightening up.

"What?"

Jezmeen felt her heart drop to her stomach.

"I know you're an amazing counselor, but seriously? Those clients should be able to connect with someone new. I mean, you just bought a business and had it professionally decorated. You've only been open for like five months."

"I know, and that's why I hired an assistant."

"Will you be back on weekends? I know you have your new house here. Your sister. Your parents."

"I've actually decided to rent out my place. I can't swing rent in St. Louis and a mortgage here. Donna will handle the clients I've already started with, and she'll take the new ones that come in, too."

"But this is all…so sudden. I just don't get it."

"I want to help the most people that I can, the best way that I can," Charles replied, looking straight ahead at the quiet road.

"I don't think I can make it without you," she said shakily, then steadied herself. "But at least you're only a phone call away."

"Unfortunately, I won't be as available as I have been here. My schedule is quite full. But, I've already asked Donna to fit you in whenever needed, and there's no charge to you."

"What do you mean?"

"It's all covered."

"She'll see me for free?"

Charles nodded his head affirmatively.

"I hate this," Jez declared angrily. "You're the best friend I've *ever* had…" Her hands shook. "Don't you know how much *I* need you. How much I care about you? *Please* don't go."

"I'm sorry, Jez," Charles replied flatly.

"Is this even hard for you?" she asked, trembling. "You don't seem an ounce upset."

"Of course, it's hard for me. But I have so many people to think about besides myself. And I just feel like God is leading me there…for now."

"So how many weeks do we have?"

"The movers are getting my stuff on Saturday."

"What? Like three days? Not even one more Sunday together? I feel like you're abandoning me, just like all the others."

"I'm sorry I didn't give you more time to–"

"I can't hear any more…" Jezmeen stood up, grabbed her purse, and hurried to her car with tears streaming down her face.

It seemed ironic to Ethan that when he had wanted to avoid Jezmeen she appeared, and when he wanted to see her, she was nowhere to be found. After reading and re-reading her letter, he'd been floored by her honesty, devastated by her past, and curious about where she was headed. He needed time with her. Time together to discern if she really had changed. If she hadn't, she'd sunk to a new level of manipulation because she included scripture.

When he looked up the passage she shared at the end of her note, he found that James 5:16 said, *"Therefore confess your sins to one another and pray for each other so that you may be healed."*

Since he'd never stopped praying for Jezmeen, that part was easy. Healing would be hard. Had she become a Christian? Or was she just reading the Bible? Both would be good. One would be better. He reasoned the only way to figure out was if he could ask her a few questions. But the rest of the week went by without one sighting of her.

He ate his lunch outside each day, hoping she'd come out and join him. And one afternoon, her car was parked on the side of the road by the Turners' house, so he walked back to the newly poured concrete patio and pretended to be measuring something, just to see if he could catch her behind the glass, but the only reflection was his.

Then he had to suffer through an awkward Sunday School class where Ariana was forced to sit next to him because it was the only open seat. Ariana was polite, but she bolted as soon as Pastor David concluded.

And Izzy kept hounding him about a Sunday lunch with Jezmeen. So when he saw Jez fighting with a box in the trunk of her car one afternoon while he was headed to his truck to get a box of nails, he shouted an offer to help. Whether she didn't hear, or she was ignoring him, Ethan didn't know, but he hurried to her trunk regardless.

"How'd you get that in there?" Ethan asked, observing the box wedged between the rim of the trunk and trunk's floor.

"The guy at the store packed it," Jez sighed, stopping the struggle and standing up straight.

"Build-it-yourself bedside table?" he asked, noting the picture on the top of the box.

"Only if I can get it out."

"Why don't I get inside the backseat and push," Ethan offered.

Jezmeen didn't say no, so Ethan proceeded with his plan. After he lifted open the small slat that led from the backseat to the trunk, he pushed the box enough that it came unwedged.

"Here, let me," he said, jumping out of the car to carry the box.

She didn't refuse.

"Where are we headed?" he asked.

"Downstairs bedroom," she replied, not nearly as chipper as she was the last two times he saw her. Whether it was the frustration from the box or something else, he didn't know.

"Hey, Jez," one of the workers in the kitchen called when she stepped inside the front door, "when you have a minute, I want you to check out the backsplash."

"Okay," she called, and Ethan could tell she was trying to sound lighter than she felt.

"This place is beautiful," Ethan said sincerely, as he carried the box down the basement steps.

"It's what a lot of money can get you," she said dully.

"I'd say the designer had something to do with it," he replied.

"This way," she said.

Ethan followed her into an airy bedroom with white walls and light blue accents.

"You can set it anywhere," she said, and then she plopped onto the plush white comforter as if she was exhausted.

"Are you alright?" Ethan asked.

"Maybe someday I will be."

"Do you need help building the table?"

"No. I'll be fine."

"Is it something with the Turners because I could—"

"No. The Turners are lovely. It's just that…a very dear friend moved away this weekend, and I feel very lost."

"Oh," Ethan said. He'd never known Jez to have any "dear" friends, and he wondered what she meant by that.

She must have sensed what he was thinking because she quickly interjected.

"You've heard me talk about him before. Charles Noble. The Christian counselor. My first real job with *Style Street.*"

"Where'd he go?"

"Back to work in St. Louis for a while. His old clients needed him," she said with a hint of sarcasm. "You may not believe it, Ethan, but I've made a lot of changes in the last few months, thanks to his influence. And I just don't know if I can move forward without him."

"So, he was like your counselor or something?" Ethan asked.

He knew Jezmeen's track record of picking up men and wondering if Charles was just the next guy after him.

"He'd never call himself that. He just said I was his friend, but yeah. He was my counselor."

Ethan sensed her honesty, so he sat down beside her on the bed.

297

"Sorry," he said. "I know what it's like to lose a friend," he replied, thinking of his first love and former neighbor, Claire. "But I know something that might cheer you up."

"Oh really?"

"Izzy has been begging me to invite you over. Think you could join us for lunch on Sunday?"

"Will your dad be there?" she asked hesitantly.

"I would imagine, why?"

"What's he think of me…since I walked out on you?"

"I don't know. We've never really talked about it."

"I guess it doesn't matter. I would love to see Izzy."

"Then come." Ethan stood up. "I should get back to work…if you're sure you don't need my help with that table," he said.

"Thanks for the offer, but I think it's only like two steps."

Ethan walked to the door, then stopped and turned.

"I forgot to tell you thanks."

"For what?" she asked, heart quickening, wondering for a moment if he'd figured out she deposited the money into his savings account.

"The note. For sharing…"

Ethan put his hands in his pockets.

"Well, see you Sunday."

Jezmeen went to the early church service Sunday morning for two reasons. The first was so she could make it on time to Ethan's. The second was because she hoped to run into Charles' sister, Nancy, and she did.

With over an hour to kill before lunch, Jezmeen waffled between going back to her apartment and changing or wandering Walmart to pass the time and also pick up a contribution for the noon meal. She decided to do the latter and then spent the whole drive there thinking about her conversation with Nancy.

It had been four days since she'd talked with Charles, and she'd expected him to text or call to make sure she was alright after her tearful departure. But he was silent, and she was too stubborn to check on him. Afterall, she was the one that was hurting.

Jezmeen just couldn't understand why he left so abruptly. It seemed like he was trying to sever all ties of communication with her. Had she done something to offend him? Was she an annoying leech, and she hadn't recognized it?

He'd cared about her at one time. She'd felt the longing he had for her—not all the time. But the wisps of longing would come and go. Surely, he wasn't like her mom...or Steven. They'd abandoned her. But Charles was upright. Stable. Secure.

Maybe she was overreacting. Once he was settled, they could find time for each other. He was a counselor who knew her whole backstory. Certainly, he would know how much a sudden departure would wound her. That's why she'd wanted to talk with Nancy. She needed someone else to reassure her that Charles hadn't completely vanished from her life.

But Nancy's answers didn't bring reassurance. Nancy didn't know when Charles was coming back for a visit, or how long he'd be gone.She said she didn't know. She claimed she didn't know he had been thinking about moving. And she acted ambivalent, sharing that Charles was constantly putting others above his own desires. Going back to his old job showed that.

When Jez asked if it was like Charles to do such a leave so abruptly, Nancy declared Charles would do anything for the good of others, but she said it in such a way Jezmeen felt as if there was an underlying message.

After that, Nancy hastily retreated, leaving Jezmeen with more questions than answers. And even after replaying the conversation, all the while wandering the aisles of Walmart, she couldn't figure it out. The only comfort she had was her new faith and the belief that she wasn't truly alone. She reasoned she'd just have to start letting her full weight rest against her Savior.

An hour later she stood at Ethan's door, carrying a pre-made fruit tray and a potted tulip plant. Easter was only a few weeks away and all the holiday flowers lined the Walmart entrance like sentinels standing guard. She figured even though Ethan was a specialist in plants and liked unique varieties, he'd appreciate the pale yellow petals.

Izzy answered her knock and nearly took her breath away with a bear hug.

"I've missed you so much," Izzy gushed, as Jezmeen awkwardly tried to hold the fruit tray and plant while being tightly squeezed.

By the time Izzy let go Ethan arrived at the door.

"Can I help you with that?" he asked.

"Thank you," Jez replied, handing him the fruit tray. Then she wrapped Izzy in another long embrace and wiped a tear from Izzy's cheek.

"I missed you so much, too," Jezmeen said softly.

"Please don't ever leave that way again," Izzy begged.

"I won't," Jezmeen whispered. Jezmeen wiped tears from her own cheeks, then addressed Ethan. "I didn't know what you were having for lunch, but I wanted to bring something. I hope this is okay."

"It's perfect," he replied.

As Jezmeen made her way into the kitchen, she noticed everything in the house was exactly the same, and it made her regret having to go back to her tiny, barely furnished, thrift-store styled apartment. Instantly, she fought back the urge to manipulate Ethan. All sorts of lies flew into her head—she was having her apartment fumigated and just needed a place to stay for a few nights, the heat was broken, and the new furnace was on backorder. If she could slither back in…

But Jezmeen knew she walked on two feet now. The belly crawling days were behind her. Charles had warned her that old patterns of behavior wouldn't disappear overnight. Rather, making one right choice after another would help her develop new ways of thinking and living. And he assured her that a truth-filled, pure, and moral life would be far more fulfilling than the shame, guilt, and depression that would come by following old patterns from the past.

Jezmeen realized again how much she missed Charles. Had she been communicating with him, she would've called to let him know where she was going for lunch and ask for advice on how to act. Instead, she spent the drive to Ethan's praying and wrestling with the loneliness she felt without Charles. Had Ethan not invited her over for lunch, she would've been virtually friendless.

"Good to see you, Jezmeen," Wayne said, standing up from the table as she entered.

"Likewise," she responded.

She set the plant on the kitchen counter.

"That's for you," she said, catching Ethan's eye. It was the first time she really looked at him since she arrived, and her heart fluttered. But she stuffed that feeling down. She'd hurt him deeply, and the only reason she was there was because of Izzy.

Ethan ushered them all to the table.

"So, Isabella Copeland, what are your latest stage aspirations?" she asked the teen, after Ethan prayed.

"Sadly, I tried out for the Muni...you know the outdoor summer musical theater shows...and got a call-back but didn't end up getting cast for any of the productions."

"I'm so sorry," Jez replied.

"I was so down, but then Ethan found out about this thing called "Theater in the Park" in New Salem, and I auditioned and got a part in this show called *A Little Princess*. I'm playing Becky, a servant girl who is really chatty but not so smart. I kind of wanted Lavinia, the typical mean girl, but oh well."

Izzy reached for a piece of pepperoni pizza.

"The bad thing is that practices go till like ten-thirty at night during tech week, and New Salem is over a half hour away.   But Ethan and my dad are going to take turns getting me."

"I can help, too," Jezmeen offered without thinking. Of course, she'd be more than happy to help. Spending time with Izzy was a privilege, but how would Ethan and Wayne take it? Like she was trying to get involved just to weasel her way in again?

"I mean, I just don't have to get up as early as Wayne or Ethan," Jez said, addressing Izzy.

"We'll be fine," Wayne interjected. Jez wondered if she'd hurt his pride.

"Well, I'm proud of you for not giving up. I bet it will be a great experience," Jezmeen said.

"My dad and Ethan prepped me on topics I wasn't to talk about with you," Izzy said casually, "like 'why'd you leave,' or 'who are you dating,' or 'where'd you go,' but they said your job was fair game."

"Isabella," Wayne chided, "all that background was not needed. Just ask your question."

"Sor-ry," she huffed, separating the syllables. "I just wanted to find out what it's like working with rich people."

Ethan gave her a stare.

"What?" Izzy retorted. "It's a valid question."

"You might be surprised to find out not all of my clients are rich," Jez replied, saving the girl from more scrutiny. Then Jezmeen let out a laugh. "That makes it sound like I have so many clients, which in reality is not true."

"But you and Ethan are both working for someone who's rich, right?"

"The Turners' are well-off, but the other two jobs I've had since *Style Street* were for middle-class clients."

"Don't you need more than one client?"

"Ideally, but I've been waiting to finish up with my online certification process to advertise."

"It's great to hear you're in school," Wayne interjected.

"I had no idea there was so much to learn. I figured they'd teach about fabrics, floor plans and color. But we're learning about furniture from different time periods, how to work with vendors and clients, what to charge, all that."

"And you like it?" Izzy asked.

"Love it," Jez replied.

"Have you ever thought about going into business with someone?"

"You mean like working for a furniture store? I know some of them sub-contract decorators."

"No, more like coming up with a 'one stop shop,'" Izzy replied.

"Huh?" Jez asked.

Ethan knew where Izzy was going and quickly cut in.

"I think it's awesome that you're following your dreams. How many more months do you have before you're done with school?"

"One. Two. It's self-paced, but I'm close to the end."

"Well, we'll celebrate. But that means you can't vanish again," Izzy replied.

"About that," Jez replied. "I've been wanting an opening to say 'I'm sorry,' and this seems to be it. I've already told Ethan, but Izzy and Wayne, I shouldn't have left the way I did. It was selfish, and insensitive. You'd think, because I know how it feels, I would've been more thoughtful."

Jez looked at all three at the table. "I promise that's the last time."

"It's okay. I'm glad you've returned," Izzy replied. Then she got up and gave Jezmeen a hug around the shoulders.

When they finished their meal, Izzy asked Jezmeen to see her room. She'd tried her hand at decorating it after Jez moved out. Wayne and Ethan stayed behind to clean up the kitchen. They hadn't been alone together for more than a few minutes since Wayne's return, and an awkward tension hung in the air as Wayne carried over their empty paper plates and threw them in the trash.

"It's good to see Jez again," Wayne said, making small talk.

"Yeah," Ethan replied.

Ethan searched the refrigerator for an open shelf to store the remains of the fruit tray.

"She looks good," Wayne said.

"Mmm-hmm," Ethan replied.

"And to think you found each other because you're both working on the same house. That is amazing."

Ethan had heard people say, "it's a God thing," about such a situation, but he wasn't ready to sound that confident, so he echoed another 'Mmm-hmm.'

"How's business going?" Wayne asked, as he carried half a box of pizza over to the counter.

"Good. Claire's mom is doing billing and scheduling appointments until I can find someone to take that administrative position. And the new guy I hired seems to be a hard worker. How 'bout you? Staying busy with clients?" Ethan asked.

"I'm swamped right now. Which is a good thing. Staying busy helps."

This was the first time Wayne shared any hint of a struggle since being back, and Ethan decided to pry him open a little further.

"How *are* you doing these days?"

"I hesitate to say it because I feel like if I do something will change, but I'm getting traction again."

"That's good, Dad."

"Work's always slow in the winter, and then I get stressed. I haven't always been great at managing my income. You understand the business side…a lot comes in during a few seasons, but you have to save for the drought. I have a budget now and lots of jobs lined up."

Wayne watched Ethan place the remaining slices of pizza into a plastic container.

"Thanks for asking," Wayne said.

"I've been wanting to know. It's just…"

"Yeah. I get it. It's hard to bring up. And I've been pretty quiet, but I know I need to be more open with you and Izzy. Supposedly that helps."

"You mean, just being honest?" Ethan asked, wondering how far his dad would take the question.

Wayne nodded his head.

"Speaking of that," Wayne began. "There's been something I've been wanting to talk to you about."

Chapter Twenty-Nine

Ethan never got to hear what his dad had been wanting to share with him because Izzy inconveniently barged in wondering what the name of the road was that they took to get to New Salem's Theater in the Park. Jezmeen left shortly after, but Ethan saw her again less than twenty-four hours later, when she joined him for lunch overlooking the lake again at the Turners.

They continued to eat lunch together all week, except for Thursday, when it rained, and Ethan stayed home, getting caught up on drafting designs for two potential clients. Their conversations weren't lively or flirtatious. No major topics were covered, and certainly no brushing of her lips against his cheek... or lips ever took place. But she kept coming, and he never refused her company.

Some days Jez was melancholy, some days more buoyant. But she never acted anymore—like she had before—and he could see *her* for the first time. Insecure, sad, lonely, kind. And the funny thing was that he liked her even more than he had when they first met, when she portrayed a sensual, confident woman.

But with their renewed relationship, Ethan felt confused. Why did he get excited when he saw her approaching? How could he think anything good could come from a past riddled with lies? Should he stuff his feelings down and hope they'd go away?

He'd attended enough church services and Sunday School classes to know that he should pray about it. And so he did. Only to receive an answer that made him uncomfortable. *Ask her to pray with you.* He'd never prayed with anyone in his life. All he could picture was clammy hands and a shaky voice. So, he put it out of his mind until something surprising happened.

The first day of May burst forth with all of the Creator's best spring decorations. A carpet of lush green grass, pink blossoms on the Red Bud, and the pachysandra's delicate white blooms displayed God's handiwork in the Turners' backyard. But Ethan's view was the hazel-colored lake while he sat eating his sandwich, when Jezmeen approached from behind.

"Another Izzy special?" she asked, taking a seat next to him.

Still chewing, Ethan nodded a confirmation. Sitting together for lunch felt comfortable. Easy.

"Thanks for having me over yesterday…again," Jezmeen said.

She unzipped her thermal tote and retrieved a sandwich of her own.

"You're a regular now."

"And I love it."

Jez pulled at a piece of crust and ate it.

"Izzy's always been really special to me. Reconnecting has been a big blessing."

Ethan noted Jezmeen's word choice with interest. Maybe now was the time to mention praying together. He was about to when Jez continued.

"Something weird happened on the drive here today."

Little waves lapped the rock-lined waterfront below them.

"I was listening to the radio, you know that station you always had on it the car, WLUJ. And the deejay said, 'If God's put it on your heart to pray with someone today, don't delay.'"

Ethan felt his heartbeat quicken. Jezmeen listened to Christian radio? And she was talking about prayer?

"Well, that wouldn't have been strange in itself, except that before I woke up, I was dreaming that we were praying together."

"That's amazing," Ethan responded. "I got the feeling we were supposed to pray together, too."

"No way," she said, looking at him for the first time since she sat down. "I don't know what we're praying for, and I'm not an expert at this at all, but all those signs are too much to ignore."

"For sure," Ethan replied, secretly grateful that God prepared the way for them to pray together.

"So, what do you think this is all about?" Jez asked.

Ethan didn't want to admit he thought it was about inviting God to be in the center of their relationship—whatever form it took.

"Maybe we're just supposed to pray for each other," Ethan said, feeling uneasy.

"Okay, let's do it," Jez said, setting the rest of her sandwich inside the thermal tote. "Are we supposed to hold hands?" she asked innocently.

"We can," Ethan said, taking advantage of the opportunity to touch her.

He reached his hands towards her, and she took them.

"They're so rough," she said, running her soft fingers over the callouses on the inside of his palms.

"Courtesy of those eight steps," Ethan said, throwing his glance to the wooden planks they were building downwards from the gazebo to the boat slip. "Only four more to go."

He rubbed his thumbs against her skin. "And yours are soft," he said. He looked into her eyes, searching for an indication of how she felt about being so close. She gave no outward sign of how she was feeling, so he continued. "I guess I'll start. If you want to say anything after I'm done, go ahead."

Ethan couldn't recall a single word of what he said when he was done, but he knew he'd covered asking for peace, direction, and protection for Jezmeen. He remained silent, wondering if Jezmeen would feel comfortable to chime in, and within a moment, she began.

God, I don't know why you asked us to pray together, but here we are.

As Jezmeen uttered those words, a cool breeze blew across the couple.

It's pretty amazing that somehow, we both are working at the Turners at the same time. God, you know I'm beginning to see how you set plans in motion, and I really thank you for allowing me to see Ethan again, so I could find forgiveness. And I really thank you for letting me reconnect with Wayne...and Izzy. You know how important their friendships have been these last few weeks. Please help all that Ethan lost in the fire to be rebuilt. Let his business grow and be all that you want it to be. And help him to stand strong with you and never fall away.

Jezmeen slipped her hands out from his grasp as soon as she uttered an "amen." Quickly, she went back to eating her sandwich, while staring at the lake, and Ethan sensed she felt uncomfortable. Sharing a sacred, spiritual space was tender, vulnerable...and beautiful.

"Where did you learn to pray like that?" he asked, keeping his eyes on her.

"Church?" she shrugged.

"You mean you hear people pray when you go to see Ace?" Ethan asked, remembering how she sat in the parking lot of her adopted son's church.

"No. I've been attending a church for a few months," she replied nonchalantly.

"Jez...that's great. What was the catalyst?"

"Charles asked me."

"The Christian counselor?"

"Yeah."

"He must be a really good friend," Ethan asked, wanting to know what *type* of friendship they had.

"He is. Well, he was."

"He's the guy that just moved, right?"

"Yep. Gave me three days' warning and just packed up and went to St. Louis. Haven't heard from him since."

"Seems weird. Especially if he just opened a practice here."

"That's what I thought. But he got some woman to take his clients until he returns."

"How good of friends were you?" Ethan asked, trying to hold back the edge in his tone.

"The best...At least I thought so. I mean, I would tell him everything. And I would try to listen, too. But I did a lot of talking," she said sheepishly. "Kind of like I am now. Before I met him, I was happy to keep everything inside. Now it seems like I can't help but let it all out."

"Were you *more* than friends?"

"Me and Charles? No," Jez gasped. "He's old enough to be my dad. I never thought about him like *that.*"

"Oh," Ethan replied, secretly quite relieved.

"But I loved him, Ethan. He was the nicest, kindest, most selfless guy I've ever met."

"At least you know there are good guys out there."

"Exactly!" Jezmeen exclaimed. "I'd really lost hope, until I met him," she continued, and then realized how Ethan could take that. "Oh, sorry. I shouldn't of–"

Ethan laughed and waved a gnat away from his face. "It's okay."

"That sounded horrible. It wasn't like you were a monster."

"I wish you could've said those first words about me," Ethan said softly, looking away from her for the first time. "But I know how selfish I was when we first met, and how my priorities were all mixed up."

"But you changed. The man I met two years ago and the man sitting with me now are vastly different."

"Thanks. That means a lot." Ethan brushed the soft grass back and forth with his hand. "And I'm starting to believe I could say the same thing about you, too."

Jezmeen's beautifully striking hazel eyes caught his. "That's the best thing I've heard all day."

"Now, if only I could see you truly lived alone, I'd really admit it," Ethan said, half-flirting, half-serious.

"My address is 474 Bruns Lane. Building A. Apartment 103. You're welcome to investigate anytime," she huffed, defensively.

"Okay. How about tomorrow night? Seven o'clock. I'll bring Chinese." He knew orange chicken with fried rice was her favorite meal, and he wanted to know the truth.

She was just about to speak when he interrupted. "No wait. Make it tonight. If someone *is* living with you, you'd have a whole day to cover his tracks," he said, trying to sound playful.

"Well, if that's the case you better make it six, just so you can see no one is hightailing it out with suitcases and furniture," she teased.

"Deal," he replied.

As Ethan pulled the keys out of the ignition, he simultaneously sniffed the scent of his cologne mixed with the sweet and sour sauce on the chicken that was sweating away in its Styrofoam container on the passenger seat of his truck. It was an unusual combination of smells, and Ethan wondered why he'd even put on the dusky cologne.

Ever since lunch, he'd felt happy—almost giddy. He had a date with Jezmeen. But even though she seemed like she was walking in a new direction, Ethan wasn't ready to let down his guard completely.

She'd been a good actress in the past. If this was all part of act two, he wanted to be ready to draw the curtain.

He opened the door to the building's first floor only to find a good-looking man, about his age, exiting. Ethan held the door for him and nodded a hello. Certainly, Jezmeen couldn't have…

Ethan's mind went places it shouldn't. Would he ever be able to trust her? Should he just turn around and leave?

"Hey," a female voice called.

Jezmeen appeared outside her apartment door and was waving.

"I saw you drive up, so I thought I'd make sure you found it okay," she said.

Jezmeen had changed from the blue jeans and white linen top she'd worn at the Turners to a yellow sundress that looked great against her brown skin. He suddenly wondered if he was underdressed in his jeans, "church" boots, and black button up shirt. Before he had another moment to analyze it further, she continued.

"It's a good thing you gave me until six, so I could get all my roommates out," she teased.

"That guy I just saw walking out was probably one of them," he said, trying to sound playful.

"What guy?" she asked, craning her neck to look down the hall.

"Good-looking. Tall. Thirties."

317

"Are you talking about yourself?" she joked.

He handed her the bag of food and followed her inside. The place was exceedingly small. One room held everything—a tiny kitchen, double bed, a round table, and a reclining chair.

"Maybe he was one of your neighbors," Ethan said, still probing.

"I wouldn't know. I've only met the one right next door, and she's about twenty-one with lots of piercings and tattoos."

"Oh," Ethan said casually while continuing to look around. She had a stack of decorating textbooks on her bed and a pile of magazines on the floor next to it. There were plates, silverware, napkins, and water glasses already on the table. No sign of men anywhere.

Jezmeen set the plastic bag on the table and asked him to follow her. She led him to a closet and then opened the doors revealing rows of women's clothes on hangers.

"I just wanted you to see I'm the only one who hangs clothes here," she said, as if she read his mind. "Feel free to search anywhere. I have nothing to hide."

"You didn't have to show me," he replied.

"Actually, I think I did."

She leaned in front of him to shut the closet doors.

"You smell nice," she said, as her body moved in front of him.

"Thanks."

She was so close, Ethan felt her arm brush his chest.

"I guess we should eat before it gets cold," she said softly, moving away.

"Well, I have to admit. I'm amazed," Ethan said after they sat down and prayed over the meal.

"Cause I'm living alone?"

"That…and everything else."

"The place is small."

"But it's yours. What happened to you these past six months?"

"God and a good therapist," Jezmeen laughed.

"God?" Ethan asked. He was hungry to learn more about her spiritually.

"Christmas Eve. A song changed my life."

Jezmeen silently reflected on the words *'Alive in me,'* as she had so many times since she'd first heard them sung.

"You want to tell me about it?" Ethan asked.

"I don't know," she said timidly.

Jezmeen ran her finger along her napkin, smoothing it.

"After the service, I felt God's presence. Alone in the parking lot. I don't know how to explain it. But His Spirit was in the car with me."

She pushed at her rice with her fork.

"While I sat there, God was reminding me of how He'd been with me my *whole* life. Even when I thought He hadn't been. He was. And He'd been using people to bring me towards Him. Actually, it started with you."

"Really?"

"You know how you'd listen to Christian radio when we'd drive in the car or when you'd draw landscaping plans in the family room at night? I couldn't help but overhear it. And then you started reading the Bible and going to church. I'd never been around anybody who did those things."

Ethan was awed. He had no idea he'd been indirectly influencing Jezmeen.

"Then when Charles invited me that Christmas Eve, all day long I felt like I just had to go. When I got there, I was so nervous. I tried to leave two times before being brave enough to go inside. And it's not like I'm totally comfortable going now, but I'm going."

Jezmeen ate a bite of rice.

"Does it ever get better?" she asked him.

"You mean not feeling out of place?"

She nodded.

"You're asking the wrong person. I feel out of place wherever I go," he teased. "Seriously though, it does get easier. When I first started going to church, I looked at it like I was going to school. I just wanted to learn. Now I know some folks, and they know me, and I actually like going."

"I don't know if that would ever happen for me. I just feel different from everyone else. Like they're all cleaned up, and then there's me."

"Well, just remember anyone can dress up the outside. I'm sure there are many other wounded warriors there. Plus, Jesus came for the sick, not the healthy."

"Thanks for the reminder."

The rest of the dinner conversation was focused on her classes, their work at the Turners, and Izzy's social life. After dinner, Ethan helped clear the plates, and when the dishwasher was full, he knew it was either time to pivot and sit down or say goodbye, so he chose the latter. He didn't want to overstay his welcome or ruin what had, so far, been a good evening.

When she walked him to the door, there was no lingering moment for anything romantic. It was "See you tomorrow," and he was walking down the hallway to the building's entrance.

Ethan sat in his car for a moment before driving away, fighting insecurity. Attraction to Jezmeen came easily for Ethan. It always had. But he'd never felt good enough for her, especially after she shouted that she never had loved him. Why was he even considering putting himself through it all again? Could she love him? Could he be enough for her?

Chapter Thirty

Jezmeen stared at her study guide. "What is the Textile Fiber Products Identification Act of 1958, and name three things that it mandates?" *Manufacturers have to label products according to the weight of each fiber, list the name under which they do business...*

She paused, searching. The last answer escaped her, and she was tired of memorizing facts. Leaning against the pillows on her bed, she heard the air-conditioner turn on, and she was grateful for the icy blast on the humid June night.

With freshly washed hair, still smelling of coconut conditioner, she felt suddenly chilly and pulled the comforter over her legs. Her phone buzzed with a text message.

"Sweaty guy is at it again," Izzy wrote.

Jezmeen laughed aloud. The night before, Jez had driven Izzy back from her late-night play practice, so Ethan didn't have to stay up. On the way, Izzy told her about one of the older teen boys in the show who danced next to her during an ensemble number. Supposedly he perspired so much, when they twirled in the song, he sprayed her with his sweat.

"Maybe you should think about becoming a director instead of an actress," Jez typed back with a smile.

"Or I should just wear this," Izzy replied, sending a picture of a person in a hazmat suit.

Before Jezmeen could send a reply of her own, Izzy said, *"Gotta run. My next scene is up."*

Jez looked at her study guide again, trying to refocus, but her mind drifted to Charles. A month had passed since he'd left, and he'd never called once. She waffled between anger, sadness, and confusion whenever she thought about the situation. What baffled her the most was the sudden abandonment. Certainly he understood the trauma she'd faced from men being in and out of her life. How could he, as a trained professional, as a friend, do the same thing? Maybe it was time to ask.

Bolstered by a burst of irritation, she picked up her cell phone and dialed. Would he even be home? It was about nine-thirty, and she knew he liked to watch the ten o'clock news, so he probably wouldn't be asleep. One ring. Two. Three. Four. If it went to voicemail, would she leave a message? But before she could think it through, he answered, sounding tired.

"Jezmeen, how are you?" he asked, trying, without succeeding, to add energy to his tone.

"Charles," she sighed. All the indignation dissipated like a popped balloon. She held back tears. "I've missed you so much."

"Likewise," he uttered with warmth.

"Did your move go alright?" Jez asked, now more concerned with how he was than her former frustration.

"Oh yeah," he replied casually. "Everything went fine. Since I left so much at my house for the renter, I didn't have that much to unpack here."

"Do you like your place?"

"Sure. It's nothing fancy. One bedroom. But it's not too far from work."

"That's great. How are your clients? Were they so glad to see you again?"

"I think so. I got some new ones, too. So, things are busy."

"And your replacement here, what's her name? Donna? She's doing well running your practice?"

"She seems like an excellent fit," Charles said with a lilt in his voice for the first time. "I check in with her at least once a week. You haven't been to see her…"

"How'd you know—oh wait you just said you talk to *her* regularly," she said with a sarcastic laugh.

"I wanted to give you time to adjust, Jezmeen. Let you realize you'd be fine without me, before we talked again."

Jezmeen didn't know how to respond, so she remained silent.

"So how have you been doing?" he asked her without much enthusiasm.

"Depends on the day. I've thought about applying at Finnegan's about six times. The Turners' kitchen is almost done, and then I'll officially be without a job."

"Have you done any marketing to get new clients?"

"Not yet. I just keep thinking I need to get my certification first."

"But aren't you close to being done?"

"Yeah, but who would want to hire me without some kind of credentials?"

"The Turners. Me. My sister. Just show people your work. It speaks for itself."

"I guess I should start getting my website developed and working on business cards and flyers. But I'm going to need income. You know how I feel about using up my savings."

"But so far, you've only had to use it for the start-up costs to move into your apartment, and the gift you made to Ethan, right?"

"Yeah, but the income from the Turners was paying my bills."

"Has Ethan acknowledged your gift?"

"No. Why would he? I can't imagine he ever knew I had that kind of money."

"You two are still seeing each other regularly…at the Turners…right?"

"He's almost done out there, but yeah."

"And how are things going with you two?"

Jezmeen laughed. "You sound like a gossipy girlfriend."

"Just wondering," he replied, the weariness back in his voice.

"Well, I've been over for Sunday lunch a bunch of times. Picked up Izzy from her play practice twice to help out. And he's been to my place."

"Sounds like there's been some healthy forgiveness."

"It's like a load off my shoulders. But Charles, I think he wants more."

"What do you mean? Is he pushing the boundaries with you?" he asked in alarm, like a bear ready to fight.

"No, not at all. It's just that—you know—I can *tell* when men like me, and he still does."

"Is that bad? Didn't you tell me that after he became a Christian, he was nothing but good to you?"

"Yes, but..."

"Are you having a hard time *feeling* anything?"

Jezmeen was silent. They'd touched on this before.

"You've been through multiple major traumas with men. When that happens, a person shuts down. It's a self-protection mechanism. It may take months, or years, for you to feel comfortable, safe, and able to tap into those emotions. To give and receive love."

She heard the beep of someone in the parking lot hitting the automatic lock on their car outside.

"But, if Ethan is the type of man you made him out to be, I imagine he'll wait…And Jezmeen, you're worth the wait."

"Oh Charles," Jezmeen whispered. "Please let's not go three weeks again without talking. It's bad enough you're an hour and half away, but at least we have the phone."

Charles was silent for a moment. "I really want you to go see Donna. Promise me? Okay."

"Why?"

"You've come so far. She'll give you the help and support you need."

"But why can't you?" Jezmeen begged.

"It's just that I'm so—"

"Busy?" Jezmeen finished. "Why did you get so busy all of a sudden? You weren't that busy here, and you were running your own practice."

"Yes, busy. I know it's not all going to make sense."

"Then explain it to me. I need that, Charles, because I *need* you."

No words passed for a moment.

"I believe our paths are moving different directions, and I think God wants me here and you there. And the me here gets tired. I'm surrounded with memories of Katherine, and the workload is…tough."

He sighed.

"So, lean into God. He's strong enough to carry you. And lean into Ethan. He can handle the weight. And lean into Donna. I think you'll find her helpful," Charles said.

"Can I still call?" Jez asked in a small voice.

"Of course. And if I can answer, I will."

When Ethan knocked on Jezmeen's door there was no answer. For a quick second he wondered if he'd gotten the details wrong. He was pretty sure he was supposed to pick her up at 5:30. From her apartment, it took twenty minutes to get to the Turners, and they were the guests of honor. Ethan rapped again a little louder. Within a few seconds the door flung open, and Jezmeen's floral perfume filled the air.

"Sorry, I'm running late," she sighed. "I couldn't decide what to wear."

Jezmeen headed towards the closet, grabbed a pair of sandals off a shoe rack, and sat on the bed to put them on.

"I love your dress," Ethan said, noting how the strapless white dress with red flowers made her shoulders look lovely. She had her hair pulled up in a loose bun, with brown wisps framing her face.

"Thanks. It was either this or that red one," she said pointing to the garment laying on the bed.

"I think this is perfect."

329

Jezmeen stood up and headed towards the kitchen table, grabbing her purse.

"Okay, I'm ready. Sorry to keep you waiting. I hope we won't be late."

"We'll be fine," Ethan said reassuringly.

"You look amazing," she said to Ethan, as she locked her apartment door.

"Thanks. Izzy helped me pick everything."

"She's got good taste," Jez said, noting his khaki trousers, white linen button down shirt, and boat shoes. "But you're missing something."

"What?" Ethan asked, alarmed.

"Your fedora," she grinned.

"I figured we'd be under the gazebo the whole time," he said seriously, and she smiled.

"Do you still worry about your birthmarks coming back?"

"Absolutely."

"Well, you wouldn't know now."

"Thanks. That means a lot. The first year after the surgery, I kept thinking people were staring. It took me a long time to realize that those days were past."

Ethan ran around the side of his truck and opened the door for Jezmeen.

"I wonder how long it will take me to think differently about myself," Jez said, once Ethan was at the wheel.

"What do you mean?" he asked, looking into the rearview mirror as he backed up.

"It's not like once you become a Christian, you stop remembering your past. And all I can think about are my mistakes, relationships, and lies. I know I'm forgiven, but it's hard to be free from all the shame."

"Jesus paid too high a price for you to carry around that heavy load," Ethan replied.

He signaled to go left at the stop sign by the exit of the apartment complex.

"So, are you looking forward to tonight?" Jez asked, trying to lighten the mood.

"Well, you know how I feel about social events, but going with you makes everything easier."

"That's a kind thing to say. I'm sorry I tortured you so many times with dinner parties at the house."

"I couldn't admit it then, but I can now. It was good for me. Every day I have to talk with clients and meeting all those new people helped me get some practice. How about you? Are you excited about tonight?"

"Of course. You know I love—"

Mid-sentence Jezmeen reached up and felt her ear lobe. "Oh shoot! I forgot to put in my earrings. And with my hair up tonight, I needed them to complete the look."

"I was going to give you this later, but I guess the timing is right."

Ethan pressed the brake as they glided to a stop at the light. He opened the glove compartment and pulled out a small white box.

"For you."

"The diamond earrings!" she exclaimed, opening the box. "But why are you giving them back? I mean, it's not like we're…"

"Together. I know. But they were a gift. Actually, they survived the fire."

"The fire on your property?"

"Yeah. Izzy had actually just dropped them off with Claire at the storefront before the fire. Claire put them in the cash drawer, and amazingly they made it through. To be honest, they were all tarnished gray, like a pond when it's frozen over. But there's a place in town that cleans diamonds."

"If you hadn't told me, I never would've known," Jezmeen said.

"You should wear them."

After putting them both in, Jezmeen drew down the passenger side mirror and inspected the earrings.

"Thank you," she said sincerely.

When they arrived at the Turners, tiki torches lit the way to the back yard. And once under the gazebo they were cheerfully greeted by Tom and Denise Turner. Jezmeen had chosen the furniture for the gazebo, arranged the potted plants, and hung the strings of white patio lights days earlier. And even though it was a June evening, the weather was a beautiful eighty degrees.

Tom and Denise introduced them to each of the fourteen other guests they'd invited, and light jazz music streamed through their outdoor speakers. Once everyone had arrived, the guests found their way to their name cards. Jezmeen and Ethan had been placed next to each other, even though neither had told the Turners about their past...or present.

A caterer had been hired, and Ethan had the best filet mignon he'd ever eaten, followed by a heavenly strawberry layer cake. And by the time the sun set, Jezmeen had socialized with all the guests with grace and ease. When the Turners offered up a toast to Jezmeen and Ethan for their hard work, Jez echoed a touching response, highlighting her gratefulness for the Turners believing in her ability. As the guests began to leave, a few took business cards from Jezmeen saying they'd call.

Even though it was late for Ethan, he wasn't ready for the evening to end. So, once they were back in the truck, he asked Jezmeen if they could make one more stop before he dropped her off. She agreed, and they headed down a country road.

"One day I took a wrong turn when I was going to pick up a load of lumber, and I stumbled across this spot," Ethan said.

He steered his truck onto the rocky shoulder.

"I didn't get out that day, but I've wanted to ever since," he continued.

Just after nine on the June evening, the horizon was already tinted a shade of licorice and scented with honeysuckle. Ethan hopped out of the truck and walked around to get Jezmeen's door.

"You wanted to show me a bench," Jezmeen laughed hesitantly.

A few feet from where Ethan had parked his truck sat a graying, weathered wooden bench.

"Wait, look," Ethan said, ushering with his hand for Jez to take a seat.

The grass was long, and it made Jezmeen's ankles itch. She sat down, then leaned over to scratch her ankles. But when she leaned back up, she looked out and realized what Ethan wanted her to see. The bench faced the lake, and on the opposite bank, the large homes lit up the inky water like lanterns.

"It's lovely," Jez breathed. "I wonder who built this here?"

"Maybe someone who wanted to observe the lives of the rich and famous?"

"Or maybe someone who saw the beauty and wanted to make himself comfortable."

"Did you enjoy yourself tonight?" Ethan asked, resting his arm on the back of the bench, not quite touching Jezmeen's bare shoulders.

"Very much. I've never really been recognized for anything before."

"And it looks like you might be getting some new clients."

"I hope so. If I don't, I'll have to get another job."

"You wouldn't happen to want to come work for Adams Landscaping?"

"What do you mean? Someone quit?"

"Well Claire, but her mom took over for her until I could find someone. And Claire's mom really wants to be done. She's been more than kind to take on the job, replacing her is way overdue."

"So, she answers your phone line, sets up appointments, follows up with customers, does payroll, that kind of thing?"

"That's it."

"How many hours a week?"

Ethan removed his arm back to his side in his excitement. "Wait, you're actually considering it?"

"I don't know? Maybe. I need work, and you need an assistant. Plus, I can do the job from home—or on the go, if I had a client."

"True," Ethan said, still surprised she bit at the proposal. "It's about thirty hours a week. But when you're done with the billing and payroll, it's basically like you're just 'on call.'"

335

"I'll think about it."

Jezmeen rubbed her bare arms with her hands.

"I didn't even realize you might be cold," Ethan said with concern. "Wait here for a second."

Ethan got up and went to the truck, hurrying back with a red and blue plaid fleece blanket. He handed it to Jez as he sat back down.

"Thank you," she uttered, and then began wrapping it around her shoulders.

As Ethan reached over to help her, their hands touched. Ethan stopped and pulled his hand away.

"Sorry," he apologized, then wondered why.

They rested silently, side by side, for a few minutes listening to the chorus of frogs and crickets hidden away in the landscape around them. He draped his arm around the outside of the blanket, pulling her in nearer.

"Do you know when I was pregnant with Ace, one of the things the doctor recommended was to bring a CD of relaxing music to the hospital," Jez said.

She rested her head against his chest.

"I picked out this ocean waves CD. The lapping of the lake against the rocks reminds me of it a little."

"What was it like? Giving birth so young?"

"Long. Scary."

"Was Steven there? Or your mom?"

336

"Nope. Neither."

"You did it all alone?"

"Yep. That's what happens when you have a self-centered mom and a loser boyfriend."

"Wow....You were brave."

"I think the hardest part was walking out of the hospital without Ace. I decided I didn't want to spend time with him after he was born. I thought it would make it harder. So pretty much as soon as I had him, he was whisked away to his adoptive parents."

"I can't even imagine how difficult that had to be."

"I think I just wanted someone there doing this," Jez said.

"You mean holding you?" Ethan said huskily.

"Yeah."

Ethan soaked in their closeness, rubbing his arm up and down on the blanket, against her arm.

"I'd like to be the one holding you like this all the time," Ethan whispered.

He felt Jezmeen tense, and he immediately doubted she'd ever be able to care for him the way he cared for her.

"I went to see a new counselor," Jez said. "Charles told me I should. Anyhow, we talked about you."

Ethan felt flattered, but then wondered if he should be worried.

"She said to be honest."

"That's really important to me," Ethan said sincerely.

Jezmeen sat up but continued to look at the dark lake.

"I don't feel anything for you."

Chapter Thirty-One

Ethan didn't know what to say. He felt duped. Even though he knew understanding women wasn't his strong suit, it seemed like their movement forward had been mutual.

"But don't take it personally," she quickly interjected.

"How am I supposed to take it?"

"It's just that I can't...well don't...I don't know...have the ability to really *feel* anything romantically," she said with embarrassment.

"Ever? With anyone? Or is it just me?" Ethan said, trying to understand.

She reached down to itch her ankle again.

"Let's just say my past is a mess, and this is one of the consequences. It's not you. I haven't *felt* anything for anyone since Steven."

"Is it curable?" Ethan asked innocently.

Jezmeen laughed heartily. "It's not like I have a disease or something. But Donna, the therapist, says building trust, acknowledging my feelings about intimacy, having boundaries, purity, all those things should help."

"Does holding you feel okay?" he asked.

"Yeah, I liked it," she replied softly.

He drew her back into his chest. She rested her head again.

"I wish I could go back and do everything different with you, Jez. I wish our relationship had started with purity. That I wasn't just another name on your list of men who used you. I'm ashamed of who I was back then."

"Yeah, well, I'm a good actress, so that didn't help."

"You and Izzy have that in common," he chuckled.

A soft breeze blew her bangs across her forehead, and he gently moved them back into place with his free hand.

"Is that okay?" he asked.

"Yeah."

He held her for a moment, forming his thoughts.

"When I first met you, I thought you were the most beautiful woman I'd ever seen…I still do. Then there were so many lies. But you delivered that letter a few weeks ago, and it gave me hope.""

Ethan rubbed her blanketed arm.

"Why? Because I said I'd changed?"

"That, and you made it sound like…

Ethan couldn't bring himself to say it. If she truly cared for him, it would become apparent. An owl hooted and a vehicle sped by on the road behind them, but he barely noticed.

"Jez, I loved you by choice when I proposed. I love you now with feeling. And it would be my privilege to do nothing more than hold you for months...or years."

She turned to face him. The darkness made it hard to see her face, but her striking hazel eyes pierced the night.

"It's too much to ask anyone. I'm not worth the wait...What if I never can give you anything more than just friendship?"

"Don't you think that's what good relationships are built on?"

"I don't know. I haven't had many."

"Me neither," he said, chuckling.

They sat quietly for a moment.

"In the end, this is your decision, Jezmeen. You've been pushed around enough in relationships. I want you to choose 'us' willingly, and not for what I can provide financially, because I'm barely staying afloat. I think God is in this, Jez, but I need you to know that, too. So, I'll wait to hear from you after tonight. You know how I feel. I'm all in. No matter what. Now it's your turn to decide."

The next three days felt like Ethan was waiting for wet cement to dry—the moments were agonizing and slow. He was thankful for a full day of work on Saturday and time with Wayne and Izzy on Sunday. When he dropped Jezmeen off, the night of the Turners' party, he told her she didn't have to join them for Sunday lunch, if she needed time to process everything. But he had hoped with his whole heart that she would be there at noon.

When she wasn't, he had to play it cool with Izzy and Wayne, even though he felt like he'd hit an iceberg and was sinking. Monday came, and when Claire's mom reminded him she was going on vacation in July, he was quite tempted to call Jez to see if she'd thought about the offer for work…and to ask if she had an answer for where they were headed.

But he kept to his word. He would wait. On Monday evening, after dinner, he sorted through his mail. Two invoice payments came in. A postcard said a dental office was seeking new customers. And his bank statement arrived. He was just about to open the bank statement when his dad's phone number appeared on his cell phone screen. Was it his night to pick-up Izzy from play practice, he wondered in alarm?

"Hey dad. Was I supposed to pick-up Izzy tonight?"

"No, I'll be heading out there in a little while. Izzy texted me that she left her pencil bag at your house, and her fancy calculator is in there. She said she did okay without it today but needs it tomorrow for school. Can I stop by to pick it up on my way to get her?"

"Sure. I'll be here."

After he hung up, he tore his thumb across the sealed envelope and looked over his May statement. His personal checking account was near empty. The business account was stable. And his savings account, usually at zero, had...Ethan held the paper back, as if he wasn't reading it correctly. $30,000. That had to be an error.

He hurried to his computer and opened the account online. Clicking onto the correct account, it confirmed the same amount. $30,000. Maybe in the last four months, he'd sold a lot of his pergola invention, he wondered. But Tryton didn't have that account number. They always sent him a royalty check in the mail. Could his dad have done it as compensation for his carelessness? But Wayne didn't have his account number either.

When Wayne arrived an hour later, Ethan had already thought of ten ways to bring it up. And after passing him the pencil bag across the kitchen counter, Ethan delved in.

"Dad, has business still been really good?"

"Yeah. I'm booked two weeks out. Why? You ready to start building the storefront? You know whenever you're ready, I'll drop everything."

"No. It's not that. But thanks for the offer."

Ethan tried a different angle.

343

"Just for fun, if you came into a windfall, what would you do with it?"

"Why?" Wayne laughed. "Did you? I'd be happy to help you if you have too much."

Ethan laughed along with his dad, hoping he'd answer.

When Wayne realized he was serious, he continued. "Well, I'd guess I'd want to rebuild your storefront first. And pay off my rehab bills. Even though insurance was covering 80%, I still owe $3,500."

So Wayne didn't have the money, Ethan realized, and he began to wonder who did?

"I wish I could help you with your rehab bills," Ethan said.

"And I wish I could help you pay for your storefront."

Wayne patted the pencil bag and then began to get up from the barstool at the kitchen counter.

"Well, I better be going," he said and started for the front door.

They stepped onto the front porch, and sconces on either side of the door lit their way out.

Wayne sighed. "Something's been eating at me for months, and I don't think it's going to go away until I come clean."

Ethan wondered if his dad was finally going to admit he knew what caused the fire.

"The day your store burned down, Izzy and I stopped by. She had those expensive earrings to give back to Jezmeen, but since neither of you were home, she gave them to Claire."

Wayne shifted his weight uncomfortably.

"I went around back to check out the leak you were telling me about, and before I left, I threw my cigarette butt somewhere. I didn't really pay attention. At that time, I was spiraling downward and just wasn't aware of what I was doing. When I got your phone call that night, I was too embarrassed to say anything. Plus, who knows? Maybe it wasn't even what caused the whole thing," he said, soothing himself. "Your report came back inconclusive, right?"

"Yeah. I don't think we'll ever know for sure," Ethan said, trying to comfort his dad. He was thankful Wayne finally got the courage to say something, but he didn't want to press the issue.

"Either way, Ethan, I wish I had come into a windfall so I could help you rebuild. It's not easy to feel like a failure in front of you."

"Hey, don't be so hard on yourself. We both know only One is perfect. If you didn't realize it, you've actually given me a lot."

Ethan swatted at a small white moth that fluttered for the outdoor light.

"I'd rather have the man who's next to me, showing me how to live a life of faith...in the ups and downs...then go back to the time when I never knew you," Ethan said.

345

"Thanks, Son," Wayne replied, pulling Ethan in for a hug.

Jezmeen was happy to see a 98% next to the grade for the textile's test. So far, she was averaging a high A for her course work. With no online classes for the evening and the last exam behind her, she felt adrift. The afternoon had been spent working on her marketing materials and looking for a website host. But the highlight of the day had been a call from one of the guests at the Turners' party. Allison Porter scheduled a client consultation for the next day.

The job didn't sound unusually complicated. Allison wanted to paint and redecorate a few rooms on the first floor of the family's two-story, but Jezmeen was thrilled to have the opportunity to bid on the project. Tomorrow she'd have work to do. Work she thoroughly enjoyed. Tonight, she had nothing to do, which meant she'd do the same thing she had the last two evenings—think about Ethan's proposal.

She had tried to call Charles on Sunday, but he didn't answer. Even though she left a message, she hadn't heard back from him, and she felt disappointed. Jez had an appointment with Donna coming up, but help was needed now. She didn't want Ethan to have to wait forever on her answer, but she was conflicted.

If they moved forward, Jezmeen knew Ethan would be true to his word. She knew he would respect her body and her boundaries. But was it hopeless? She'd always dreamed of moving near the ocean and being free of men—independent...and alone.

Loneliness seemed to follow her everywhere she went. It was like the neighborhood cat that always came back when it was hungry. She longed to be part of a family. Sunday lunches were the best, and she hated to miss the day before, but it would have been unfair to Ethan to show up without resolution to his question.

Grabbing her cell phone off the floor next to the recliner, she decided to try Charles again. Maybe she could catch him at home on a Monday night. After six rings, it went to his voicemail. She hung up without leaving another message and sighed.

No doubt that meant she should go to God. She knew it in her heart, but it was easier to talk to someone whose voice she could hear instantly. Jezmeen uttered a quick prayer. *God, You know how conflicted I am. I don't want to hurt Ethan again, and don't know if I ever want to be in a relationship. Am I capable of loving someone the way you want me to? Please give me wisdom. Amen.*

Jezmeen walked over to the kitchen table, retrieved her Bible, and returned to the recliner. She opened it haphazardly, and it fell to Psalm 25:4. *Show me the right path, O LORD; point out the road for me to follow.* Then she heard knocking on her front door.

Chapter Thirty-Two

"Ethan!" Jez exclaimed, as she opened the door.

"Sorry to bother you so late. Mind if I come in for a minute?" Ethan asked, breathlessly.

"Sure. Is everything okay?"

"Just trying to get to the bottom of something."

She led him down the small hallway and into the main area of the studio apartment. Grabbing her Bible off the seat, Jezmeen ushered for Ethan to sit in the recliner, and she headed for the bed.

"Excuse the outfit," she said, realizing she was sporting plaid lounge pants and a baggy white t-shirt. "I haven't led the most exciting life today."

He seemed too distracted to pay attention to what she was wearing.

"So…what's up?" she asked, easing onto the white comforter.

"I got my May bank statement today."

"And you rushed over to tell me that," she chuckled again uneasily. Had he figured out she deposited the money? Why else would he have come over?

"Jez, I thought you were broke," he said, the floor lamp next to him casting a golden glow on his troubled face.

"Would I be living in a one-room rental, furnished with thrift store finds, if I wasn't?"

"Maybe you're just frugal."

"Why are you asking?" Jez asked. She had given up lying, but she wasn't sure she wanted him to know the truth. He might try to give the money back.

"$30,000 was deposited into my savings account."

"Could it be your royalties from Tryton?"

"They don't have my account number. No one has it, except for you."

"What do you mean?" Jezmeen asked, trying to play dumb.

"Don't you remember that when you bought all the furniture for the house, I deposited that exact same amount, and you or I could withdraw what we needed? Just *you* or *me*."

"So, you think I have that kind of money just laying around, and one day I just decided to give a whole chunk of it to you for no reason?"

Jezmeen pulled a pillow over her stomach and tried to calm her beating heart with a slow inhale.

Ethan sat back in the chair, slowing his words and demeanor for the first time since entering.

"Oh man. Did I totally mess up here?"

He ran his hand through his wavy brown hair.

"Maybe it was a bank error," he muttered almost to himself. "I am so stupid. And sorry. I shouldn't have rushed over here like this. I told you I would let you have time and space…to figure things out, and now I've blown it."

His voice dripped with distress, and Jezmeen's heart went out to him. She couldn't let him suffer needlessly. Even if telling the truth meant he might not accept the gift, at least she'd tried.

"Did you ever think about going into detective work?" she asked.

"Why? Because I stink at it?"

"No, because you figured it out."

"Wait…I did? You really put the money in that account?"

She nodded her head in affirmation.

"But how did you get that much—Why did you do it?"

"Somehow, I always managed to surf the wave of a free ride. Which means I've been able to save most of my income for the last twelve years."

"So, when you told me that you were broke and paying off student loans, that was a lie?" Ethan asked, remembering a conversation they'd had a year earlier.

"Unfortunately, yes."

"Why did you do it?"

"Lie?"

"Not that. Why did you give me so much money?"

"Well, I spent it, so I figured I'd return it."

"But I had to have furniture. It wasn't like you owed me."

"Sure, but I didn't buy you thrift store finds like these," Jezmeen replied, pointing to her kitchen table and reclining chair. "And you didn't *need* all the high-end artwork or vases or candles. I was reckless with what you gave me to manage. And then when I heard about the fire…"

"Certainly, you had to be saving for something."

Jezmeen thought about Monica's offer to buy the *Style Street* franchise, but she didn't feel melancholy. That would have been a huge financial risk, like running a marathon before she'd ever done a sprint.

"One day I planned to move to a beach, get a little cottage on the coastline…but who says that still can't happen?"

Jezmeen smiled, and Ethan's heart beat a little faster. He loved seeing her smile.

"I can see you're trying to understand my motives. I know it's a lot of money," Jez said. She thought about how it took her almost two years to save that much. "I saw how hard you worked to make everything in those greenhouses grow. You put *so* much time into those plants, and your business. To think you couldn't rebuild because you didn't have the funds, and that I had something to do with it…I just couldn't sit on my nest egg and not help out."

She pushed the pillow on her waist and watched it deflate, then inflate slowly.

"So, you want me to use that money to start again?"

"Yes."

Ethan leaned his head back against the light blue chenille upholstery for a minute.

"I don't think I can take it."

"What? Why not?"

"It's too much."

"But, Ethan, I felt like God told me to do it."

"Wow," Ethan said, amazed. He sat in silence for a moment.

"Okay Jez, I can't take it unless you're getting something from the investment, too. I've been holding onto an idea…but it all depends on your answer to what you want to do about 'us,' and I really don't want to pressure you."

"You'll never believe what I read right before you knocked on the door," Jezmeen laughed.

Two late nights with Ethan meant Jezmeen had to work hard to stay awake in church. They'd spent hours brainstorming their new joint venture, and she'd typed up ten pages of notes. When Ethan admitted the idea had begun with Izzy, she was pleasantly surprised. Somehow that made it all the more perfect.

Jezmeen followed the congregation's lead, as they stood to sing a closing hymn. Brushing a strand of hair behind her ear, her hand grazed the diamond earring from Ethan. He'd said they been covered in soot, but now they sparkled radiantly. The pastor's sermon focused on Christ's blood washing believers clean. Just like the diamonds, her stains had been removed. That moved her to tears of gratitude.

After the song ended and the pastor closed in prayer, she headed to the bathroom thinking about God's goodness as she walked. Since November, she'd sought counseling, moved into her own place, worked on forgiving herself and others, started an online degree program, and righted a wrong. Even more gratifying was her celibacy. No longer using men for what they could provide or how they could be manipulated was freeing. Her pastor talked about being a new creature in Christ, and she felt like one.

She still missed Charles. He'd been the first man who'd ever loved her with pure intentions, and the void was hard to fill. On the way out of the restroom, she stopped for a drink at the fountain, and as she bent down, she overheard a conversation that made her ears perk up. Charles' sister was talking to someone nearby in low, hushed tones.

"So how is Charles *really* doing?" a voice she didn't recognize asked.

Jezmeen knew they were right around the alcove where she was drinking, so she just stayed stooped down, hoping to remain discreet.

"Well, he's tired," Charles' sister said.

"Working with prison inmates all day and doing group therapy at night would do that to you," the unknown voice interjected. "Why in the world did he want to go back to all that when he finally opened a private practice?"

"He's never come right out with it, but I'm pretty sure it was a woman."

"He was going back to St. Louis for a woman?"

"No, he was leaving Springfield because of one...I think he'd fallen in love."

"What's wrong with that? Did he feel guilty that not enough time had passed since Katherine's death?"

"No, it was the woman's age. She was like twenty years younger than him."

Jezmeen was tired of crouching down, but she didn't care. They were talking about *her*.

"Is that such a bad thing? After all, celebrities do it all the time."

"I think he was trying to get out of the way because there was someone else he felt was better suited for her. He prayed about it all and felt like he was doing what God wanted him to do."

Jezmeen didn't need to hear anymore, and she didn't want to be caught once the conversation came to a close. With agile steps, she went in the opposite direction of the two ladies and hurried out of the church.

When she got to her car, she rolled the windows down all the way to let out the hot air. Charles worked with inmates? Why hadn't he ever told her? He said he worked with adults and teens, but that's all she really knew about his counseling practice. And he'd fallen in love with her. Somehow, she'd always known.

Oh, Charles, Jezmeen thought. *Why didn't you just tell me? I would've told you to stay.* But if he had stayed, would she have clung to God…and Ethan…just the same? Or would she have run to him, as she had lately, with all of her problems? *He did it all for me,* she realized, and then wondered if she was talking about Charles or God.

6 Months Later…

Jezmeen and Ethan had been counting down to the first weekend in December with great anticipation. Trinity Landscaping and Interior Design was opening, and they'd needed every hour over the last six months to make it happen. Constructed atop the burnt embers of the old store, Ethan, Wayne, and one of Wayne's friends, worked every night and weekend, when the weather allowed, building the new structure. And this time, Ethan installed a sprinkler system.

When Ethan first proposed the idea that they combine their businesses and offer a one-stop shop for interior and exterior design, Jezmeen was intrigued. Because she had less clientele, she would run the store, doing Claire's old work, plus build up her own customer base until she had enough jobs to hire someone to take on the administrative side of things.

The name was Wayne's idea, and not only did it remind Jezmeen and Ethan that God was the glue between them, but also that the Holy Trinity was ever present. They designed the store to be shared. Ethan's half would display flowers and shrubs, once he had time to build the greenhouses and cultivate the seeds, while the other half was Jezmeen's to stage. Jezmeen took full advantage of her area, purchasing an inviting table and chairs for client meetings and creating a personal workspace with a desk and filing cabinets.

Weeks earlier, they'd spent a Saturday evening addressing invitations to their grand opening, and Ethan encouraged Jez to invite all her connections through bartending. Certainly, she'd gotten to know some of the capitol town's most notable residents. And she realized all those years spent bartending were being used by God now in a new way.

While they worked side-by-side, Ethan treated her with pure respect. Sometimes they held hands, occasionally he rubbed her shoulders, and every day they shared a hug goodnight, but he let her lead, which made her aware of how slow she was taking it. But he insisted he didn't mind, and as their friendship grew, so did her trust. And alongside trust, love blossomed.

Not extravagant, passionate love, but gentle, kind, and stable love. A love to be depended on in all seasons. A love for a lifetime.

In November, when Ethan's landscaping jobs slowed down and they both moved to working inside the storefront, there'd be times she'd just well up with gratitude. The formerly awkward recluse was exactly what the formerly promiscuous drifter needed. Long before Jezmeen realized what God was doing, He'd brought them together so two could become one.

On the Saturday morning of the grand opening, Jezmeen and Ethan both fought nerves. Would people come? Could they sustain this dream? Were their fledgling efforts enough?

Without his own plants to sell, Ethan and Jezmeen brainstormed what he could offer at the grand opening. And they decided upon poinsettias. One day they'd grow rows of trees, including spruce trees for Christmas, but for now they'd sell the white and red poinsettias that they received at a wholesale price from a vendor.

Ethan would also offer coupons for landscaping, mowing, and even Christmas light removal. Jezmeen, on the other hand, would be offering half-price color consultations for people who wanted help picking paint for their walls, and she'd be running a drawing for a free room design.

With contests and refreshments, coupons and plants ready, Ethan and Jezmeen, along with Wayne, Izzy, and even Ethan's mom, Suzanne, prayed together and were ready to greet their guests by 9:00 AM on the gray, cloudy, fourteen-degree day.

With gusto, they unlocked the double doors into the store and were pleasantly surprised to find five cars already in the parking lot. For the first hour, Ethan and Jezmeen fielded questions from potential clients in their own respective areas of the store, while Izzy and Wayne checked out customers and Suzanne handled refreshments.

But at ten o'clock, Ethan approached Jezmeen. At Ethan's side was a beautiful couple with a young child.

"Jezmeen," Ethan said, "I'd like to introduce you to my former neighbor, Danielle, and her husband, James Patton."

The beautiful blonde was holding a small child, but she reached out an arm and shook her hand; then James offered his as well.

"I haven't seen Danielle in what—" Ethan asked, looking at Danielle, "four years?"

"Something like that," Danielle replied with a pleasant smile.

"I owe my start to James though," Ethan replied, now throwing his gaze at the tall, handsome man next to Danielle.

"James was a former representative for the state of Illinois. He bought my old house and took an *HGTV* crew around the backyard, which started this whole thing. The *HGTV* episode got my pergola invention before the eyes of the owner of Tryton Building Products."

"Well, thank you for that," Jezmeen said kindly.

"My pleasure. I don't think I really knew at the time how big of a deal the *HGTV* thing was," James replied.

"We were so excited to read about your new joint venture," Danielle broke in. "Once we saw the article in the paper a few days ago, we knew we had to come and see Trinity Landscaping and Interior Design *and* meet your fiancé."

Jezmeen felt for the engagement band that was back on her ring finger, as of Thanksgiving. Ethan had asked in a simple, yet heart-felt proposal, and Jezmeen easily said "yes" knowing that this time she'd actually walk down the aisle without hesitation.

"You seem like you complement each other so well," Danielle said.

"We're a good blend of opposite and alike," Jezmeen replied. "How long have you two been married?"

"Three years, and we had Benjamin fourteen months ago," she said, lifting the chubby towhead to be seen.

"He's beautiful," Jezmeen said. "Thank you so much for stopping by. Please make sure to sign up to win a free design project and get some punch and cookies for Benjamin."

Ethan ushered them towards the refreshments, and the next hour passed quickly. Claire and her fiancé Tyler stopped by to visit a little before noon. And Ethan learned that they'd officially set a summer wedding date. Although they'd have the ceremony in Springfield, a celebration would be held in Tianjin, China when they returned in the fall. Tyler planned to continue at Nankai University, while Claire still had employment as an English as a Second Language teacher in Tianjin as well.

During the afternoon, there were periods with fewer people, and the time moved slowly. By closing time, Jezmeen was ready to get off her feet. With only a few customers in the store, and about fifteen minutes left until five o'clock, Jezmeen heard the chimes on the door ring, and her breath caught as she saw Charles walk in with her new therapist at his side.

Jezmeen had continued to see Donna every other week during the fall, and she'd developed a close bond with the gentle woman. Donna had told her she was coming. Charles was the surprise. It had been over six months since she'd seen her dear friend, and her soul stirred with excitement and gratitude over his appearance.

After overhearing Nancy's conversation at the water fountain, many months earlier, Jezmeen immediately called Charles. She intended to give him an overly perky report about her relationship with Ethan, with great exaggerations of her stability. But when he didn't answer, she, instead, left a message saying she was doing well, she wouldn't bother him anymore, and she thanked him for his friendship.

She purposely made an effort, and it took effort, not to call him again. There were many times she wanted to dial his number with a concern or worry, but instead she took her burdens to God. Jez hoped that her call would make Charles realize she was okay without him, and that he could come back.

Making a beeline for the couple, Jezmeen greeted them both with happy hugs.

"Charles, Donna, thank you so much for coming," she gushed.

"We're both thrilled for you and Ethan," Donna said. "Have you had a good turnout today?"

"This morning was crazy. It's slowed down now, but yes, it's been a great day," Jezmeen replied.

"Where's Ethan?" Donna asked. "I'd love to meet him."

"Of course," Jez replied, and she steered them to where he was talking with a customer. After Ethan ended his conversation, Jezmeen made introductions all around.

"Well, Ethan," Donna said, "it's amazing to see how God has helped you rebuild all that was in rubble."

"A year ago, I was clearing ashes, and today I'm standing on them," Ethan replied.

"It's a beautiful place," Charles said, casting his gaze around.

"Thank you," Jez and Ethan replied in unison and then laughed.

"I'd love to see your area," Charles said to Jezmeen.

"I think I'll browse the poinsettias," Donna said, and their group broke apart, Ethan with Debbie and Charles with Jezmeen.

As they walked, Charles chatted about her racks of wallpaper and fabrics. Then he saw her interior design certificate from Ashworth College hanging on the wall.

"Well, congratulations," he said, beaming at her with pride. "You did it."

She let the weight of his words sink in. Finishing her courses with straight A's, she earned a glowing recommendation from one of her professors, which she shared on her new business website. When they reached the wall with flooring samples, Charles stopped and looked at her.

"Donna tells me you're doing well," Charles said softly.

"I am."

"She's a good counselor."

"Just like you."

"Thanks, but remember, we were just two friends getting together for coffee," he winked, knowing the truth in her statement.

"How are things going for you?" Jez asked. "It's been so long…"

"Well, I have a few weeks off at Christmas, and let me tell you, I'm really looking forward to it."

"Do you have any plans to come back permanently?"

"Actually, I do. Hopefully, if they can find a replacement for me in St. Louis, I'll be back at the end of January."

"That's great," Jezmeen said with a rush of relief.

"Donna's done a wonderful job maintaining my client load and hers, but it's getting to be too much, so the timing is just right. My sister tells me you're going to a new church?"

"Yeah. Ethan and I started going to his church around the time we got engaged."

"Engaged again," Charles smiled. "This time feels right?"

"Definitely," Jezmeen said confidently.

"You're like a new person," Charles glowed.

"A new creature in Christ."

He took her hand in his and gently squeezed it. "My soul is satisfied," he smiled. "Well, I better get back to Donna. We drove together."

"Oh?" Jezmeen said, cocking her eyebrows.

"She's a lovely, lovely woman," he said with a twinkle in his eye.

Charles started towards the front, but Jezmeen stopped him with her words.

"Mr. Noble, every ounce of you lives up to your last name."

"Thank you," he said, choking on the words.

"And Charles," she said quietly, "I will *always* love you."

` With leftover containers of Chinese on the coffee table and a movie playing in the background, Jezmeen could barely keep her eyes open, as she leaned against Ethan's arm on the sofa. The day had been a success, and she shut her eyes in contentment.

When she woke up, the movie had finished, and some comedy show played in the background. She moved her neck side to side, sore from laying on it in one direction for the last hour, and her eyes met Ethan's.

"Nice nap?" he asked playfully.

"Hope I didn't drool," she kidded, half-way serious. "What a day," she commented.

"I think we both have more leads than we have time."

Jezmeen curled her leg underneath her body and turned to face Ethan on the couch.

"Sounds like a good problem," she replied.

"As long as I don't have to do too many Christmas light removals, or I'm taking you along. After all that was *your* idea," Ethan teased.

Jezmeen felt the sweet presence of the Holy Spirit in the room.

"It was nice that VJ came by today," Jez said, making small talk. "And it's obvious he's completely smitten with that worship leader...Ariana?"

"Yeah," Ethan laughed. "I think they're a good match."

Jezmeen took Ethan's hands and laced his fingers with his.

"How about us?" Ethan asked, looking down at their hands.

"Are we a good match?" Jez questioned.

Ethan nodded in affirmation.

"Absolutely. Without a doubt, God gave me the best gift when you walked into Finnegan's," Jez replied.

Jezmeen freed her hands and ran her fingers lightly across his cheek. Ethan raised his downcast eyes to meet her gaze.

"You're not only the man I need, you're the one I want. I love you more than I can express, Ethan."

Ethan's eyes grew moist.

"Over a year ago, I was sitting here, you pulled back my hair, and you kissed me on the cheek," Jez said, and Ethan instantly remembered. "That was when I knew."

"Knew what?"

"Knew there was hope. Something inside me stirred. I felt..."

Jezmeen gently ran her hand through Ethan's wavy hair and along his jawline. Then she cupped his face in her hands, brought her lips to his, tenderly kissing him, and her whole body tingled.

Discussion Questions

1.   As the book opens, Ethan is reciting, "Love is a choice." Later he says he loves by choice and with feeling. Which of these statements, do you think, is more accurate?

2.   Izzy, Wayne, and Ethan have Sunday lunches together. Do you have any weekly family traditions?

3.   When Jezmeen is hired at *Style Street*, it is hard for her to connect with Monica, the owner. Later we find out Monica has narcissistic tendencies. Have you ever been around someone like Monica?

4.   Jezmeen becomes homeless after she breaks up with Ethan. Why do you think she leaves him? Do you think homelessness would look like Jezmeen's situation in "real life?"

5.   Ethan struggles with devastating circumstances after becoming a Christian. His assistant, Claire, tells him, "You learn the most in the wilderness. When you get to the Promised Land, you'll be strong and lean and healthy because of all that walking." Do you agree?

6.   Jezmeen is greatly moved because of a Christian song at the Christmas Eve service. Why do you think music is so powerful? Has a song ever affected you in a similar manner?

7.   Why does Charles leave Springfield? Do you think his actions made a difference in Jezmeen's life? Have you ever made a big sacrifice for someone?

8.	Ariana reveals she has trichotillomania. Have you ever met anyone with this disorder? Why do we tend to hide the struggles we're going through from others?

9.	Ethan ends up taking over some of his dad's responsibilities throughout the story. Have you ever had a role reversal with a parent? What did you learn from it?

10.	Did you like how the romantic relationships fell into place at the end of the book, or would you have paired them differently?

Author's Note

Did you know that just like the character Ariana, I too struggle with trichotillomania? For many years, I only pulled my split ends when I was nervous or bored, but since I turned forty, I've found the habit worsen.

Writing especially heightens the hair-pulling. As I've analyzed why, I've realized some of my anxiety comes from the aspiration for each novel to be well-crafted and well-received. I care about spreading the message of God's grace, love, and salvation. When I was studying vocal performance in college, the feeling was similar—a nervousness that comes from desiring my "offering" to be enjoyed.

Because writing is such a solitary discipline, it helps to hear from readers! Did you like "Freeing Grace?" Were you satisfied with the ending? I'd love to hear from you, in any fashion. Honest reviews on Amazon are always appreciated, or my email address is powellstudio1@gmail.com, and you can also give me feedback there.

I've plucked five pieces of hair while typing this note to you. It just goes to show that, like Ariana, I am far from perfect. Thankfully, God says His grace is sufficient, and His power is made perfect in our weakness.

www.ingramcontent.com/pod-product-compliance
Lightning Source LLC
Chambersburg PA
CBHW032132190626
46814CB00005BA/1665